# BIG LEAGUE DREAMS

# BIG LEAGUE DREAMS

ALLEN HOFFMAN

SMALLWORLDS

ABBEVILLE PRESS
PUBLISHERS
NEW YORK
LONDON
PARIS

JACKET FRONT: "Hank Severeid." The Sporting News, St. Louis, Missouri.

EDITOR: SALLY ARTESEROS
DESIGNER: CELIA FULLER
PRODUCTION EDITOR: MEREDITH WOLF
PRODUCTION MANAGER: LOU BILKA

FIRST EDITION
2 4 6 8 10 9 7 5 3 1

LIBRARY OF CONGRESS CATALOGING-IN-PUBLICATION DATA
HOFFMAN, ALLEN.
BIG LEAGUE DREAMS / ALLEN HOFFMAN.
P. CM. — (SMALL WORLDS : [2])
SEQUEL TO: SMALL WORLDS.
ISBN 0-7892-0191-7
1. JEWS—MISSOURI—SAINT LOUIS—HISTORY—FICTION.
2. RUSSIAN AMERICANS—MISSOURI—SAINT LOUIS—HISTORY—FICTION.
3. SAINT LOUIS (MO.)—HISTORY—FICTION. I. TITLE. II. SERIES:
HOFFMAN, ALLEN. SMALL WORLDS : 2.
PS3558.O34474B54      1997
813'.54—DC21           97-11068

*For Avi, Nehama, Ellie, and Atara*

# THE BRIDGE

CROSSING THE RIVER NEDD AS HE DEPARTED KRIMSK, the rebbe had the visionary experience of treading in the footsteps of Napoleon. Looking down at the water, he saw a cloud reflected as a pyramid and knew that Napoleon had crossed the river like a modern, steadfast pharaoh. The knowledge that he was emulating mighty pharaoh gave the rebbe confidence that he was traveling in the correct direction, for he understood that Israel's post-Temple exile had not gone far enough. To ensure that it would, the Krimsker Rebbe, Yaakov Moshe Finebaum, wanted to imitate the Shekinah, the glory of God's presence, by burying himself in the depths of exile and thus spreading the messianic redemption. On the throbbing steamship that crossed the Atlantic Ocean to the demonic Other Side, presentiments of diaspora impurity encouraged him.

A glance at the map told the rebbe that the city in which previous Krimsker immigrants had settled—and promised help—was the correct place. St. Louis, buried in the middle of the continent, sat astride a river. These similarities with the old home comforted him and held the promise of a new Krimsk. In contrast to the simple Nedd, the new river had such an astonishing name, the Mississippi. On the train west, the rebbe eagerly anticipated crossing the Mississippi, in the belief that this initial encounter would inspire the same prophetic talents that his departure from Krimsk had.

Repeated inquiries elicited the response from the conductor that the train was on schedule and would approach the river at sunset. To the rebbe's surprise, they did not get off the train. The train itself began to climb onto a massive masonry and iron bridge, which carried it across the river. And the river? Yaakov Moshe rushed to the window, leaning close to the pane, to examine the Mississippi in mystic intimacy, but the Eads Bridge was so high that he could barely see the barges floating impossibly far below. The river, like an ocean, stretched away as far as the eye could see. The rebbe ran across the car to the window on the opposite side, and the Mississippi stretched away even farther and grander. Suddenly he realized that the seemingly small chains of barges lost on its mammoth surface could hold all of Krimsk, Krimichak, and the pond in between. Seeing his terrified amazement, the conductor came over to announce with unbounded American pride that the American Mississippi River is greater than the Nile in ancient Egypt.

The rebbe turned back to the unbelievable sight. In the interim the setting sun had shifted slightly, and the great majestic Mississippi reflected the red dying rays; the rebbe gazed upon a boundless stream of blood like pharaoh's lesser Nile during the ferocious first plague. Yaakov Moshe turned away from the window and fell into his coach seat.

Reb Zelig, clutching the Torah, leaned toward him to ask if they should recite the blessing upon seeing a wonder of nature. The rebbe leaned forward and kissed the holy scroll's blue velvet cover, which was the color of real life-giving water and not the bloody life-depleting crimson that drained a continent through the empty void beneath. With tears in his eyes, he turned to the sexton and said, "In America there is no Sabbath, only magic," but Reb Zelig could not hear him because the bridge echoed and re-echoed the metallic clatter of the wheels, mocking any attempts at speech.

## ST. LOUIS, MISSOURI
## 1920

### SHABBOS
### (THE SABBATH)

The Sabbath is one-sixtieth of the World to Come;
a dream is one-sixtieth of prophecy.

There is no dream that does not contain some nonsense.
—Babylonian Talmud, Tractate Brachot

# SAINTS AND REBBES

In 1764 French fur traders founded the city of St. Louis. Wishing to win the favor of the French king, Louis xv, the founders named the new settlement after the king's patron saint, Louis ix, better known as Saint Louis, who had been dead for almost five hundred years.

Louis ix himself was an inspired if somewhat unsuccessful traveler who launched the Seventh Crusade but never arrived in the Holy Land because he was captured in Egypt. His greatest success consisted in getting himself ransomed and returning alive to France. Undeterred by this failure, he undertook the Eighth Crusade, in which he managed to escape capture but not death. In legend he fared much better, becoming Saint Louis, after whom the city was named.

The Krimsker Rebbe felt no affinity for Saint Louis, although he might well have; both men were ascetic, deeply revered, righteous spiritual leaders who were more respected than emulated. And of course both found themselves in the snares of Egyptian bondage; Saint Louis's had been real but finite, whereas the rebbe's was metaphoric but ongoing. The rebbe was aware that greed had prompted the city's founders to evoke the memory of Saint Louis. That was understandable, for the rebbe knew that after the French Revolution none other than Napoleon—who had played such a symbolic role in the rebbe's departure from Krimsk—needing money to finance his European wars, had sold the lands included in the Louisiana Purchase to the United States. For the Krimsker Rebbe, however, as for Saint Louis before him, money was an evil, but so obvious an evil as to be a crashing bore.

What interested the Krimsker Rebbe were the American Indians. Although the Native Americans were new to the white Europeans, they were the old part of the New World. And the New World to the Indians wasn't very new at all; for them, only their white visitors from the Old World were new. So the rebbe sought the Old World connection at the heart of the New World. The rebbe, after all, understood that there is nothing new under the sun. Some Indians worshiped the sun, some the moon, and all revered the mighty Mississippi, the Father of Waters, a sort of liquid patron saint, just as in ancient Egypt the enslavers of Israel had worshiped the sun and the River Nile. So if there is nothing new under the sun, what is old under the sun could prove a great mystery, a veritable happy hunting ground for the Krimsker Rebbe. And the rebbe knew that both hunting and mysteries are often evil and almost always dangerous.

# CHAPTER ONE

THE WHITE-BEARDED OLD MAN OPENED THE FORD'S
back door and with surprising ease hoisted a large trunk
into the automobile. Remarkably erect and robust for his
seventy years, he was not even sweating in the warm morning sunlight. As a concession to the St. Louis climate and
this morning's physical task, he had removed his suit jacket
but not his hat. He would like to have taken that off, too,
but he was slightly embarrassed to appear on a public
street in a skullcap. The tree-shaded suburban neighborhood knew him as the Krimsker Rebbe's sexton, and it
wouldn't have mattered to the Germans, Irish, and Italians,
who inhabited the numerous duplexes and occasional apartment house and were really very fine neighbors, friendly,
polite, and respectful. It mattered to Reb Zelig, however, because this was America, and whenever he could avoid calling attention to the difference, he preferred to do so. He had
shortened his side curls and had tucked them behind his
ears; he wore a modern short suit jacket and broad-brimmed
felt hat. Outside the neighborhood they often mistook him

for an old-fashioned farmer. That is, when he was alone. The Krimsker Rebbe himself wasn't embarrassed to go anywhere in a skullcap—he didn't tuck his long side curls behind any ear either—and his long frock coat trailed ostentatiously behind him like a Civil War relic.

When they had suddenly left Krimsk in 1903, Reb Zelig never had expected to understand the Krimsker Rebbe, and the rebbe did not disappoint him. But Reb Zelig had been puzzled more than usual recently when the rebbe insisted that he, Reb Zelig, must say the mourner's kaddish for the deposed and executed Tsar Nicholas II. Reb Zelig mentioned to the rebbe that they were no longer in Russia, and Nicholas had been deposed before his death. The rebbe flicked his wrist impatiently and said, "Nu, you can ask a better question. Ask why a goy like you should say kaddish for a Jew. Ask me, and I'll tell you the answer. You killed him, and there's no one else to say kaddish for him, so you might as well do it."

In Krimsk, Reb Zelig would have assumed that the rebbe was referring to great kabbalistic secrets and mysteries. But such esoteric lore, essential as it was in the Russian village of Krimsk, seemed so very alien in St. Louis. Reb Zelig even wondered if the rebbe knew what he was talking about. Still, Reb Zelig had dutifully begun to say the memorial prayer, informing inquisitive congregants that the rebbe had told him to do so for the victims of the Bolshevik Revolution, who had no one left to say it in their memory, a story that was pretty much true as far as it went. Occasionally Reb Zelig wondered what the rebbe had really meant, but even in America he wasn't about to take that much liberty with his rebbe as to ask him directly.

Most of the time the rebbe seemed aware of his surroundings—even when he went around the Osage Indian reservation with his phylacteries on his head and arm as if he were in the beis midrash back in Krimsk. Once Reb Zelig had asked the rebbe why he found the Indians so fascinating.

"Here," the rebbe said, pointing to the Osage encampment, "and only here lies the secret to America. Here and nowhere else." It all seemed a little strange to Reb Zelig, but he was only a sexton, not given to unraveling great secrets. Not given to killing people either, much less former tsars. Some day maybe the rebbe would explain that to him, too.

But tomorrow morning it would be the Osage Indians who were perplexed; tomorrow would be the Sabbath, and no Jew wore his phylacteries on the Sabbath. The Indians had never seen the rebbe on a Sabbath. In fact, Reb Zelig himself was slightly perplexed that they were about to drive down to the reservation. The rebbe had always insisted on returning home to St. Louis for the Sabbath, no matter how far or how fast Reb Zelig had to drive. Perhaps there was a very special ceremony that the rebbe wanted to observe. Reb Zelig would find out soon enough, but now that he had the automobile loaded, he had better put on his jacket and tell the rebbe that they could get started. They had a long journey and wanted to arrive well before sunset, when the Sabbath would begin.

# CHAPTER TWO

REB ZELIG WENT TO HIS ROOM BEHIND THE BEIS midrash, put on his suit jacket, and then went up the back stairs to knock on the kitchen door of the rebbe's apartment. The rebbetzin opened it.

"Reb Zelig, have a safe trip and good Sabbath," she said.

"Thank you. May you, too, have a good Sabbath," he answered.

"The rebbe is in the study. He's expecting you."

Reb Zelig nodded and walked down the hall to the study. Although the door was open, he knocked and waited for the rebbe's permission to enter. None came, and he knocked louder. Still he received no response. Thinking the rebbe might have gone to some other room, Reb Zelig called, "The rebbe should be informed that it is time for us to leave." He turned completely around, hoping to hear an answer from one of the bedrooms or the living room, but to his disappointment, he was greeted by silence in all directions.

He knocked again and entered the dark study. The curtains had been drawn together in preparation for the rebbe's departure; although no one else used the room, whenever he left on any overnight journey, it was ceremoniously closed.

Perhaps, Reb Zelig thought, the rebbe has already gone downstairs and is waiting for me in the automobile. That happened occasionally when the rebbe was impatient to go somewhere. Reb Zelig did wonder why the rebbe had left the study door open. As he turned to close the door behind him on his way out, he noticed with some astonishment that the rebbe was sitting motionless on a chair in the corner, leaning forward with his hands resting on his knees. No doubt the rebbe had closed the curtains himself and then simply sat down. The strange, disquieting, and disrespectful image that came to Reb Zelig was of a large bullfrog crouching motionless in the shadows beside a pool. The sexton flushed in shame at his irreverent imagination. To overcome his embarrassment, he pushed the door open and rushed over to the rebbe.

"Rebbe, it's time we were leaving!" he burst out altogether too loudly.

He received no answer. Although it was gloomy in the corner farthest from the door, Reb Zelig knew that the rebbe's open, obtusely glazed eyes were not even blinking.

"Rebbe," the sexton pleaded frantically, just as childless women importuned the Krimsker Rebbe for a blessing to become fruitful, "Rebbe, we have to get started."

The rebbe said nothing.

In frustration, Reb Zelig paced to the door and back before trying again.

"The car is loaded. We have all the food we need. I checked myself to be certain that we have the necessary Sabbath loaves and wine. We're all ready."

When he received no response, Reb Zelig pulled the thick, heavy, suffocating curtains open. The brilliant full-morning sunlight flooded the room, blinding Reb Zelig and causing a momentary stabbing pain in his head. His eyes closed reflexively; kneading them with his knuckles, he turned away from the window before attempting to open them again. When he did so, he blinked several times and saw that the rebbe remained in the same position, lost in reverie. In the bright light he looked faintly ridiculous. The rebbe's pupils had contracted to mere pinpoints like a cat's; the intractable, stubborn rebbe had adjusted without surrendering an inch. He had not even blinked. The disturbed sexton grabbed the wide lapels of the rebbe's frock coat and forcefully shook them.

"We're all ready. There's nothing to keep us here," Reb Zelig said roughly.

The shaking proved successful. The rebbe was staring at Reb Zelig with all the dismay and contempt that he had for ruffians. The sexton stopped as suddenly as he had begun. The rebbe's lapels remained crumpled, floating as high as his chin.

"There's nothing to keep us here," Reb Zelig repeated quietly.

He smoothed the rebbe's lapels as he spoke.

"The river," the rebbe said matter-of-factly.

"What river?"

"The mighty Mississippi."

"We don't even cross the Mississippi," Reb Zelig said, slightly bewildered.

"What color is it?"

"How should I know? The color it always is, I guess. What color should it be?"

"The color the Creator gave it," answered the rebbe, and he suddenly stood up.

Reb Zelig examined the rebbe closely and concluded that he had returned to normal and it was time they were on their way. He reached to close the curtains.

"No, leave them open. We're staying home for the Sabbath," the rebbe said.

"We are?"

"Yes."

"But, rebbe, the automobile is loaded."

"Unload it. We have to be *here* for the Sabbath. You may go now," the rebbe said quietly but curtly.

"We shall pray as usual then?"

"How else should we pray?" the rebbe mused aloud.

Reb Zelig didn't answer as he left the room. Why couldn't the rebbe make up his mind? He went down the hall to the kitchen.

"Are you leaving now?" the rebbetzin asked.

"No, we're not going," Reb Zelig said quietly.

The rebbetzin heard his annoyance.

"Oh, you're not?" she asked, hoping to draw him out. She knew that the rebbe would never tell her.

"No. If you need some things to prepare the three Sabbath meals, make a list, and as soon as I unload the car, I'll pick them up," he answered.

"Yes, thank you. I appreciate that. You don't know either, do you?" she asked.

"No. I wonder if he does," Reb Zelig ventured irreverently.

"Oh, you can be sure he does," the rebbetzin announced with finality.

Reb Zelig went to his room to take off his jacket before returning the large steamer trunk to the house. He could feel that the morning had grown considerably warmer.

The rebbetzin's faith in the rebbe continued to amaze Reb Zelig, but then she didn't have to go about finding a quorum of ten congregants for the Sabbath prayers this evening. On an average Friday night they barely managed a minyan, and since they had been planning on spending the Sabbath with the Osage Indians, Reb Zelig had notified their few regular congregants to attend services elsewhere. Now what was Reb Zelig to do?

He supposed that he would have to call up those who had telephones, but even if he could contact them, what if they had made plans that they couldn't change? This wasn't Krimsk, where the rebbe's wish was everyone's command. He would drive around to a few others after he did the rebbetzin's shopping, but he wasn't very hopeful about their praying "as usual" this Sabbath. At least they would eat as usual, but why couldn't the rebbe go through with the Sabbath as planned? Friday morning! What a time to go changing Sabbath arrangements! And the rebbe had done so at the very last moment when he had suddenly sat down in the corner, collapsing into a near trance. The rebbetzin claimed that the rebbe knew what he was doing. Reb Zelig certainly hoped so.

Well, one thing Reb Zelig did know: it was getting hotter by the minute, and the longer he waited to unload the automobile, the more difficult it would be.

Reb Zelig carefully draped his suit coat over the back of a chair to keep it from getting wrinkled and immediately felt a twinge of conscience over what he had done to the rebbe's lapels. After all these years, that he should do a thing like that! What was happening to him? He had been the calmest man in Krimsk. But why did the rebbe say those things about him? That wasn't right. And what was this crazy business about the river? But enough of this; he'd better get to work.

And then Reb Zelig did a very strange thing. He took off his broad-brimmed felt hat. He had worked outside in the street on much hotter days than this without removing his hat. Suddenly feeling both defiant and determined without quite knowing why, he wanted to unload the automobile in his skullcap and side curls. Let the whole world flow by like a river—what did he care? He wasn't a murderer, was he?

# CHAPTER THREE

MATTI STERNWEISS LIFTED HIS HEAD OFF THE PILLOW and rubbed his eyes with relief and embarrassment that the tenacious horrors he had just witnessed had been only a nightmare, after all. He let his head fall back onto the pillow, then—lest he doze off into such terrors again— pushed the sweat-soaked sheet off his body with a determined thrust of his stubby, muscular arm and sat up. He stretched his legs over the side of the bed and watched his naked soles contact the cool linoleum floor. As if reassuring himself that he was now on hard, firm ground, he lightly traced small circles with the balls of his feet. A bitter, ugly taste lodged in the bottom of his throat, as if the dream had melted, depositing the choking residue of death. For a moment Matti thought he might throw up, but mastering the impulse, he decided to rinse his mouth. On his way to the bathroom, Matti saw a morning breeze rustle the filmy white curtain and glanced out the window, half expecting to see a flaming shiny metal airplane falling from the sky. To his relief, however, all he saw were the stately, patient sycamores with their shaggy bark and large shady leaves bordering the quiet street.

The actual crash had occurred over a thousand miles away in Morristown, New Jersey, a place even Matti had never passed through in all his baseball travels, and he had seen more than his fair share of small towns. Several days earlier in New Jersey, at precisely eight in the morning, people on the ground had heard a motor backfiring in the sky and had looked up to see the New York–to–Chicago mail plane flying very low. The all-metal monoplane suddenly tilted forward and, spewing flames, plunged toward the earth.

At first the onlookers thought the aviators were parachuting to safety from the "blazing meteor" (that was how the newspaper described it). But when they counted three, then four, then five white objects sailing out of the monoplane, they realized that the pilots were saving the mail at the risk of their lives. The plane itself crashed in a tremendous explosion that sent a ball of fire cascading higher than the treetops. When local farmers arrived, they couldn't even extricate the bodies, which the terrific impact had thrust deep into the mangled mass of metal.

Just thinking about it was enough to make Matti's skin crawl. He hurried into the bathroom and stuck his head under the faucet, gargled with cold water, then brushed his teeth—not so much to clean them as to leave a pleasant taste in his mouth, but Matti knew that was only a temporary screen. Underneath, the inescapable, heavy bile sat inside him like a frog that had temporarily dunked its head under water but sooner or later was sure to come up.

Closing his eyes to dry his face, Matti suddenly

remembered the other fire, the one he had kindled in Krimsk as a boy on that fateful Tisha B'Av night that led to the Krimsker Rebbe's departure for America. He had been in the witch Grannie Zara's cottage when crazy Faigie Soffer had screamed so loud that the entire neighboring Polish village of Krimichak must have heard her. Refusing his pleas that they leave, she insisted on their destroying Grannie Zara's beloved cat Zloty. Matti had managed to coax the great cat with the overly large paw into the cupboard along with the other cats and set it ablaze. As the villagers approached, Matti and Faigie had fled into the night. Matti also recalled the strange harmony of the interior of Grannie Zara's home: everything was in perfect order, measured and precise. The cottage, of course, burned with the cats, and the unsettling harmony was reduced to shapeless ashes. And now, Lieutenant Max Miller's harmony of flight had been destroyed by the motor's backfiring, and he had plunged to his fiery death. Matti shook his head at the terrible irony: just like that—a few backfires—and the aviators' glistening heavenly chariot suddenly became their sealed and charred metal coffin. The hurtling plane had even succeeded in burying itself several feet deep in the ground!

Matti looked into the mirror; wet strands of hair matted his forehead. Still in his pajamas, he reached for a comb. Instead of arranging his hair, however, he sat on the edge of the tub. Comb in hand, he mulled over the fatal accident once again. Lieutenant Max Miller, the finest mail pilot of them all, had just completed six full years of flying without a serious accident—twice as long as Matti had been a catcher for the St. Louis Browns baseball club, and Matti thought that he had learned everything there was to learn! After six flawless years, what could have gone wrong so suddenly as to have entombed Lieutenant Max Miller in his own plane?

Matti had never been one to dwell on someone else's tragedy. Certainly he had never chewed things over and over until they were tasteless. He had always decided what he wanted to do, and then done it. Of course, Matti was aware that some things had changed recently. He had never been in love before. There had been girls, but he had never felt the way he did now about Miss Penny Pinkham, and he had never been on the verge of fixing a baseball game either.

Matti had never been superstitious—not even back in Krimsk, where superstition had been a way of life. What others considered auguries and omens were just so much nonsense to him. Why shouldn't they be? He had gone over things carefully—analyzing everything—and had concluded that he should do it. In fact, he had decided that this Friday afternoon's game against the Detroit Tigers was the one to fix. But now this crazy dream had shaken him. No, he didn't think he was falling prey to superstition or guilt; he had thought it all through, but he was shaken, and only a fool wouldn't take that into account. Matti was no fool. Tomorrow there would be another game that would be almost as good as today's, and by then Matti would be his old self, all mastery and intelligence, a model of concentration.

His mother called, asking if he was all right. "Fine, Ma, I'm fine. I'll be out in a minute." He stood up and combed his hair and then flushed the toilet although he hadn't used it. Old ladies always listened for such sounds.

Back in his room he dressed quickly, but as he reached

for his wallet, the breeze rustled the curtains again, and he knew that this wasn't the day to put his plan into action. He couldn't think about today's game because the breeze suddenly wafted him back to New Jersey and the farmers who couldn't remove Max Miller from the all-metal plane. There was nothing for them to do but to pick up the mail.

Some of the sacks had burst when they hit the ground, and the letters had been scattered across a field. The farmers wandered about, gathered them together, and turned them over to the postal authorities. The newspaper said that a surprising number of the letters were for people in the Midwest and had been sent all the way from Europe.

Matti suddenly wondered whether one of them might not be for him, from Krimsk. At that he smiled. Who in the world would write to him from Krimsk? Krimsk was mercifully far, far away; even Matti's widowed mother didn't correspond with anyone back in Krimsk. Most of Krimsk had immigrated to St. Louis soon after the rebbe arrived. In St. Louis, however, the Krimsker community had not remained very close. The rebbe would have been the natural magnet to hold the group together, but he was such a prickly individualist that only a handful of older Krimskers bothered to attend his synagogue. Much of the time the rebbe seemed to be more interested in the American Indians than in his own Jewish coreligionists.

Matti and his mother had not been to his synagogue in years, although Matti supposed that the rebbe still remembered him. Not that Matti attended any synagogue very regularly; on the High Holidays he accompanied his mother to a more American synagogue, and that was all. No, he couldn't even remember the last time they had been to the

Krimsker Rebbe. Occasionally the rebbe's sexton, Reb Zelig, drove by, and they exchanged a perfunctory nod of acknowledgment. Matti even thought that once he had caught sight of Reb Zelig in the stands at the ballpark, but that was several years ago, and although the man had looked like Reb Zelig, Matti was never sure. After all, why would Reb Zelig watch the St. Louis Browns? Even if he wanted to, Reb Zelig wouldn't have time; he conducted some sort of used clothing business to support the rebbe's synagogue. In St. Louis, as in Krimsk, the rebbe's financial probity was legendary; the Krimsker Rebbe refused to accept donations. And look where it got him in America. Matti imagined that his house of worship must look like an oriental bazaar, with various items of apparel draping the empty seats.

Thank heavens, baseball had absolutely nothing to do with Europe. Baseball was the American game. Matti felt certain that poor Max Miller must have been a real baseball fan. He was some kind of hero, throwing out the letters like that. Matti was sure that no one in Europe would have done such a thing. The brave young aviator's death seemed like such an American tragedy. Matti loved America, and as much as he bothered with theological thoughts anymore, he believed that God had blessed America—but apparently not quite enough for Lieutenant Max Miller. That troubled Matti; the talented pilot seemed to have been so deserving of success.

Matti was also sure that in Krimsk they had never even seen an airplane. Why did they need one? Who gave a damn about Krimsk anyhow? He had better start concentrating on catching today's game, or the St. Louis Browns would lose it honestly to Ty Cobb and the Detroit Tigers without Matti's making a cent.

# CHAPTER FOUR

AFTER HIS SEXTON HAD LEFT, YAAKOV MOSHE FINEBAUM, the Krimsker Rebbe, returned to his seat in the corner and concentrated, but he could not recapture the image that had stunned him so suddenly: the Mississippi River as he had seen it on his arrival seventeen years earlier, flowing red with blood.

He turned to look out the window into the yard and saw the ripening apples pulling the pliant branches toward the earth. The grass was full after the summer's growth, and the tall, spindly weeds poked higher than the fence bordering the alley. He opened the window, and the full, rich morning heat of late summer carried the aroma of growth coming to fruition. The Krimsker Rebbe felt welling within himself the stimulation and fear of awesome expectancy. This was definitely not the Sabbath on which to leave town.

# CHAPTER FIVE

A⊤ NINE O'CLOCK BORUCH LEVI RUDMAN PULLED UP
in his new Hupmobile in front of "his" synagogue, that is,
the one he had purchased for Rabbi Max. Since his return
several weeks ago from Krimsk, he had been attending the
seven o'clock morning service. This morning, however, he
had slept late, a very unusual occurrence, which made
Boruch Levi very uncomfortable.

By this hour he should already have been down on the
levee at his enormously successful junkyard and rag shop.
After all, he had been away for most of the summer, and he
had some catching up to do, but he wanted to consult privately with Rabbi Max about Isidore Weinbach's memorial
tea party this coming Sunday afternoon, honoring Weinbach's father on the anniversary of his death.

The idea of a memorial party in a formal rose garden
with tea in china cups—with saucers yet—and sandwiches
trimmed of their crusts was absurd, and Boruch Levi was
as embarrassed as anyone else to be involved in such a
ridiculous perversion of tradition. At authentic memorial

repasts, at Shabbos kiddush immediately following the morning service or at the "Third Meal," eaten between the Sabbath afternoon prayers and the Saturday night service, Jews sucked salty herring off the rigid, symmetrical bones and drank strong whiskey from short, thick glasses as had their fathers and grandfathers before them for generations. But Isidore, formerly Yitzhak Weinbach of Krimsk, no longer entered a synagogue, and worse, he and his wife had adopted a complete tradition of rose gardens, an aesthetic that excluded herring and whiskey. Since they no longer observed the traditional dietary laws, they could not serve the kosher Jews of Krimsk anything more substantial. Sometimes Boruch Levi wondered why the real estate mogul even bothered with the silly event, but he supposed that a father was a father and memory remained memory even with the weak crust trimmed from tasteless goyish white bread.

Ever since Boruch Levi's recent triumphal summer visit to Krimsk, the American brand of remembrance seemed all the more embarrassing, even a mockery of the parent it was intended to honor, but ever-loyal Boruch Levi—even more so after Krimsk—willingly organized the annual event and would continue to do so as long as Isidore Weinbach could resist his wife's impulse to grace the rose garden with those truly trayf abominations that sat upon the great oak table of her dining room.

Although he had long ago paid back the money he had borrowed, Boruch Levi felt himself indebted to Isidore Weinbach. The debt went beyond mere money back to that final astounding Tisha B'Av in Krimsk. On their way into Krimsk to commit mayhem, the riotous peasant mob had torched the large unused synagogue known as the Angel of Death. As if possessed, the Krimsker Rebbe had dashed into the flaming inferno to save the holy Torah and moments later had emerged spinning like a top with a fiery figure who clutched the sacred scroll to his chest as if it were a child. Believing the smoldering figure to be the devil himself, the Polish peasants fled back to their neighboring town of Krimichak. The "devil" turned out to be a young itinerant student radical, agitating against the Russian tsar, and the rebbe had rewarded him on the spot with his own daughter's hand in marriage. The rebbe had also announced that Reb Zelig, the Angel of Death's custodian, was to become his personal sexton, and—most amazing of all—he was to accompany the rebbe and the surviving Torah scroll to America!

Within weeks, the Krimsker Rebbe had realized every one of these goals. Marrying his daughter to a perfect stranger was even more astonishing because she had been betrothed to Yitzhak Weinbach, even then a great financial success as a match manufacturer. Yitzhak had protested, but to no avail; it was as if the rebbe had been possessed on that fateful day. If Yitzhak had felt betrayed in love, Boruch Levi had felt betrayed in guidance: the previous night, when Boruch Levi had sought permission to emigrate to America, the rebbe had been horrified at the suggestion and had explained to Boruch Levi that "even the stones in America are trayf." Boruch Levi, having lost all faith, had sought help in emigrating from the rebbe's other victim, Yitzhak Weinbach. Yitzhak accompanied Boruch Levi to America, aiding him generously and continuing to serve as his financial patron in his first St. Louis years. Even after

Weinbach launched his own spectacular career, he remained in touch with Boruch Levi and never made him feel that he was the slightest imposition.

Boruch Levi had never forgotten that help, and he, too, along with the rest of the Krimsk community, took pride in Isidore's staggering commercial success. Although Weinbach had arrived in America with a tidy sum, within ten years he had become a millionaire. How else could he have become president of a bank?

Almost all of those leaving Krimsk had gravitated to St. Louis, because that was where the earlier arrivals had settled. They were from such a small town that New York had seemed too big; somehow they had managed to filter through to the Midwest. Until recently Boruch Levi had thought there was something almost magical about his New World home, St. Louis. Founded in a great bend on the western side of the Mississippi River, the city had extended to the West like a great seashell or fan, whose parallel structural lines led directly to the generative source of the river. All of the city's great thoroughfares came together downtown by the river because that is where they started. The city's geography enabled a man to see where he had come from and where he was headed.

Boruch Levi, along with many others from Krimsk, had personified the progressive urban development. His junk shop was still on the levee by the river, but now he lived in the city's West End in a graceful neighborhood between Delmar Boulevard and the open expanse of Forest Park. Each day as he drove through the city, he enjoyed every moment of the lengthy commute, for he felt it demonstrated the linear magnitude of his success. Downtown he would detour from his direct line to drive by Yitzhak Weinbach's bank. Ever loyal, Boruch Levi wanted to assure himself that everything was all right at his friend's bank. And now, as an act of allegiance, Boruch Levi was on his way to arrange for Yitzhak Weinbach's memorial garden party, where kaddish would be said for Yitzhak's late father, may he rest in peace.

Rabbi Max never entered banks, and that gave Boruch Levi pause; he had come to the spacious brick synagogue building to ask the self-styled "poor man's rabbi" to lead the afternoon memorial service and to deliver some spiritually uplifting words in Isidore Weinbach's formal rose garden.

Boruch Levi would never have had such a preposterous idea before his visit to Krimsk. Who was more extreme and uncompromising than he himself, the King of the Junkmen? Boruch Levi had worshiped at the altar of obstinacy for years. Furthermore, he didn't believe that his unaccustomed efforts as peacemaker would succeed, but nonetheless he had this powerful impulse, almost a passion, to bring Isidore Weinbach and Rabbi Max together. In their perversity they seemed to have much in common; their wounds were self-inflicted, and through mutual contact the spiritually impoverished and financially impoverished could enrich each other. As with old bottles, rags, and junk metal, Boruch Levi understood that their potential value could be realized through connecting the appropriate markets.

As Boruch Levi approached the synagogue building, he was surprised to find the front doors wide open an hour and a half after the morning services had ended. The sanctuary was dark and empty, but beyond the open basement door the stairway light was shining invitingly.

Boruch Levi descended to the basement, where to his

dismay he found Rabbi Max funneling wine from a small cask into a motley assortment of bottles. Concentrating intensely on his measurements and struggling to balance the weight of the bulky cask so as not to waste any of his precious creation, the rabbi wasn't even aware that anyone had entered. Boruch Levi called the rabbi's name. With no surprise or embarrassment, Rabbi Max glanced up, annoyed at having been disturbed.

"Rabbi Max," Boruch Levi said, an almost naive hurt in his voice, "you promised me that you wouldn't ever do this here."

"Shalom, Boruch Levi. Welcome. Just let me finish with these small bottles. They're a nuisance, but very popular."

The rabbi finished, then put down his cask and motioned for Boruch Levi to come to him. The rabbi stood behind a picket fence of bottles, over which they faced each other uneasily. Boruch Levi's disdain increased as he approached.

"Do you know that the front doors of the building are wide open, and so is the door to the basement, with the light blazing on the stairway to guide the world down to this?" Boruch asked in proprietary disgust.

"There's nothing to worry about. Your friends the police aren't like you. They don't come around very early in the morning. They wait to arrest me on the street," Rabbi Max answered casually, enjoying his sponsor's discomfort.

"Who's talking about the police? Never mind the police. The hell with the police," Boruch Levi fumed. "What about the Jews? It's a disgrace. This is supposed to be a synagogue. What if some Jew should come to see you, Rabbi, and find you like this? It's a disgrace for the Jews."

Rabbi Max remained calm. "There's nothing to worry about then," he said, pointing to the strange collection of bottles in various stages of production. "These," he repeated with an almost paternal pride, "these are my little hasidim. Faithful, true, and full of life. And like good Jews everywhere, persecuted by the authorities." Rabbi Max chuckled at his little joke.

Boruch Levi held his tongue at the barb aimed at his hasidic Krimsker background.

"Rabbi, it's a scandal, and I am ashamed of you."

Rabbi Max smiled ironically in agreement. Boruch Levi chose to ignore this further taunt.

"You don't have to carry on like this. You can perform as a rabbi and make an honest living." Boruch Levi paused to take a breath before he made his suggestion. "I want you to lead the afternoon services in Isidore Weinbach's rose garden. Sunday is the memorial day of his father's death, and he wants to say kaddish, the memorial prayer."

Rabbi Max stood looking at Boruch Levi as if he had suggested that Rabbi Max officiate at J. P. Morgan's or John D. Rockefeller's conversion to Judaism.

"Oh you do, do you?" the rabbi asked.

"Yes, I do," Boruch Levi insisted without giving an inch. "And I think it would be nice if you said a few words either before or after the service. It might be a good idea to mention the roses. God created them, too. It won't take more than a half hour. That's all."

"That's all?" the rabbi asked, his voice rising as he lost his composure.

"Yes, *that's all*. This has to stop. You have to start acting like a mensch."

The rabbi had maintained some control until Boruch Levi had uttered the last word, "mensch."

"Like a mensch!" Rabbi Max shouted. "I'll tell you why I'm doing what I'm doing here on one condition, that you promise not to tell another living soul. Do you agree? Good. I'll tell you. The night after the Volstead Act became law, I had a dream in which my holy mother, may she rest in peace, appeared to me and begged me to become a bootlegger."

A maniacal, impish grin spread across the rabbi's flushed face. Boruch Levi had a momentary desire to wipe it off with a backhand slap, but he thought better of it, turned around, and climbed the steps.

# CHAPTER SIX

ON HIS WAY OUT OF THE SYNAGOGUE, BORUCH LEVI carefully closed the doors behind him. He normally would have slammed them hard enough to break every bottle in the basement. He would also have proceeded to fight tooth and nail to throw Rabbi Max out of his, Boruch Levi's, synagogue and back into the street where he had found him, but things had changed. Boruch Levi sensed that in closing the heavy ornate doors he was ending a period in his life. His visit to Krimsk had taught him more respect for the complexity and difficulty of life, and he could no longer charge through everything with his former explosive self-assurance and blind certainty.

There was no doubt that Boruch Levi was angry at Rabbi Max—a steaming, roiling anger at having been taunted, betrayed, and humiliated as Rabbi Max reduced his life to a satirical parody. Rabbi Max was very fortunate that Boruch Levi had gone back to Krimsk; otherwise, the "poor man's rabbi" might have found himself lying in a puddle of poor man's hooch with a terrible headache. Although his anger was real, Boruch Levi managed partially to overcome it because his primary emotion was exasperation with Rabbi Max for not having the common sense to accept genuine friendship. (Whose friendship could ever be more genuine than Boruch Levi's?)

Although Boruch Levi was now one of the enemy, it hadn't always been that way. Several years ago Boruch Levi had received word from Krimsk of his mother's death. That same night he once again dreamed of burning cats, the same dream he had on that final Tisha B'Av in Krimsk. Not knowing what to make of the recurring dream and sensing that he needed some spiritual guidance to inter-pret it, he turned to Rabbi Max, unique in his coarse informality, tolerance of lax religious practices, and com-passion for the poor.

Only the rabbi's distrust of the rich exceeded his envy of them, and consequently they did not flock to his irregu-lar ministry. In his original storefront, the poor and only the poor felt at home, for Rabbi Max went beyond the hasidic enthusiasm for identifying the holy sparks in the secular and the sinful; the rabbi loved equally to burlesque the holy by calling attention to the contradictions, absurdi-ties, and general arrogance that so often accompany the divine. People said that it was a good thing the dead were laid out horizontally at the funerals the rabbi spoke at; oth-erwise no one would know whether they were at a funeral or a wedding. Rabbi Max once stated that the only true religious Jews he had ever met were all Bolsheviks, and that it was a pity that they had to burn in hell as heretics.

On those few occasions when as a poor, struggling junk peddler Boruch Levi had felt a need for religion, he had entered Rabbi Max's hole-in-the-wall. Occasionally inspired, often entertained, he had always felt welcome.

"It's not so bad," Rabbi Max had commented after hearing Boruch Levi's dream of the burning cats. "Personally, I hate cats; they make me sneeze. On the other hand, the Talmud says that you can learn modesty from a cat since it crouches low when it makes, but I don't see what that has to do with your particular dream unless you have a burning sensation when you make. No? That's good. You should be well. At any rate, you had this dream the last time you were with your mother. Maybe she's trying to tell you something. They don't have phones over there in that medieval swamp, so when she was alive she couldn't reach you in person. Now at least she can get in touch. See what happens tonight."

That night Boruch Levi's mother appeared to him and begged him to become religious and to observe stringently the Sabbath and the dietary laws. In the morning he ran to the rabbi, who listened quietly and said, "It might have been worse. It might even be for the best. This way you won't work on the Sabbath, and maybe you won't become too rich."

Rabbi Max was both right and wrong. His hasid didn't work on the Sabbath, but he did become rich. As Boruch Levi prospered, he helped Rabbi Max in every way he could, including buying the respectable brick building. But the more he did, the less Rabbi Max appreciated it. He told Boruch Levi that from the shame of accepting support from the rich, he could not sleep nights. Taking advantage of the legal provisions permitting the manufacture of wines for religious ritual use, Rabbi Max went into business in his own kitchen with the same lack of discretion in crime as in his sermons.

The rawest rookie on the police force could and did arrest him as he sold his religiously inspired homemade spirits from door to door. When a scandalized Boruch Levi bailed him out the first time, Rabbi Max, laughing at what he termed Boruch Levi's naïveté, explained to the uneducated rag dealer that according to the Talmud, Prohibition was thoroughly nonsensical because even the rabbinic sages did not have the authority to proclaim a restrictive decree too harsh for the people to live with. Boruch Levi suggested that the rabbis and the Talmud had nothing to do with it, but the Congress of the United States and the Treasury Department certainly did. In response Rabbi Max chided Boruch Levi for putting the goyish Congress above the sages, since the former were known alcoholics whereas the latter were merely suspected bootleggers.

Boruch Levi saw that nothing could be done with this mad, high-spirited passion. To protect the good name of the Jewish community, he took it upon himself to send the synagogue some good pre-Prohibition whiskey from the saloons he had bought out immediately before the Volstead Act became law. In addition, Boruch Levi exacted a promise from Rabbi Max that he would keep his bootlegging out of the synagogue. A promise, Boruch Levi had just discovered this morning, that Rabbi Max had not kept.

Before leaving for Krimsk, he had warned the rabbi to stop the bootlegging; with Boruch Levi gone, there wouldn't be anyone to bail him out of jail for the Sabbath. In fact, Boruch Levi had sent five hundred dollars in cash to tide the rabbi over during the summer. Of course, they both knew that Rabbi Max would be in jail by Wednesday and that the wonderfully loyal Inspector Doheen would be sure to have him released for the Sabbath.

The thought of his friend Doheen brought Boruch Levi back to the present. He recalled with satisfaction his own part in protecting the chief of police during last week's Prohibition raid. No one loved the chief more than Inspector Doheen, not even Boruch Levi.

Boruch Levi knew how to appreciate both love and hate; Rabbi Max didn't. For a real rabbi, one had to look at the Krimsker Rebbe, something that Boruch Levi had not done in seventeen years. Even in the middle of America, the rebbe didn't care what others, rich or poor, Jews or goyim, thought of him.

As he sat behind the wheel of his car, Boruch Levi sadly realized that Rabbi Max had known that Boruch Levi's rediscovering the world of his youth in Krimsk would end their relationship. The rabbi had been poisonously opposed to the visit, mocking his desire to return to that "dung heap of stagnation."

Now Boruch Levi needed a new rabbi. He felt himself maturing, but he seemed to be growing back into Krimsk. That wasn't the way things were supposed to happen in America. He was perplexed.

# CHAPTER SEVEN

IN HER JUNKYARD BORUCH LEVI'S SISTER, MALKA, pulled a large handkerchief from her overalls and wiped her forehead to give herself more time to think. In her grimy hands the fresh cloth became smudged and dark. She had been standing in the hot morning sun, sorting a month's accumulation of tires, when a peddler with his horse and wagon pulled into her yard with a load. She hadn't been expecting him, since the peddlers collected during the day and came to the junkyards in the afternoon to sell their day's accumulation.

"That looks like nickel to me, and that's worth some money," the peddler said.

Malka pensively tapped the ground with one of the oversize unlaced army boots that she always wore when working in the yard.

"Look at that metal. Zinc, too, and those bottles are perfect! You dream about a load like this."

"I don't dream about anything," Malka said.

She really didn't.

"That's too bad; dreams are sweet things, if I say so myself."

Carey was not one of Malka's regular customers. He generally sold to Bierenbaum or to the Greek. Obviously unable to get his price yesterday from either one, he had left everything on the wagon overnight and was trying his luck with Malka this morning. He had a day, maybe two days' work there.

"What do you want?" she asked with no sense of urgency and little interest, as if she were annoyed at having as important an activity as sorting tires interrupted by such nonsense.

"Well, dreams are cheap, and I want to unload so I can go about my business. I'm willing to take twenty dollars for the lot and be finished with it," he said, stroking his horse's muzzle, as if this humane act would demonstrate his honesty and virtue.

Malka figured that at his price she could turn a profit, but she suspected that his regular buyers hadn't offered him any more than fifteen, and he would take that from her rather than lose face by going back to one of them. The day was slipping away from him. The question was whether he could get his hands on any more nickel. If he could, she wanted him to bring it to her.

"You often have dreams like this?" she asked, nodding in the direction of the wagon.

"No, ma'am. This, as you can plainly see, doesn't happen very often," he answered.

"I'll give you fifteen dollars for it," she said with a finality that didn't leave any room for bargaining.

Carey suddenly looked distressed. He pushed his hat back in consternation.

"It's worth more than that," he protested weakly. Gaiety and confidence had deserted him at Malka's non-negotiable offer.

Malka shrugged her shoulders. "Not to me it isn't."

Carey looked down and kicked the dirt.

"Make up your mind. I've got work to do."

"I'll take it, but it's worth more," he said.

Malka reached into the upper pocket of her overalls, took out a wad of bills, and peeled off a ten and five.

"Dump it over there," she said, pointing to an area near the scale house.

As she handed him the bills, she caught the faint scent of liquor on his breath. To be drinking so early meant that Carey must have had a tough time with his regular yards. After doing no better here, he'd be needing another drink soon, and that gave her an idea. She let him get on his wagon and go fifteen feet so he could fully taste the bitterness of failure before she called to him.

"Hey, Carey, c'mere—Yeah, now!"

He climbed off his wagon and came back to her. She didn't take a step in his direction. She stood with her brawny arms across her ample chest and looked him straight in the eye.

"You know what's going on in this town, don't you?" she asked.

"Much as most, I guess," he answered vaguely.

"How much did you think your stuff was worth?"

Carey looked suspicious. Malka was not one to raise her price after a deal had been struck and paid for. In fact, she wasn't one for bargaining; it was her price—take it or leave it.

"Twenty dollars, like I said," he answered without much spirit.

"Well, maybe, in which case I would owe you five more dollars, wouldn't I?"

Carey looked very uncomfortable now, as if he were a mouse with which a cat named Malka was playing.

"I guess so," Carey said.

"You know I would," she fairly boomed.

She reached into her money pocket and fished out a five-dollar bill that promptly became smudged with grime in her stubby, tire-sorting fingers.

"You know I would," she repeated, "but of course I can't let you have it. Not for this load I can't. It's not worth more than fifteen. But you might have something else I could use for these five dollars."

The peddler, not a bad-looking man, remained suspicious. The thought crossed his mind that she might be propositioning him, but he rejected it; Malka never looked at anyone other than her elegant gimp of a husband. That match, Carey thought, must have been made in heaven, since no one down here could have come up with it.

"All that's on the wagon is all there is," he said innocently.

"Carey, you know what's going on in this town. You're a knowledgeable man, and you might know where my husband goes to do his betting."

Carey's eyes suddenly flickered with a flash of interest at the dirty bill waving in her hand, and Malka was certain that he knew. He didn't answer right away. Instead, he kicked at the ground.

"If you don't know, I understand, but a few cool drinks on a hot day like today would be a sweet dream come true,

Mr. Carey. And once I put it back in my pocket, it won't come out again."

"Heinie," he said softly, as if his throat were very, very dry.

"Where?" she asked severely.

"He runs a cigar store around the corner from the post office on Eighth Street."

He reached for the money. She gave it to him.

"All right then. It's a deal," she said.

Slightly ashamed and slightly fearful that hard-bargaining Malka might change her mind about paying such good money for something so worthless to him, he quickly shoved the bill into his pants pocket.

"Say, is he a Jew?" she asked.

"No, a real Kraut, just like his name, but he's not a bad fellow at all."

"Thanks," she said.

"Listen, nobody has to know about this? About me, I mean?"

"Nobody," she said.

Carey nodded and started to go. Malka turned back to face the small hill of tires. She smiled broadly, voraciously sucking air into the gap between her large front teeth as if fueling a furnace, and wiped her brow, this time in growing confidence. Never a passive person, she had finally taken her first step toward solving her problem.

As she returned to sorting through the tires in search of ones with enough tread to be sold to filling stations and resold as spares, she felt herself calming down. She couldn't do anything else anyway until this afternoon, when her brother would be in his office. Stepping into the house for coffee or for lunch, she would call his secretary and make an appointment. Until then she would try to stay in the yard; the heavy manual labor had a soothing effect on her, even in the heat.

She had already flipped a surprising percentage of tires aside into a smaller pyramidal pile. To an untrained eye there might not seem to be any difference, but she knew that they still had life in them and would make it back onto the road, just like before. That seemed to augur well for her marriage, and ignoring the heat, she went at the hill of tires with a vengeance.

# CHAPTER EIGHT

MATTI STERNWEISS HAD SUCCEEDED IN THRUSTING ASIDE his nightmare, and his singleminded concentration had resulted in a three-to-one Browns victory over the pennant-contending Detroit Tigers. Although he was pleased with his performance on the field, he had only postponed making the fateful decision. Oblivious of everyone else in the immediate aftermath of victory, Matti studiously weighed himself in the Browns' locker room. He was hoping that the numbers would come out even, but the smaller weight balanced perfectly between the two and the three. Squatting behind home plate for nine innings on a sweltering St. Louis September afternoon, Matti lost on the average five pounds a game. This Friday afternoon he had lost five and a half pounds, nothing exceptional about that.

Not usually given to omens, Matti was aware that his fractional weight was irrelevant to the decision that he was weighing at the moment: whether or not he should fix tomorrow's game against the Tigers. How else could he afford to marry Miss Penny Pinkham? The small weight stuck between the whole numbers seemed to symbolize his own inability to decide.

Matti looked around at the tumultuous celebration of victory: sweat, excitement, pride, and a godlike exaltation tempered with a mortal weariness. Around the winning pitcher's locker a crowd of reporters and well-wishers pressed Thatcher Jones for the details of his great feat, striking out the legendary Ty Cobb three times. Matti knew that they were talking to the wrong man. He looked back at the scale; it hadn't budged.

"Hey, Sirdy," a good-natured, jocular voice called to him. "Quit trying to Jew the thing down. That's where it is, and that's the way it's gonna stay."

Without turning around, Matti recognized the voice of tomorrow's starting pitcher, Dufer Rawlings, one away from his twentieth victory. Aware of the irony that the key to his throwing the game was interrupting his deliberations, he turned toward Dufer with a pensive smile. After seventeen years in America, he had never succeeded in developing a shy, crooked smile; it remained pensive and lugubrious, pure talmudic anxiety from Krimsk. But the smile was sincere; no one, not even Matti—or "Sirdy," as he was known to the baseball world—could look at Dufer Rawlings and not smile. He was just about the most likable fellow you could ever meet. Always a smile, always willing to do a favor, not a mean bone in his body. Hadn't he always willingly accompanied Matti to the Pinkhams and talked him up to Penny's father and brothers?

"Yeah, Dufer, I guess you're right. That's where it is," Matti agreed.

Although Matti was standing on the scale five inches

off the floor, he still had to look up at the young giant. As usual, a hank of light brown hair cascaded over one side of Dufer's handsome forehead. Dufer flipped his head slightly to get it away from his eye. On his way to the showers, he wore nothing but a towel wrapped around his waist. If Apollo had parked his chariot outside the ballpark and walked into the locker room for a shower, he might have been mistaken for Charles Dufer Rawlings's brother. If the sun god had had a shock of straight hair tumbling down onto one eye, he might have been mistaken for his twin. Matti knew that the resemblance ended there. Apollo, an Old World deity, was an anti-Semite. Everybody over there was. Dufer wasn't, his remark about "Jewing down" notwithstanding; that was how they talked.

"You know you look like Apollo, you big lunk," Matti said.

"Who's he play for?" Dufer asked seriously.

Matti smiled at the pitcher's innocence. This marvelous Iowa farm boy didn't know enough to hate Jews.

"A Mediterranean club. Don't worry about it. He hasn't got your speed."

Dufer's handsome brown eyes brightened at the mention of his marvelous fastball. Matti yawned.

"You're not too tired, are you? You got something for tomorrow, don't you?" the pitcher asked in his most somber manner.

"You bet, Dufer," Matti said energetically. "Have I ever let you down?"

Dufer smiled and shook his head.

"Not you, Sirdy. You never let any of us down. We all know it, too—" He nodded in the direction of Thatch

Jones. "We know the score. You're okay." He gave Matti an appreciative pat on the back and headed for the showers. "I'll even save you some hot water if you hurry!"

Matti thought he detected a shadow of doubt in Dufer's eye, but before he had a chance to analyze it, Zack Freeling, the Browns' manager, was standing next to him. The short, graying manager listened to Thatch expound on his memorable accomplishment. The pitcher's voice was almost hoarse, but suffused with the delight of triumph.

"The first time, I got Cobb on a good fastball low and away, and then I came back the second time to get him on a sharp hook that had a real good hop on it."

"Good game, Sirdy," the manager said, without looking at him.

"Thanks, Skipper," Matti said.

The manager turned to his catcher. "Is anything he's jawing about over there right?"

Matti modestly shook his head.

The manager shrugged and smiled. "And compared to Dufer and MacGregor, he's a genius."

Zack Freeling carefully eyed the catcher to see if he would join in his joke, but Matti didn't respond. It wasn't in his interest to disparage the pitchers who were his meal ticket.

"Of course, if they could use their heads, too, then you wouldn't be here," the manager said somewhat caustically. "How did you do it?" he asked Sirdy.

"In batting practice I noticed that Cobb was cutting his stride, and in the field he didn't follow through on his throw," Matti answered.

The manager nodded in admiration, and his eyes

flickered in enlightenment. "Cobb's got a side pull and can't get around inside," he said, almost whistling in fascination.

"Today he couldn't," Matti smiled.

The manager looked at Matti with a shrewd expression of his own.

"Never underestimate him, eh, Sirdy? You're something else. You could manage this club right now. Tomorrow's a big one. If they don't win tomorrow, they'll never catch the Indians."

Matti nodded.

"Get some rest, Sirdy. It won't be any cooler out there tomorrow."

Matti watched the manager walk away. Freeling was a smart, cynical little man. If Matti stayed in baseball for a few more years of catching in the big leagues, followed by twenty of coaching and managing in the minor leagues, and everything went right, that's all he would be, too.

Matti had to keep his eye on Freeling. Although the manager needed him, he also felt very nervous about a catcher who was smarter than he was. Unlike Dufer, Freeling wasn't too fond of Jews. When they were in the ballparks where they got down on Matti with cries of "sheeney" and "kike," Freeling would say curtly, "Keep your mind on the game," as if he were embarrassed to have Matti on his side. Matti detected in Freeling's eyes more than a glimmer of identification with the vociferous patrons of the national pastime.

"They don't bother *me*," Matti would retort with an arrogance calculated to irritate the manager.

He had to laugh. In the old country they killed Jews for sport without saying hello. Here these Yankee Doodle

Dandy clowns thought that a few names were so god-awful. They could yell themselves hoarse. Some things you have to put up with.

Freeling would take credit with the owners for Cobb's three strikeouts. Occasionally he told Matti not to be in such a rush, he would get his. But Matti was in a rush, and when he looked at Freeling, "his" didn't seem to be worth waiting for, even if he could afford to wait. Matti wanted to marry, stay home, and enjoy his wife. Enough of all the traveling that once had thrilled him; besides, the manager didn't make more than Matti did. As Freeling once confided to him, "It beats having to make an honest living. I'll say that much for it." Kike or not, Matti was the only one on the Browns team to whom Freeling thought it worthwhile to speak. Beyond a polite smile, Matti never responded to his mock confidences.

Matti moved over to the stool in front of his locker and sat down to rest a minute. Normally, he savored that weary, private moment before showering when he stared at the symbols of his success—bulging catcher's mitt, spikes, and hat in his locker and the soiled, crumpled uniform at his feet. Then he would joyously marshal his strength, fling his flannels into the large laundry basket in the center of the room, and go in to soak under the hot water.

Today, though, he just sat. He could see the scales before him. He wasn't getting any younger. The Browns weren't going anywhere this year, anyhow; without solid pitching even George Sisler's incredible hitting couldn't carry the club. They had had a lousy start and had not more than a so-so shot at third place. When the starting catcher, Swede Jansen, broke his leg in Chicago, Matti had taken over, and the club started winning. With him calling all the shots behind the plate, Dufer and MacGregor had a good chance of winning twenty games apiece. The two had marvelous arms, and even Thatch wasn't bad. Had Matti been behind the plate all season, they might have been right up there fighting for the pennant with the Tigers and the Indians.

They weren't, though. As usual, the marvelous George Sisler was generating excitement at the plate, leading the league with a near four hundred average, but for St. Louis fans, Sisler of the Browns and Rogers Hornsby of the Cards were not news. The papers were making a big thing about St. Louis's chances of having two twenty-game winners. Matti would never be rewarded for that success. Dufer and MacGregor would barely be remunerated. Ball players made peanuts. The owners raked it in, and they didn't share it. A short, slow catcher who had a hard time hitting two thirty wasn't going to get a cigar when it came time to talk contract. Not when that polar bear Swede Jansen hit over three hundred. If the Browns were smart, they would trade Jansen for a good hitting outfielder, fire Freeling, and make Matti the playing manager. But not much chance of that.

Who besides Freeling really knew how important Matti was to the club's success? And he wasn't telling very many people. If Matti were manager, the pitchers would follow his lead, but many of the other players probably would not. Matti had never asserted himself as a leader. Perhaps it was a mistake, but he had never had the confidence. He just wanted to stay on the team. He did things to ingratiate himself. Selflessly and tirelessly, he would quietly coach the other players, but he still suffered his share of jokes and pranks. No more than others, but too many for a managerial candidate. Freeling always seemed to enjoy the jokes on Sirdy.

Take his detested nickname, "Sirdy." As a rookie three years ago, everyone had called him "Matty," just like the great Christie Matthewson. Most of the game he rode the bench behind Jansen, but when they had two days of doubleheaders against the Yankees in August, Matti had made it into the last game. With Lou Gehrig on second, Babe Ruth knocked one off the center-field fence. Matti blocked the plate, even though Gehrig barreled into him as the throw came home. Matti knew that his career was at stake, and he refused to give an inch. Gehrig sent him sailing into the air, but Matti held on to the ball for the out although he landed on his head. Dizzy, he insisted on staying in the game. He knew what was going on, too. When the next batter tapped the ball back to the mound, Ruth had strayed too far down the line from third. Matti yelled over the crowd for MacGregor to throw to third to pick off Ruth. But the collision with the locomotive-like Gehrig had smashed Matti's tongue back into Yiddish-speaking Krimsk. Instead of calling third, he had screamed, "Sird! Sird! Sird!" Much to his teammates' amusement, he had become "Sirdy" Sternweiss.

The next day the nickname appeared in all the papers—no doubt, Freeling's doing. It stung, for if the truth be told, Matti was one of the few Browns who had finished high school, and he spoke and wrote better English than anyone else on the team. He had worked long and hard to master the strange tongue that he had encountered at the age of ten. Occasionally, Freeling referred to him as "Professor Sirdy."

The others would laugh, but they all knew Freeling was ridiculing them, too—if not publicly, then privately, and certainly to the front office. The manager's job was not so very secure either. The joke among the players was that Freeling worked harder upstairs and in the pressbox than he did on the field.

Should Matti fix the game? Perhaps he could think things through better under the showers. He wearily flipped his uniform into the basket. As he walked past the crowd around Thatcher's locker, he heard Ty Cobb's conqueror saying, "No doubt about it. We miss Swede's bat in the lineup. With him behind the plate, we would be right up there with the Tigers and Indians fighting for the pennant."

That dumb son of a bitch, thought Matti. With the Swede they would be in sixth place right now, and come winter, the club would be wanting to cut Thatch's salary. Instead of fourteen wins, he would have seven at best, with fourteen losses to go with them. I should work for that ingrate? The hell with him! Better take mine while I can.

Such thoughts encouraged Matti toward his fateful decision against the Browns, but he could not bring himself to throw the game. He was afraid of getting caught. How was he to evaluate the risk? And was the reward worth that risk? Penny Pinkham's lovely face, framed by the freshly starched white nurse's cap, came to mind. It was worth any risk. Matti had an overwhelming desire to see Penny this evening and propose marriage. With her companionship, he knew that the issue would be resolved.

But today was Friday, wasn't it? On Fridays he ate the Sabbath evening meal with his widowed mother. Penny wouldn't be expecting him; he would have to call and tell her that he was coming over later. Explaining Penny to his old Jewish mother would be another problem, but Matti was confident that she would come around. After all, this was America!

Standing in nothing but a towel, he called the clubhouse boy and told him to telephone the Pinkhams' home. Matti did not enjoy speaking to Penny's brothers or her father. In addition, having the clubhouse boy announce the call always impressed everyone.

"A call from the St. Louis Browns' clubhouse. Just one minute, please," the boy announced and handed the receiver to Matti.

"Hello?" Matti said, his voice so filled with excitement he didn't sound like himself.

"Charles? You will be able to come this evening, won't you?" The lively, melodic voice of Penny Pinkham quaked with anxiety.

Matti felt a rush of blood to his head that threatened to blind him in shame and anger. Speechless, he continued to hold the receiver to his ear.

"Charles? Charles, that is you, isn't it?" Penny asked in embarrassment. Receiving no response, she asked fearfully, "Who's there? . . . Sirdy, is that *you*?"

Matti slowly hung up the telephone and turned around.

"Hey Mack!" he yelled gruffly to the tall pitcher, who was on his way out of the clubhouse in his street clothes. "Come here a minute, will you?"

The lanky left-hander hurried over with a friendly smile. "Hey, Sirdy, you called a great game today," he said.

"How long has Charles Dufer Rawlings been running around with Penny?" Matti asked harshly.

A look of severe discomfort creased Alex MacGregor's thin face.

"Sirdy, I promised to be downtown at six," he said, begging to escape.

"Tell me, Mack," Matti insisted.

"Don't ask me that, Sirdy," Mack said, his eyes avoiding Matti's.

"Then don't ask me when you're going to win twenty games," Matti said in icy anger.

Mack's face registered hurt and shock; then he looked directly at Matti in reproach, as if to ask how the short catcher could suggest any connection between something so holy as his winning twenty games and something so profane as a woman. He saw that this strange little genius, who knew more about his pitching than he himself did and more about American League batters than anyone who ever lived, wasn't kidding.

"You aren't going to do anything foolish, are you?" he asked, preparing the way for his admission.

Not promising anything, Matti just stared at him.

"All summer," Mack said quietly.

"Ever since I brought him over there to help me out?" Matti asked.

Mack nodded. "Yeah, I guess so," he said quickly, wanting to get away from the particulars. "Sirdy, you know Dufer. He wouldn't hurt nobody. It wasn't his fault. He wouldn't do that to a friend."

"No?" Matti asked cynically.

"Hell no, he wouldn't. She was chasing after him like all blazes. She's nuts about Dufer. Sirdy, it was her fault."

Ignoring Mack, Matti stood there, suddenly enlightened as to what the shadow in Dufer's eyes was all about, why Dufer never seemed to be carousing with the other players on Friday nights, and why, for the last month, Penny had found it impossible to get off duty every Saturday night.

"Don't do anything foolish, Sirdy. There's a lot of fish in the sea, believe me. And they're all alike." Mack tried to ease the pain and assure his twenty victories. He was only two short.

"Thanks, Mack," Matti said curtly and turned toward the showers.

"Don't mention my name to nobody," Mack whispered.

"Have I ever let you down?" Matti called over his shoulder.

"Not you, Sirdy. No sir, not you!" Mack called back loudly, with a hearty conviction that he hoped would convince both of them.

"No sir, not me," Matti muttered to himself with bitter irony.

# CHAPTER NINE

MATTI SHOWERED AND DRESSED QUICKLY. ON HIS WAY out of the clubhouse, he bumped into Dufer. Don't get mad, Matti thought to himself, get even.

"Dufer, what are you doing tonight?" he asked innocently.

"Not too much," the near-twenty-game winner answered.

Matti studied Dufer for nervousness, uneven voice, or any of the other telltale signs of prevarication.

"I thought you might want to join me at my mother's for supper tonight. Some good home cooking might be what you need before tomorrow."

"Gee, thanks, Sirdy. She's a great cook, too. You bet she is, but I thought I'd better take it real easy tonight so I'll be ready for the Tigers. They're a rough bunch."

"All right, we'll make it some other time."

"Sure thing, Sirdy. I'd appreciate that. Give your mother my best."

"Sure," Matti said and continued on his way. He was

impressed. No doubt about it, the witless Dufer Rawlings had carried it off perfectly. He could lie as well as he could pitch, a real all-around natural.

Dufer had never turned down a free meal before, much less a home-cooked one. Matti was embarrassed. He was so smart, and he still wanted to believe that it wasn't so. Matti wondered whether Dufer could tell a cheating lie like that to one of the other players. Was it so easy because "Sirdy" was a Jew? If a small Jew had no business with a lovely Christian Miss Pinkham, then Dufer was neither cheating nor betraying but rather upholding the laws of decency and nature. After all, Matti reminded himself, as the Talmud puts it, he who steals from a thief is not culpable.

The way his Jewishness was showing was not lost on Matti. The next thing you know, he would be running around with the nutty old Krimsker Rebbe and dancing with the Osage Indians instead of playing ball against the ones from Cleveland.

But the interesting question of Dufer's attitude toward Sirdy's Jewishness would have to be filed away for investigation at a later date. Matti had to decide a more immediate and crucial question: how much money could he safely put down on the Tigers for tomorrow's game without any chance of getting caught? Greed, Matti knew, was his enemy as well as his ally. If it weren't for greed, he would never be doing such a thing, but if he tried to reap too great a profit, then someone somewhere would become suspicious.

Matti liked his chances up to ten thousand dollars, the sum total of his parents' savings from fifteen years in the butcher shop and the money Matti himself had managed to save from his paltry baseball salary. In fact, ten thousand dollars was five times his annual salary as second-string catcher for the St. Louis Browns. The money would have to be bet at four or five different places so it should not attract too much attention. Yes, that was a good round figure. Large enough to be interesting to Matti, but small enough not to be very interesting to anyone else.

If the syndicate were fixing things, they would make a fortune. After all, the rich get richer. Matti was not rich yet, although deep in his heart, he was certain that in America Matti Sternweiss was destined to die wealthy. He had always been a master of strategy, and now the clever attack had ten thousand dollars written on it, no more.

In fairness to the syndicate, if it weren't for their suggestion, he might never have attempted what had come to seem so obvious. On their last road trip to New York, he had been approached by an ex-fighter, Abe Levin, whose name had since popped up in the rumors about last year's World Series. He was reputed to be well connected with the Arnold Rothstein gambling syndicate. Levin told Matti that he was interested in using him for "charity" and invited him to be his guest for dinner at a folksy Jewish restaurant, where he introduced him around as if he were Babe Ruth and Lou Gehrig rolled into one.

As barefaced as it was, Matti had enjoyed the flattery and adulation. Over coffee, Levin asked what he thought of the Series the year before. Matti and everyone else in the American League knew that last year's Series wasn't on the level, but all he answered was that the Cincinnati victory came as quite a surprise. His host answered laconically, "Not to everyone." Yes, Matti said that he had heard that, too, but what about the rumored grand jury investigation in

Chicago? Might not indictments come as quite a surprise, too? "Not to everyone," Levin admitted. He added contritely that the whole business had been very sloppy, but in spite of that, they weren't going to get anyone higher than the players. Levin's joyous certainty that only the little fish would wind up in the net seemed an unsavory augury to Matti. The coffee suddenly tasted as bitter as a prison term.

"I'm a second-string catcher," he responded.

"No, not now. Since Swede got hurt, you're first string, but if you don't collect now for turning the club into a winner, you never will." Levin had hammered the table for justice.

The whole thing was idiotic. Half the Chicago White Sox team was under investigation. Given the character and education of the simple farm boys, under any sort of severe direct examination they were sure to crack. Especially if the rumors of a double cross were true. One rumor had it that the syndicate never came through with the remainder of the dough. The other, that the former first baseman, Chick Gandil, didn't deliver to his own teammates. Either way, Chick was in trouble; everybody had him on the other team.

"You want Chick to have a minyan in Alcatraz?" Matti asked.

"Too many were involved, and they were stepping on each other's toes. But with the Browns' bozo pitchers, you can control the game. With just one man in one game—you. Nothing bad can happen."

Matti looked at him noncommittally, then shook his head. "It's not for me," he said.

"There's a lot of money in it," Levin promised.

Matti shook his head again.

"In advance, and it would be a game against a good

club. One that would be favored over the Browns anyway. We aren't talking about a risky long shot; we're talking about a sure thing. No one would suspect a thing."

"No, it's not for me."

"Why not?" Levin asked in earnest disappointment that suggested poor Matti just did not realize what a true and righteous friend Abe Levin could be.

"Baseball's been good to me," Matti said in quiet simplicity.

"It could be better," the ex-fighter rejoined enthusiastically, as if he were upping the bids.

"I hope so," said Matti with an innocent smile that said he wanted no part of it. "Thank you for supper, Mr. Levin," he added.

"Abe, call me Abe. Sure, kid. And they say you're the smartest man in baseball," Levin said in bitter jest.

Matti shrugged modestly, as if to suggest that it was not his problem. That was for others to decide.

On the teeming streets of the Jewish Lower East Side, Matti thought to himself that baseball had been good to him—but not good enough for him to marry Miss Penny Pinkham. Abe Levin made sense. Especially the part about the Browns' bozo pitchers and one man in one game. Only one part didn't make sense; Matti didn't need Abe Levin, a proven incompetent and an admitted fair-weather friend. Matti could do it alone with much less risk. He went down the street whistling like—well, like ten thousand bucks.

Even as he jauntily counted his projected winnings that night, he was aware that the fix involved some risk. Matti could never go to any bookmaker and bet against his own team. Nor could he send someone who would be recognized as his agent. He trusted his cousin Herbie, who had taken over his father's butcher shop, but the only book where Herbie could place a sizable bet knew that he was Matti's first cousin. Matti needed someone who bet often enough so that he would be a welcome customer in any number of shops. Ideally, he should be a foolish, unsuccessful bettor whose thousand or two on a favored team would not change the odds and whose winning would be attributed to dumb luck. After all, any dummy could bet on a favorite. Above all, it had to be someone whom Matti could trust and control.

Finding him had proven more difficult than Matti had thought, but Matti had been patient. He had always been patient—until he met Miss Penny Pinkham. But even though Penny was the initial stimulus for this wild project, Matti kept calm. He had no desire to become the cantor in Chick Gandil's synagogue behind bars. When Matti had almost despaired of finding the right man, it came to him in a flash. The perfect accomplice had been there all along under his very Krimsker nose.

## CHAPTER TEN

THE AMERICAN METAMORPHOSIS OF BARASCH LIMP LEGS fascinated all of Krimsk in St. Louis; even Matti succumbed to the general interest. In Krimsk the cripple had been the model of self-effacing, sober loyalty, a veritable human watchdog at Beryl Soffer's match factory. He had even remained at the match factory for several years after the rebbe had led the migration from Krimsk. Then Boruch Levi had sent his sister Malka a fine dowry, enough money for a first-rate wedding and passage for the new couple to America. To everyone's surprise, Barasch Limp Legs accepted the proposal and appeared in St. Louis on the bride's beefy arm.

Barasch arrived in Beryl Soffer's old hand-me-down clothing, looking like the Barasch Limp Legs of old, but almost immediately a new, unimagined personality emerged. A gambling, womanizing, drinking dandy, he always wore a tie and a vest with a gold watch chain, and he specialized in the houndstooth check patterns favored by lively young bachelors and drummer salesmen. In addition, he sported a neat derby that managed to stay on his head through the bobbing gyrations of his unchanged gait. There were limits to New World magic; in America he remained a cripple, but even that no longer seemed so disabling, and it certainly did not appear ludicrous, merely unfortunate.

In Krimsk, where he had always wanted to please, his sycophantic actions had appeared horsey, grotesque, foolish, and awkward. In St. Louis he did not try to curry anyone's favor; as befitted one on the frontier, he was very much his own man and after his own fashion took to heart Jefferson's Declaration of Independence: he loved life, reveled in liberty, and pursued happiness. Enjoying the good things in life with a frolicsome verve, he exhibited a patrician detachment, a particularly American aristocratic mien.

There were moments when a crippled foreigner pursuing his pleasures might meet with laughter, even ridicule, but he refused to let such things wound him. He treated such incidents with a dignity and distance that gave little pleasure to his persecutors. He had that invulnerability that protects the aristocrat in the marketplace: he is believed to be different by his possession of some unique knowledge of life, and therefore the normal standards—and barbs—are inappropriate.

This dignity never deserted him, even in the most undignified situations. In bordellos, he was continuously drawn as if by an unseen magnet to any wispy blond young woman; such a female reminded him of his Krimsk employer's wife, Faigie Soffer. The delicate midwestern women who stirred this remembrance were treated to a rare gentility. Only at that brutally sensitive moment when the wave of passion receded, giving way to remorse and memory's bitter return, did Barasch lose his composure and moan, "Faigie, Faigie! Oy, yoy, yoy."

The providers of his pleasure and pain were offended to have the truth told that they were the wrong persons and further insulted to have it uttered over their naked bodies in such Old World melancholy. On his future visits they would exact their revenge by greeting him with, "Want to make a little 'Faigie, Faigie, oy, yoy, yoy?'" Even that taunting Barasch could handle with a distant, gentle, honest dignity; that was, after all, what he wanted. And if he did not return, those blond, wispy women missed him and envied the mysterious Faigie, for he was a strong, respectful lover, and very, very gentle. "Faigie, Faigie, oy, yoy, yoy." Yes, that was their Bernard.

Although he responded to "Barasch," he called himself Bernard. Local Krimskers, naturally, continued to call him "Barasch" to his face (Matti, of course, very calculatingly called him Bernard), but behind his back, he became known as "Bernard Limp Legs." Had he heard the nickname, it would not have bothered him; it would be their problem, not his. Krimskers called him "Bernard Limp Legs" not as a nasty jibe so much as a well-earned tribute. They were rooting for him. He was living, drinking, whoring, gambling, elegant proof that they had come to the right place at the right time. You want to know what America is? Just look at our Bernard Limp Legs! God bless America!

Matti shared this enthusiasm and had been delighted with the idea of having the most amazing New World success of the older generation as his betting accomplice. With his dignity and humane charm, coupled with his unabashed pursuit of gentlemanly vices and that awful wife, Malka, Barasch was the perfect partner. Or so it had seemed.

Matti gave Barasch a few tips on which games the bookmakers' odds might be beaten at. More often than not he was correct, but to Matti's surprise, Barasch did not get very excited about winning. Matti was perplexed; unlike every other man he knew who loved to gamble, the results neither elated nor distressed Barasch. The act of gambling itself seemed to fulfill him, and his lack of success proved it. Behind Malka's back, Barasch bet small amounts on baseball without the least understanding of the game, much less of the teams playing any given game. Barasch's betting on baseball was the equivalent of another man's buying a lottery ticket. With one important exception, however: people purchase lottery tickets in the hope of winning.

Why, Matti wondered, did Barasch gamble? Perhaps the thrill lay in Malka's disapproval. She didn't mind his going to prostitutes; she even supplied him with the money. This aspect of their relationship shocked Matti as deeply as it did most of the local Krimskers. But, Matti reasoned, if slovenly Malka laughed slyly at Barasch's other women, his drinking, and his dress, those other endeavors might not provide the essential ingredient that gambling did— the piquant thrill of cheating on his suffocatingly vulgar, possessive wife.

Matti suggested to Barasch that together, with his information and Barasch's placing of the bets, they could make a real killing. At the word "killing," Barasch blanched, as if Matti had suggested that they commit a real murder.

"I thought you might want some money so you could

afford your own pleasure without having to depend on your wife," Matti said.

"No, I couldn't do that. Malka works so hard for us," Barasch explained, a statement that thoroughly dumbfounded Matti and left him in despair.

Matti had pretty much given up the whole project when early one morning, his phone rang. Half asleep, he answered, and a voice that at first he did not recognize asked him, "Is that young, slight blond nurse the reason you need so much money?"

Caught off guard by the early hour and by Barasch's earnestness, Matti answered truthfully.

"Then I think we have to get your project moving," Barasch replied.

Matti never understood why Penny Pinkham should have had such an electrifying effect on Barasch. So far as he knew, Barasch had never even spoken to her. But Barasch was now burning to fix the game, although Matti could not convince him to put down any of his own money on the sure thing.

Barasch maniacally insisted that whenever Matti called him, he use rigamarole code words about Krimsk such as "the match factory," "Krimichak," and "Froika's violin." In fact, at times Matti feared that Penny Pinkham had entered Barasch's head and unhinged his mind. At such moments, Matti suddenly thought he was glimpsing the clownish Barasch Limp Legs of Krimsk. Barasch's magical transformation seemed to unravel right before Matti's eyes. Matti remained convinced that Barasch's honesty and dedication—his Krimsk hallmarks with Beryl Soffer—would serve him equally well with his new American master, but these strange developments made Matti uncomfortable. He felt relieved that he was about to put their plan into motion. Yes, he had better find a private phone to make the fateful call. The sooner they finished with this, the better for both of them.

# CHAPTER ELEVEN

As Matti entered a grill across the street from the ballpark, the proprietor greeted him warmly. A combination of nerves and nine innings behind home plate contributed to a dry throat. He had sipped over a quart of cool water in the locker room, but what he really felt like having was a cold beer. Downstairs, they had a speakeasy.

Prohibition puzzled Matti; it was one of the few things that made him feel alien, even like a worldly European. Instead of serving beer upstairs, as they always had in the clean, bright, well-ventilated grill, they all ran to drink it in a dark, dirty basement at twice the price—like little children closing their eyes and playing blind man's buff.

Could America be so simple? Perhaps, Matti had thought, they are so simple that they don't hate the Jews. Prohibition had amused him; suddenly it did so no longer. Matti was annoyed and not very tolerant of America's "noble experiment." After his conversation with Penny, Americans no longer seemed so childlike and innocent. It was worldly Matti who had been going around with his eyes closed, stumbling about like a fool. Matti sensed that if he opened his eyes to Prohibition, it would be more than a silly inconvenience; it would be something ominously corrupt that not only infested the subterranean darkness but also spread it.

Matti settled for a soda and took it with him into the office. He closed the door for privacy. Often he had called Penny from here. Sipping the icy drink, he stared at the black telephone and then at his pocket watch. It was a touch too early, so with evident relief he called his mother.

"No, my friend can't make it, Ma. He's busy."

"What's so busy that he doesn't eat supper?" she asked.

"You'll have to ask him. I'll be over by seven," he said.

He spoke to her in a loud voice, so that anyone listening would be able to hear clearly. After hanging up, he casually finished the soda, then checked his watch. This was it. By now Malka should be out in the junkyard, receiving the peddlers' daily collections. Matti had seen the ragtag procession with their handcarts, the more fortunate with their horses and wagons, lining up next to the scale house, waiting their turn to approach Malka. She, with her big black purse under her arm, weighed their loads and paid in cold cash right on the spot, regally refusing to discuss her prices. She had better be out of the house, or Barasch would never be able to leave, not once she knew he was speaking to Matti.

Matti could hear the phone ringing in the kitchen.

"Hello," Barasch said.

"Bernard?"

"Yes, speaking."

"Bernard, I'm calling from the Soffer match factory," Matti said, identifying himself as Barasch had insisted.

"How's everything at the factory?" Barasch asked. Matti could hear the excitement in his voice.

"Not so good. Tomorrow afternoon at ten after one, Weinbach will have the upper hand," Matti answered. "Can you hear me?"

"Tomorrow afternoon Weinbach has the upper hand at ten after one," Barasch repeated.

"Yes, that's it," Matti said. He added, dropping any attempt at disguise, "Be careful. Don't let her see you go out."

"Don't worry about a thing. She's not even around," Barasch fairly bubbled.

"She's not down in the yard receiving the peddlers?" Matti asked suspiciously.

"No, I had the children turn them away. No one's in the yard."

"Then where is she?"

"As long as she's not here, what do we care? Just relax. Tomorrow afternoon Weinbach has the upper hand at ten after one, right?" Barasch recapitulated.

"Yes, that's it," Matti said with no enthusiasm.

"Good, I understand. Good-bye," Barasch said with enough enthusiasm for both of them.

The conversation should have ended there, but Matti quickly called, "Bernard," before Barasch could hang up.

"Yes?" Barasch asked, somewhat surprised.

"*Gut Shabbos.*" Matti hung up. He stared at the black earpiece in his hand as if it could give him a clue as to why he had at the last minute felt compelled to wish Barasch a good Sabbath. What did the Sabbath that would begin at sundown have to do with anything? Was it because they both seemed to be on their way back to Krimsk—Matti thinking about Jews and goyim all the time, and Barasch lurching around like Beryl Soffer's private scarecrow? What would Barasch make of such nonsense? Matti smiled ironically. Barasch would attribute any strange behavior to Matti's pure, innocent, unrequited love for Miss Penny Pinkham. Matti wasn't about to tell him about his surprise phone call to his true love.

Matti replaced the earpiece in its cradle and decided that he felt like a beer, even if he had to descend into that rathole for it. Barasch was in such a rush, he would probably have all the bets down before the beer got to the filthy table. But where was that horse Malka? She was a crafty one, and her absence bothered him.

# CHAPTER TWELVE

MALKA HAD MADE A TELEPHONE CALL, CHANGED FROM her coveralls into a black dress, climbed into her beat-up Dort truck, and driven out of the junkyard without bothering to close the gate behind her, something she never forgot to do.

At the moment, she didn't give a damn about the yard; the peddlers could wait until tomorrow morning for all she cared. If they went to some other junk dealer, she could always raise her prices and bring them scurrying back. Her pride and joy, her physical delight, the father of her children (her "little red-haired bastards," as she herself publicly referred to them) worried her to distraction. How could she raise her price to bring Barasch back when she didn't even know what the price was? For no apparent reason he seemed hell-bent on destroying himself, the wonderful and noble creation that she referred to as her glorious "Commodore Vanderbilt."

No one was prouder of Barasch's unexpected metamorphosis than was his ungainly and unchanging mate.

She too found her bent-wing butterfly a symbol of New World blessings, taking a stubborn, perverse, patronizing pride in his ability to Americanize so successfully.

She worked hard in her fitful, inconsistent, cutthroat manner and made a good living for them. Although he did not work, he never had to ask her for money; she gave generously, even affectionately. Working in an old army overcoat and unlaced boots in the junkyard, she could turn away from the brass pipes she was sorting, call Barasch over, and present him with a ten-dollar bill, saying, "Just look at you, go downtown and get yourself a new pair of shoes. Some Commodore Vanderbilt I have."

This last epithet was particularly dear to her; although Barasch had been among the last of the older generation to arrive, he spoke the best English and occasionally passed himself off successfully as a Dutchman who had fallen off a windmill as a boy. In her voracious way, Malka employed the story for her own purposes. Lifting the blanket from her massive, pale flesh, she would command him to enter by saying, "Maybe the little Dutch boy wants to try the windmill again?" And her Barasch would accept with a gracious, "Yes, my dear."

High as his perch was, here he was well-rooted, with a sturdy limb, and he never slipped. He was consistent, always treating his wife with dignity and respect. In their conjugal unions she was capable of many moods—from wild, pig-eyed passion to cool, ironic detachment, as if two old neighborhood acquaintances had bumped into each other at a department store basement rainwear sale. Then she might become casually conversational and inquire, "What do you say?" Barasch would always say, "May God bless us with healthy, kosher children," continuing his forceful efforts toward that end. An answer that even the shameless Malka did not ridicule until she bore five stout, ruddy babies, who all looked like her, with square jaws, pig eyes, and hair the color of rusting iron in the junkyard outside the window. (Years later, as they grew to majestic heights, his genetic contribution would become noticeable.)

When carrying the first child, she taunted him that he had never dreamed he was so potent. He told her that he had already proven himself with Faigie, Beryl Soffer's wife. Malka burst into ribald, preening laughter and lifted up her skirts, and the invitation to the "Dutch boy" of windmill fame gave way to one for "*Beryl* Limp Legs to come guard your yard."

Sex was the real thing. She was more than amused; she was proud to have shared her Barasch with Faigie Soffer, the grand dame of Krimsk, and to share him with the American-born goyish professional ladies of the night. She wisely permitted him to roam and to romp; after all, he was a gentleman. But in her slovenly way, she was confident, and with good reason. She knew that she could always better the competition's offer. When the juices flowed, and there was no drought in those regions, she thrust and clutched and ravished him with kisses that came close to dislodging his head. Of course, the next time, she might command him to enter and hold him in an inescapable bearlike embrace and then proceed to "fart like a windmill," to her sly, chuckling delight. Love was always so astonishing to Malka!

In public, too, she was proud as a peacock of her man. She never missed a chance to sit next to him at a Krimsker gathering—he in his elegant sartorial splendor and she in a plain rag, as if someone had dropped a poorly cut kitchen curtain over a bulky wood-burning stove. With her legs wide apart and a heavy purse on her lap—as if to advertise that she had all the merchandisable goods in any market—she would survey the throng with a gap-toothed smile that suggested it was their good fortune that cannibalism was out of style. Through all the aggression and power, the rapacious scorn and ribald challenge, a femininity—situated between her thighs to be sure—never left her even as she waxed rich in the purse above.

Malka understood excess better than anyone alive. If Barasch returned drunk, she sobered him up in a business-like way with cold water. Not cruelly, but not kindly either. "Thank God you're a cripple, Barasch Limp Legs. How the world would suffer!" she would guffaw between buckets. But suffer from what? From Barasch who as a whole man would be capable of Herculean feats of debauchery? Or from Barasch the whole man who would have no need to treat the world with such unbalanced, immoderate excess? Not one given to idle speculation or dreams, she never did say.

Although Malka willingly subsidized Barasch's wastrel pursuits, she would not tolerate one thing about Barasch—his suffering. She could not stand to see him in physical pain or the object of ridicule. When the damp cold attacked his maimed joints with arthritis or rheumatism, she would carry him in her arms like a baby into the truck and from the truck straight into the sweltering steam bath, oblivious of the other customers, who, grabbing their sheets about them, would howl with indignation. She would leave a healthy tip with the attendant to make sure that Barasch would be massaged and coddled until she came back at the end of the day to help him home. When it came to ridicule, a junkman or driver who unwisely made some remark about a "gimp," a "limp," or a "crooked scarecrow" tasted her anger and, if close enough, felt her pummeling blows.

Malka gripped the steering wheel as she recalled one distant Sunday afternoon when she was walking on her gentleman's arm to visit a Krimsker acquaintance in St. Louis. Suddenly two less than virtuous women across the street recognized Bernard and burst forth in girlish giggles and catcalls that ended in their chanting, "Bernie, Bernie, he's our boy! Faigie, Faigie, oy, yoy, yoy!"

There was no mistaking whom they were yelling at, nor who they were. Barasch tried to calm her by patting her arm and telling her to pay them no mind, but his wife and protector was not to be denied. In her shapeless black tent, she leaped into the street with deadly bovine grace and was upon the two buxom, corn-fed girls. With the momentum of her sudden and unexpected arrival, she dealt the first a blow to the face that broke her nose and sent her sprawling on the sidewalk. The second made the first of two mistakes in not fleeing, and lost two teeth. She crumpled to the ground at Malka's feet and then committed her second error; she started to get up. By gripping her beribboned hair, Malka assisted her ascent until she was high enough to receive a ferocious kick in the backside that sent her sailing through the air. Like a monstrously large rag doll, she flew over the recumbent figure of her associate.

Breathing heavily from the outrage—the exertion itself compared to her daily workout throwing metal in the junkyard had proven minimal—she returned to Barasch's arm.

"Darling," Barasch said, "they're just silly children."

That very night she lifted the blanket and ordered, "Beryl Limp Legs, how about a little 'Faigie, Faigie, oy, yoy, yoy'?" He answered, "Yes, dear," and that night he fathered their first healthy, kosher child, a pig-eyed lusting prince of the junkyards, as she, Barasch's devoted wife, mixed and served her loving husband a medley of passion, farts, medical history, and low comedy.

Such sweet marital memories brought tears to her eyes, and she squinted through them to see the road. How wonderful it all had been! She pulled the truck to the side of the road and stopped to wipe her eyes, but before she could do so, the tears had already turned to bitter stinging anger as she thought of Matti Sternweiss and his effect on her man. Since Barasch's friendship with Matti had begun, he seemed to return to the way he had been in Krimsk. She, too, had noticed the ungainly equine Krimsk gait. How could she not have noticed? His derby was dented and filthy from tumbling off his head into the dust, and he kept retracting his upper lip and baring those large teeth with a snorting sound. When she spoke to him about his appalling regression, he responded with an uncouth, horsey laugh that she had not heard since the night he had proposed in Krimsk.

Uncomfortable as she was with his deteriorating appearance, she was equally distressed with his constant running off to the bookie to play Matti's incessant tips. Often successful, Barasch inevitably bet the winnings and never finished with so much as a cent. And Malka knew that these small but dangerous bets were part and parcel of Barasch's degeneration at the hands of that sordid, arrogant little Matti Sternweiss. That baseball clown had to be stopped, and Barasch had to return to his role as the ideal American gentleman.

Well, thought Malka, not quite everyone saw Barasch as a symbol of New World blessings. Her sexually puritanical brother Boruch Levi, who was responsible for Barasch's immigration and indirectly responsible for his well-being and high lifestyle—he had set up Malka in her own junk-yard—disapproved of him totally. Once, observing the transformed Barasch as he gallantly charmed a social gathering, Boruch Levi muttered to his sister with disgust, "Over there he licked asses, here he pinches them." Delighting in her brother's revulsion, she smiled and replied, "Yes, brother, that's true, but don't forget that here it's a rich soup for all of us. Over there, there was nobody to pinch my ass, and there certainly wasn't anybody to lick yours!" With a scowl that would cause every junk peddler in the city to cringe, Boruch Levi walked away from his sister's vulgar mouth.

Malka laughed now as she put the truck into gear, just as she had laughed that night; but it wasn't a laughing matter any longer. She had dressed this afternoon as a "lady" so as not to offend her brother, the pious aristocrat of the junk business. Although she had welcomed him home after his visit to Krimsk—only a madman would want to go back there!—she had never really apologized for the incident before he left. This afternoon she would even apologize if necessary; there was nothing he loved more than that. Yes, she would do what was needed to soothe his injured pride. Afterward, she could always bruise it again easily enough, but for now she had better be respectful, very respectful.

As she turned onto the levee, the cobblestones caused the truck to bump and shake. She slowed down to protect the beat-up old truck and quiet the palpitations of her own heart. Rough, brawling Malka was fearful. She had protected her man against all comers, but could she protect Barasch from himself?

# CHAPTER THIRTEEN

Although he had arrived late, Boruch Levi had put in a very productive day on the levee. He had supervised the loading of two boxcars with wiping rags and a third with roofing. Two more cars of scrap metal left the yard for the mill. Skipping lunch, he sipped two coffees from the diner next door while doing business on the phone with various junk shops in southern Illinois. In the midst of his buying and selling, he had managed to squeeze in a call to the Krimsker Rebbe's sexton. Mentioning that he had just visited Krimsk and had regards for the rebbe, Boruch Levi spontaneously asked whether he could do anything for the wondrous spiritual leader. To his delight and surprise, Reb Zelig requested that he attend prayers at the rebbe's beis midrash this very Friday evening.

Boruch Levi had established contact with the rebbe for the first time since leaving Krimsk almost twenty years ago, and he had been invited to the beis midrash. This also solved the problem of where Boruch Levi himself would pray and made him confident that he would resolve the problem posed by Rabbi Max's insubordination. In an optimistic mood, he settled into his office and assumed his favorite position.

Boruch Levi loved to sit back in his rolling swivel chair with his feet up on the desk as his workers filed through the office on their way home. His reclining position reflected both the boss's royal prerogative and his denigration of the white-collar world of accounts and pencils. For all his financial success, Boruch Levi had never mastered English, although he could read rudimentary street signs and write his own name. With his precocious memory and aptitude for figures, he had no need to. The business was in the buying and the selling. For that you needed a good quick head. The scale house was more important than any desk. Boruch Levi never put his feet up on the balance arm of a scale. That was where you fed your family. The office was simply a perquisite of success, somewhere between a good cigar and a fine automobile.

More than mere possessions, Boruch Levi valued his close friendship with Michael O'Brien, chief of police. He also cherished his place in the synagogue next to the holy ark on the eastern wall (although there were undeniably some minor problems at the moment in that sphere). Once he had established such bonds, they remained fixed, and he would remain faithful though the sky turn to brass and the earth to iron. Boruch Levi—the right hand of both powers, secular and divine. Seated at his desk on a Friday afternoon, or next to the chief himself on the way to a raid, Boruch Levi inspired in any onlooker the biblical phrase, "the proud man's contumely."

For all his social pretense and scornful haughtiness, Boruch Levi had a perverse, brutal honesty that saved him from his most pompous self. He still enjoyed rags, scrap metal, and used bottles. They constituted an economic reality that he understood above all others. In the junkyard he was a full captain, and nobody's lieutenant. If society's esteem—which Boruch Levi craved and pursued—did not extend to junk, too bad for society. Boruch Levi, for all his airs, was not about to reject his basic identity. There was no dilemma for him. Proud and loyal, he honored that particular cornucopia—in this case waste and scrap filled—that bestowed upon him its riches.

Business was going very well, and his relationship with the chief and other top police brass—how he loved those shiny, orderly double-breasted buttons—couldn't be better, especially after last week's raid. The chief's hand had improved, and he was back at his desk at headquarters.

His wife and child were fine, thank God. Both in Krimsk and in St. Louis, his marriage to Golda was a source of satisfaction and pride. She was a quiet, religious woman who kept a good home, cared for her family, and cooked the traditional dishes. Golda wasn't from Krimsk itself, but from Sufnitz, the largest town in the region—according to Sufnitzers, the only town. They thought themselves cosmopolitan and viewed Krimsk as a hapless backwater on the River Nedd. In Sufnitz, Golda's father and grandfather had been teachers, and Golda was very well educated; she could read and write both Yiddish and Hebrew. In the old country her family never would have consented for Boruch Levi to stand under the marriage canopy with her. Although he did not descend from a line of scholars, he had inherited poverty in abundance. In America he had acquired wealth if not education, whereas Golda's family retained their impressive scholarship, their disabling poverty, and their numerous daughters. So in St. Louis the match had been made. In the old country, poor scholars were matched with rich men's daughters, whereas in America rich men married poor scholars' daughters. The Krimsker wags said that it was the complete Old World–New World match and that Boruch Levi should have paid the matchmaker double, because he was as rich as she was poor, and she was as educated as he was ignorant. Golda was a worrier and a bit timid; Boruch Levi attributed those blemishes to her having grown up as a child too close to so many books, but after all she was only a woman, so it didn't matter. He did not appreciate such traits in his son Sammy, but he knew that Yitzhak Weinbach thought the boy sensitive and intelligent. Yitzhak even thought that Sammy would make a good lawyer. That might not be bad at all.

Only the thought of his sister made Boruch Levi scowl. Malka had phoned his secretary to say that she would be coming by to see him. If she was driving down to the levee and not dropping by the house on Saturday night, as she had when she greeted him on his return from Krimsk, she must want something very substantial. He couldn't imagine that her problem was financial. Junk prices were up, and anyone with any sense was making a few dollars. No doubt Malka, even with her sloppy management, was making her fair share. She could buy and sell all right, and on the scale she was a real operator, even if she didn't always open the yard early enough or know exactly what she had in inventory. She had her business talents, thank God, but the things she could say! His sister had a mouth like a torn pocket.

The memory of the insult she had delivered earlier in

the summer, before his trip back to the old country, still rankled. With Barasch and the children she had come by on a Saturday afternoon to say good-bye, and as usual she had started a quarrel. This time she suggested that had Boruch Levi really been a decent son, he would have managed to visit Krimsk while Mama was still alive and not five years after her death. He had answered that it had been Malka who had left their mother in Europe to suffer during the war; he had sent enough money for her to come to America with Malka and Barasch. Malka replied that she was sure Mama had heard about Boruch Levi's violating the Sabbath in St. Louis and didn't want to see her beloved son carrying on like a goy. He had answered that the Sabbath was only one day, while Mama had had to suffer Malka's flying skirts seven days a week.

Flushing crimson, Malka had turned away; Boruch Levi had called to his eight-year-old son Sammy that it was time to go to the synagogue for the afternoon prayers. They had been wrangling on the second-floor balcony, and Malka remained there with the rest of both their families. When he had reached the street, she called his name in a voice loud enough for the whole street to hear. He stopped and turned to watch his sister raise her skirt above her waist and thrust her backside down at him, calling with derision, "Brother, dear, you can kiss my ass!"

Had his child and wife not been watching, he would have rushed upstairs and given her a few slaps worth remembering. As it was, he turned his back and continued on to the synagogue.

Boruch Levi's trip to Krimsk had gone very well. Distributing almost fifteen thousand dollars in charity—half of it his personal gift, half raised from other successful for-mer Krimskers—he had been received as a prince. Every-one had come running to welcome him the first night at Beryl Soffer's. He delivered letters, gifts, and personal greet-ings from the Krimsker community in the New World, but he also talked, listened, and observed.

Krimsk, now Kromsk, was part of the proud new Polish republic, since the Polish general Pilsudski had succeeded in repelling the invading Bolshevik forces. Fortunately for both Krimsk and Kromsk, the ravaging warfare had oc-curred across the River Nedd, so that except for the name of the town, very little had changed. Without being asked, on the very next day Boruch Levi imperiously summoned the Krimskers for private audiences and began donating money for dowries, business loans, grants to take chroni-cally ill children to see specialists in Warsaw, stipends for talented young boys to pursue secular or religious studies, and a substantial donation to repair the decrepit but well-populated old folks' home. Krimsk insisted that he sit on the beis midrash's eastern wall, and when he entered the old folks' home, the residents, struggling with crutches and canes, all rose with tears in their eyes and blessed him as if he were a baron like Rothschild of Paris or Gunzburg of Mos-cow. He for his part responded aristocratically by shaking hands and exchanging a few words with every individual. He left with tears in his eyes and decided that while in Krimsk he must show himself worthy of their praise by wearing a suit and tie every day and not playing cards.

Originally, in addition to distributing charity, Boruch Levi had hoped to indulge himself in those luxuries that he had not been able to afford but had dreamed of as a boy:

leisure, play, rich food, and strong drink. His newfound dress and decorum, however, created an unanticipated seriousness of presence and purpose. He visited with many people, and although the discussions contained the sweet, romanticized remembrance of his unhappy youth and the equally satisfying glorification of his successful present, they often focused on the difference between Krimsk and St. Louis. If everyone was so wealthy in St. Louis, why did they work on the Sabbath? If kosher meat was so good and plentiful, why didn't they eat it rather than the food of the goyim? And the most basic question: if Jews were not persecuted for being Jews, and there was no problem living like a Jew, why didn't they live like Jews? In Poland, as in Russia, there were economic and social rewards for surrendering one's Jewishness, and yet few did so; in America, where the rewards seemed meager, so many did!

Sweating in his suit and tie—Kromsk summers proved no cooler than Krimsk's had been—he sweated more when asked these troubling questions. He had never stopped to think about them before. Everything seemed so obvious standing in Krimsk's dusty, unpaved streets, and everything had seemed equally obvious while motoring along in his Hupmobile at thirty miles an hour down the broad boulevard that bordered on St. Louis's Forest Park. He just didn't know, and when they asked him why he had returned to religion—the earliest Sabbath violations had been excoriated in the mails back to Krimsk; later the subject discreetly disappeared from most correspondence altogether—and why only he had bothered to visit them, he told the truth. His mother had appeared to him in a dream requesting him to become religious. Boruch Levi didn't tell them, however, that in St. Louis he had told almost no one of his dream. Just as he felt comfortable, even proud, to relate so miraculous a dream in Krimsk, he had been uncomfortable and embarrassed to reveal such an odd, mystical event in St. Louis.

It all seemed to come back to the same problem: Krimsk was Krimsk and America was America, even though the two seemed to be inhabited by the same people. As for why he had returned to Krimsk, he did somewhat better answering that; he had come to visit his mother's grave. After such a dream, it seemed the obvious and appropriate thing to do. And, too, he told them that he wanted to show off in his hometown, which knew him as an impoverished, uneducated half-orphan, what a success he had become by giving large amounts to charity. He surprised himself with his honesty, but he could not resist giving some of the few answers he happened to know.

Initially he had feared questions about the Krimsker Rebbe, since he had lost touch with him, but he confidently answered queries about where the rebbe lived, whether he gave interviews and bestowed blessings, and the state of health of the rebbe and the rebbetzin. Boruch Levi even told them proudly about the rebbe's selection as a member of the Governor's Council on Indian Affairs and his rejection of the prestigious position. Krimsk enjoyed and understood that, too, all right; who was more talented than their wonder-working rebbe, and who had ever fled from all honors and wealth as their holy rebbe had?

Strolling through Krimsk, Boruch Levi found himself thinking about the Krimsker Rebbe. Only the rebbe remained constant. He had been an enigma in Krimsk, and he was an enigma in St. Louis. Why had he secluded himself for five years in Krimsk? Why had he left for America? Why did he study and live among the Indians in the Osage reservation? No one knew, but at least he had remained the same. In both Krimsk and St. Louis he had excelled intellectually, and in both places he had refused honors and wealth. Boruch Levi intuitively felt that the rebbe and only the rebbe knew why Krimsk and St. Louis were so distant that when a man stood in one he could not imagine or remember standing in the other. No wonder they did not ask more penetrating questions about the rebbe. What was there for them to ask? But there was something for Boruch Levi to ask—the difference between Krimsk and St. Louis. Only the rebbe, the constant, harmonious, and holy rebbe seemed capable of integrating the two worlds.

With these surprising and admiring, almost worshipful feelings toward the rebbe, Boruch Levi began to ponder the events of that last fateful Tisha B'Av in Krimsk. The rebbe had counseled him not to go to America. But then the rebbe had suddenly decided to go to America himself! The rebbe appeared to have lied to him, and in response Boruch Levi rebelled against God, the rebbe, and his mother, may she rest in peace. But now Boruch Levi thought that something must have happened that night of the rebbe's return to his congregation, or perhaps at the moment when the rebbe witnessed the Angel of Death synagogue burning and the Torah being rescued—something that led the rebbe to change his mind about America. If that was so, the rebbe had not betrayed him but had been faithful to his newer prophetic insights.

Boruch Levi's stay in Krimsk lengthened, and he tarried at leisure in the shade of old walls near which he had played and under trees he had climbed. As he skimmed stones in the pond and prayed in the beis midrash on the eastern wall—there were limits to his reflective humility—he was struck by his affinity for Krimsk. After all, only he had returned. Although he relished his success in America and was growing anxious to return to the world of paved streets, trucks, trains, Victrolas, telephones, and indoor plumbing, he could not deny that Krimsk was part of him and part of him was Krimsk, even if he could not integrate or even understand the relationship between the two. In that sense, he was as different from all the others who remained in Krimsk as he was from those in St. Louis. Perhaps Boruch Levi really did belong in Krimsk, and the Krimsker Rebbe had recognized that unique quality when he had commanded Boruch Levi to stay. Boruch Levi felt a growing need for the rebbe but feared that the rebbe might not welcome him again, since Boruch Levi had not taken his advice earlier.

Such reflective analysis made him uncomfortable. Krimsk offered other revelations that were less painful and often fascinating. Boruch Levi delivered gold watches from Barasch to Beryl and Faigie Soffer's two sons. Their healthy, normal younger boy was a source of great pride to the parents, but it was their older son, Itzik Dribble, who interested Boruch Levi. Itzik had developed into a tall, broad-shouldered man, but anyone who had seen him seventeen years before would still have recognized him instantly as Itzik Dribble. He had been limp along the edges as a child, and now that his edges had expanded so considerably, his dribble and droop were more pronounced. When he was a child, his spineless blond hair had hung limp upon his head; as a man he had a yellow beard that hung slack and meaningless from his face. Everyone knew that this idiot was the reason Beryl had remained in Krimsk, and for many who had gone to America, Itzik Dribble typified Krimsk, languishing hopelessly cursed and deficient through no fault of his own. Suddenly, seeing him in Krimsk, Boruch Levi was reminded of America's incredible mindless physical growth. Why? For what purpose? Itzik Dribble and America seemed like some child's balloon, inflating to grand proportions but without an inner structure to give it definition.

Both Beryl and Faigie expressed intense interest in their former watchman Barasch. Beryl cried when he heard how his "pure brother" had gone astray. He literally collapsed into a chair, and Faigie ran to bring him a glass of water. Beryl begged Boruch Levi to try and guide Barasch back to the religious path that he had walked in Krimsk. Wasn't Barasch a fine person? Beryl asked Faigie, and although she certainly agreed, Faigie, in her quiet way, seemed to breathe a sigh of relief when she heard of Barasch's scandalous carryings-on. Boruch Levi didn't know what to make of either reaction.

Dressed as an American—and therefore invisible as a Jew—Boruch Levi had strolled one afternoon across the bridge to the Polish town of Krimichak, which seemed as tired and unchanging as Krimsk. Perhaps even more so, because no one had left. On the way back over the River Nedd to Krimsk, he met a tired herdsman leading his cattle back to Krimichak from the meadows. The elements had tanned and parched his face into a leathery surface that made him look older than his forty-five or fifty years, but his carriage was still erect and his body strong; Boruch Levi greeted Wotek by name. The herdsman stopped in amazement and after some difficulty—and much encouragement—he recalled Boruch Levi, the junk peddler with the hopelessly swaybacked nag.

Wotek carefully eyed Boruch Levi's clothing and wondered aloud whether he had been made a baron in America. Then he wondered how long he had been gone. Boruch Levi mentioned that he had left soon after Grannie Zara had died and the large synagogue had burned. Those events Wotek remembered very well: the flaming devil with burning coals for eyes rushing straight from the flames. He spat three times in recollection of such a frightful apparition and then three more times in remembrance of the witch Grannie Zara. Then he added, "You know, they burned Zloty and the other cats. We didn't know that then. That was wrong, too."

Boruch Levi walked back to Krimsk, but that night he didn't sleep even though he had the softest featherbed in town. Was he afraid his recurring dream of the burning cats would return? It didn't, but Wotek's information seemed to confirm his suspicions that in the night of Tisha B'Av the rebbe had told him the truth about the seductive dangers of the Evil Inclination. At the time of his interview with the rebbe, the two fateful fires had not occurred: later that night the witch's home and the cats burned—and it wasn't until the following afternoon that the Angel of Death synagogue had gone up in flames as the young man miraculously emerged with the holy Torah intact. Boruch Levi suspected that in Krimsk the rebbe had not betrayed him so much as fate had surprised them both. The rebbe had informed him correctly that Boruch Levi would always make a good living. The question, the rebbe had said, was "not what kind of living, but what kind of life?" And here, once again back in Krimsk, Boruch Levi was wondering what kind of life. He thought that the rebbe would not be surprised if he knew that Boruch Levi was lying in bed in Krimsk pondering such things. Still, he wondered who the "they" were who had burned the dead witch's house with her cats inside; "they" had ignited both Krimsk and Krimichak.

In Krimsk, Boruch Levi persistently inquired about the "flaming devil with flaming coals for eyes," the man named Grisha to whom the rebbe had presented his daughter, Rachel Leah. They had married and departed from Krimsk not long after everyone else, but no one knew where they had gone or what had happened to them. There were rumors: they had gone to the Holy Land, they had been killed in the World War, Grisha had become a high-ranking Bolshevik and a friend of none other than that madman, Lenin. But nothing had been heard from them since their departure, and no one really knew anything for sure.

The night before Boruch Levi was to leave, Beryl Soffer gave a party in his honor. Everyone came, many with letters for him to deliver, and all blessed him as the most wonderful benefactor Krimsk had ever known. Later, when he was packing in his room, he heard a soft knock and opened the door to find Froika Waksman. On his visits to his old house, he had met Froika, who now lived alone in his family's old home and worked as a shoemaker, just as his late father had. Froika was saying kaddish for his mother, who had died in the winter. As an orphaned bachelor, Froika had time, and

Boruch Levi had had some searching talks with the young man. Froika had a good head on his shoulders and wasn't lazy; a man like that could go a long way in America, and Boruch Levi had offered to sponsor him. Froika had hesitated and said that he would let Boruch Levi know.

"Have you decided to leave?" Boruch Levi asked now.

"Yes," answered Froika somewhat reluctantly.

"But you don't seem certain."

"I am certain that I want to leave Krimsk," Froika said definitely.

"Then what's the problem? I'll certainly help you."

"I don't want to go to America. I would appreciate your help in going to the Land of Israel," he answered.

Boruch Levi was slightly surprised. They had discussed St. Louis and Krimsk; Palestine had never been mentioned.

"The Land of Israel?" Boruch Levi queried.

"Yes, I think sooner or later the goyim will destroy Krimsk. If not the Bolsheviks, then the Poles themselves—or someone else. I know you disagree, and I hope you're right, but that's what I believe, and that's why I want to leave Krimsk. Until you came, I had hoped to go to America like everyone else, but after talking with you, I don't think I want to," Froika said with a trace of embarrassment at disparaging his potential benefactor's new homeland.

"Why not?" Boruch asked.

"Well, if I'm leaving Krimsk because of the goyim, I don't think I should go some place where I will become one of them. Better I should go to a place where I shall be certain to remain a Jew."

"Don't I live like a Jew?"

"Yes, Boruch Levi, but you are different. You said so yourself. I'm not. I'm a simple Krimsk shoemaker," Froika answered.

"Yes, Froika, I shall do what you want on one condition. You must take your violin with you." Boruch Levi remembered how Froika's mother madly believed that her tone-deaf son would bring immense glory to the family by playing the violin in St. Petersburg before the tsar. In real life, Froika's cacophonous attempts with the instrument had sounded more torturous than the burning cats' screams that pierced Boruch Levi's nightmarish dreams.

Froika laughed. "That violin is reason enough to leave. It was so awful. That instrument of torture was the one thing you remembered about me as a child." But as he spoke, he realized that Boruch Levi wasn't laughing with him.

"You're not joking, are you?" he asked Boruch Levi.

"No, I'm not. That's the one condition: you take the violin."

Boruch Levi's square jaw was set. Froika had no doubt that if he wanted the man's help, he had to take the hideous violin.

"Why?"

"In America you would do very well as I have, and if you wanted to return here, you could, but Palestine is a poor country. If you go there, you will never return." What Boruch Levi didn't add was that his decision had something to do with the burning cats. That prophetic dream's relationship to all of this was unclear, and he wasn't about to tell Froika about the dream anyway. "That's the way it is; take it or leave it."

Froika shook his hand. "I'll take it. I'll take the infernal thing to the Holy Land, but if I ever play it, it's on your conscience and not mine," he said half seriously.

Boruch nodded judiciously, even pompously. "I'll send you the money. Whatever you need."

The next morning he visited his mother's grave for the last time. The wagon with his luggage waited outside the cemetery to take him to the train at Sufnitz. As he exited through the gate and climbed onto the seat alongside the driver, he felt that in St. Louis he had two irrevocable links to Krimsk. He would remain true to his mother, and that meant his sister Malka was all the more his responsibility. There would never be any escaping that. The other link was the Krimsker Rebbe, that enigmatic holy man.

Now as he sat in his office awaiting his sister, he sensed that today would be an opportunity to keep faith with his mother. It might be difficult, but he welcomed the challenge. How to keep faith with the Krimsker Rebbe was not so obvious, although he had already contacted Reb Zelig and would be praying with the rebbe this evening. Out of old loyalty, of course, he would never let his ex-rabbi remain in jail over the Sabbath. Even if Rabbi Max was a fool, he was a rabbi. For the poor he was a good rabbi, but didn't the fool understand that God had granted the rich their riches, too?

Boruch Levi looked up to see his sister enter the office.

# CHAPTER FOURTEEN

Malka settled herself into a chair near her brother's desk. His studious inattention to her meant that he was still steaming at the insult that she had delivered before his trip. This gave her such joy that she almost forgot why she had come. Stifling a smile, she put her purse on her lap, all business and propriety. She didn't want to call attention to the actual insult for fear that he would explode and then she would never get what she wanted, but she knew that she had better acknowledge his moral leadership.

"How is the synagogue?" she asked by way of an oblique apology.

Without looking at her, he emitted a low grunt that suggested that her interest was insincere and that she need not worry about it.

"The family?" she asked.

Again she received the same reply.

"Thank God," she said. "As Mama, may she rest in peace, used to say, health is everything."

Boruch Levi turned his unsympathetic scrutiny upon his sister. He couldn't stand her mentioning their mother. How such a fine, saintly woman could have borne such a vulgar, shameless creature as Malka was one of the more fantastic and less pleasant mysteries of creation.

"Boruch Levi, I am here because I need your help."

He didn't say anything, but she could see he was interested. There was nothing he liked better than lording it over everyone else as the great protector.

"I'm worried about my Barasch. He has been acting strangely lately, and I don't like it."

"What's the matter? He hasn't been running around like a meshuggenner?" Boruch Levi growled.

Malka looked her brother straight in the eye.

"I know that Barasch is not to your liking, brother, but I was no princess and had no choice the way you did with your highborn Golda, a teacher's daughter no less. I was ugly, ignorant, and poor. I did what Mother told me to do, and after her death I'm still obeying her."

Boruch Levi turned away to avoid her deprecating and accusing confession. Malka smiled behind his back. When all was said and done, her brother had no instinct for the jugular.

"What's wrong?" he asked.

"I think Matti Sternweiss is the problem," she said.

"That little bum? That ballplayer?" Boruch Levi said in grandiloquent scorn. He said "ballplayer" with considerably more derision than he said "bum."

"Yes," Malka replied, only too pleased to help him focus his anger on a common enemy.

"He's a nothing," Boruch Levi said.

"Yes, but as Mama used to say, 'He's a nothing, but even a cat can still cross your path and ruin your life.' Since he became Barasch's best friend, I have no rest. Barasch is always running off to the bookie."

"You want me to talk to Barasch or Matti?" he asked.

"Neither. I want you to talk to the bookie."

He took his feet off the desk and sat up. "The bookie?"

"Yes, and I don't want Barasch to know anything about it."

"What did the bookie do? Let me talk to your man; I'll straighten him out, and I'll see to it that Matti spends more time in the ballpark," he stated with authoritarian certainty.

"No, I'll not embarrass him!" Malka shot back. Her face flushed in anger.

Boruch Levi received his shameless, taunting sister's hot reaction with sarcastic amusement. That jewel is her pride and joy, after all. Like they say, it's the right rag for the right *tuchis*. He laughed, and Malka flushed in embarrassment.

"I don't want my man shamed. I don't care what happens."

"I didn't know he embarrassed so easily."

She opened her great purse and took out a man's handkerchief. Tears flooded her eyes as if she were peeling onions; she wiped them with no sign of emotion.

"There's a lot you don't know, Brother. If you want Mama's grandchildren to grow up with the man she picked to be their father—"

She poked at her eyes with the handkerchief.

Even though he knew the tears were for his benefit, still she was a mother, and she cried for her children.

Where the hell would Barasch go anyway, that he could get such service?

"All right, I'll see what I can do."

"I want you to take care of it," she insisted.

"All right, I'll take care of it."

Malka stopped crying and put the handkerchief back into her purse. Not one to waste time on pleasantries, she stood up.

"Soon," she demanded. "I don't like the betting business. That's a bottomless pit. If it ruins me, Brother, you know on whose doorstep I'll turn up, so save us both some trouble."

Although she had confidence in his loyalty, she could not refrain from offering Boruch Levi a form of motivation dearer to her own heart—financial self-interest.

Boruch Levi scowled. "If he wants to ruin you, he'll ruin you. Who's his bookmaker?"

"He runs a cigar store around the corner from the post office on Eighth Street. Barasch calls him Heinie."

"A Jew?"

Malka shook her head.

"What about Hebrew lessons for your sons?" he asked.

"Well, my children are not the descendants of scholars," she taunted with a smile, but her brother's set jaw suggested to her that for now she had better stay on his good side. "We aren't too close to a synagogue, and they help in the yard, but they should learn how to make a blessing. That wouldn't hurt them. What do you suggest?"

"I'll send Reb Zelig to see you. Just see that they behave. He's no youngster."

"Reb Zelig? The Krimsker Rebbe's sexton?" Malka asked in surprise.

"Yes."

"I thought Rabbi Max was your rabbi."

"Things change."

"You get tired of bailing him out of jail?"

"No, I can't leave a rabbi in jail over the Sabbath. Not even him. He's been making the stuff in the synagogue. What kind of business is that?"

A very good business, thought Malka to herself, but she heard that flinty tone in her brother's voice and held her tongue. Let him focus on her problem, not his.

"Thank you. Have a good Sabbath and give my love to Golda."

"Good Sabbath," he answered.

As she left, Malka saw her brother nod, and knew that what she wanted was as good as done. She decided to stop off downtown on the way home to buy Barasch two new shirts. No, maybe three, now that there was no chance that her man would lose them off his back.

Before Malka had arrived, Boruch Levi had been thinking that he would give the chief of police a call to see how his wounded hand was doing. Now he decided to take a ride by headquarters on his way home. Since this bookie Heinie wasn't a Jew, he had better consult with the chief or with Inspector Doheen. Whoever this Heinie was, he was going to be in for one hell of a surprise. Boruch Levi was sure of that.

# CHAPTER FIFTEEN

By the time Boruch Levi arrived at the chief's office, the chief, still recuperating from his bullet wound, had gone home for the day. His secretary, however, immediately rang the chief of detectives, Inspector Doheen, and handed Boruch Levi the phone.

"Hello, Inspector Doheen. Is the chief all right?"

"He's doing fine, but he's still on the mend. Has to take it easy."

"Good. Good," Boruch Levi said.

"Yes, in a week or two he'll be as good as new. Is everything all right with you, Levi?"

"Everything is all right with me, but I have a family problem that I wanted to talk to the chief about," Boruch Levi said somewhat uncomfortably.

"Come by my office, and let's see if I can help," Doheen said sincerely.

"Thank you, Inspector. I think I will, if you have time."

"I'll make time. Don't you worry about that," Doheen said respectfully.

Inspector Doheen, chief of detectives and senior intelligence officer of the police force, had always been respectful. The tall, lean, dark, dour Irishman made many of his other more sociable and fraternal senior officers uncomfortable with his morose, distrustful air. They joked among themselves that the chief had picked him precisely because he neither looked nor acted like an Irishman, not even in uniform, so in plainclothes no one would guess that he was a policeman. In fact, they knew very well why he had been chosen. Doheen seemed more loyal to the chief than to the general good, that Hibernian brotherhood known as the Force, which they served loyally in the hope of advancing even higher to the position of chief or even to commissioner. Doheen apparently lacked such vaunting ambition. He did not even drink because it aggravated his dyspepsia, which his peers attributed either to his piety (he attended mass daily) or to his inability to escape his own saturnine presence, which was always enough to give any of them indigestion.

Initially skeptical of Boruch Levi's affection for his beloved chief, Doheen came to admire the Jew's loyalty, sobriety (he drank with the best of them but never to excess), desire to serve, and devotion to family and religion, particularly his unstinting and unapologetic observance of his Sabbath. As the years went by, Doheen came to appreciate that Boruch Levi did not want the usual greedy favors. Bailing out his bootlegging rabbi for the Sabbath was a different matter. "I understand, Boruch Levi; the others don't, but I do. I'm religious myself. We're all sinners— even the clergy are human beings—and because they fall now and then doesn't mean they're not of the cloth and can't help guide the rest of us unholy sinners. Why, there was only one Jesus. A man has to have respect for the Church, I say."

Last's week's incident demonstrated even more clearly that Boruch Levi's true reward was the same as Doheen's own—service to their chief. Prohibition had led to raids on the burgeoning breweries, stills, warehouses, and speakeasies, but not on all of them, of course. The chief's standard operating procedure permitted small operations to pay off, but the larger, rowdier, more violent and more brazen syndicate operations were not to be tolerated. The chief himself loved the excitement and headlines these raids produced and insisted on participating. Doheen, worrying more about the chief's safety than his own, permitted Boruch Levi to accompany the chief as an unarmed bodyguard. Doheen had seen Boruch Levi masterfully defend his interests on the levee against some very rough characters. With the junkman along, he could concentrate on directing the raid and not have the aging chief's safety as his primary concern.

On last week's warehouse raid, a lone gunman had holed up behind some beer barrels. Beyond an open space, the police crouched behind large crates. Although cornered, the crook refused to surrender, and in the first exchange of shots he hit the chief in the hand. Boruch Levi, who was by the chief's side, yelled for everyone to stop firing. Even the gunman obeyed. Boruch Levi called out, "You son of a bitch, you shot the chief. Now that's enough! You had your fun. Come out of there right now, or I'm coming to get you!"

After waiting a second, the unarmed Boruch Levi vaulted over the crates, sprinted across the open space, dived over the barrels, and pounced upon the gunman before the man knew what had happened. In vengeful fury, Boruch Levi snapped the gunman's pistol arm as if it were a dry stick and proceeded to pummel him. Doheen heard Boruch Levi's sudden, heavy blows beating a damaging tattoo on the man's face, thudding into flesh and bone. By the time Doheen and the others arrived, the unconscious gunman's face had been smashed into a bloody, bruised pulp and Boruch Levi, fists still clenched, was scowling over him, "You son of a bitch, you shot the chief."

Inspector Doheen motioned for Boruch Levi to enter, rising from his desk to shake his hand. "Come in, come in," he said so warmly that the two young detectives who had just arrived to brief him looked at each other in surprise at such an outpouring of affection from the dour inspector. When they saw who it was, they respectfully stood up.

"Gentlemen, will you excuse us for a moment?" the inspector said.

The two smiled at Boruch Levi as they passed him. He merely nodded curtly. Doheen closed the door.

"Boruch Levi, I drove the chief home myself. He had to rest. He's no youngster."

Boruch Levi nodded.

"You look a little concerned," the inspector said sympathetically.

"I have a strange problem with my brother-in-law," he said uncomfortably.

"Mine's an alcoholic, damn him, but let's sit down and see if together we can't handle yours."

Boruch Levi told Doheen about Malka's visit and her insistence that the bookie be spoken to without Barasch's knowledge. Embarrassed by his sister's foolishness, he looked up.

"You can't choose your family, although in your case you couldn't have done better than your sainted mother. Boruch Levi, don't let such nonsense bother you. I give you my word that your brother-in-law won't be able to lay a bet anywhere in town, and he won't know why either. I'll take care of it myself. Right away, too. It's as good as done. Don't lose any sleep over it. You just go home and enjoy your Sabbath," Inspector Doheen said.

# CHAPTER SIXTEEN

SCRUBBED AND DRESSED IN HIS SABBATH TWEED KNICKER suit, Sammy hurried down the steps and across the lawn to greet his father, Boruch Levi. Although it was still before the Sabbath, Sammy quickly took advantage of the opportunity to wish his father a good Sabbath. When his stern father's words began with a Sabbath greeting, they tended to be less harsh and demanding.

"Good Sabbath, Sammy. No, don't go to the synagogue yet. Wait for me. We'll go together."

"We're going together?" Sammy asked in timid surprise.

"Yes," his father answered. "If you can stay clean, you can wait out here. Otherwise, come inside."

"I'll be careful. I'll stay here."

"Uh-huh." His father nodded and effortlessly hurried inside.

Although Sammy couldn't hear any creaks or groans, much less thumping, he knew that his father was charging up the wooden steps to their second-floor home. Sammy listened with a competitor's ear. Everyone else except the two of them made some noise on the stairs. They moved differently. Sammy, with the light willowy build and oval face of his mother's family, had a dancer's demonstrative grace. His coordination seemed to be related to his lack of weight. His solidly built, square-jawed father, however, suggested power even when he was standing still. When he moved quickly, there was no wasted, showy motion, just an incredible efficiency of force like the steel ball bearing that Sammy liked to roll down the steeply slanting garage roof. The shiny ball flying perfectly straight and fast inspired in Sammy respect and fear, as did his father. At least with the bearing, the boy could touch the reflecting, hard exterior, wondering at its strength and untempered coldness.

His father didn't tell him very much but always expected him to understand things. Sammy often knew what his mother was thinking, rarely what his father had in mind. Sammy sensed something strange about the world: fathers treated eldest sons as if they were small replicas of themselves, but the sons seemed to inherit more from the mothers. His bullying and brutish cousins, Aunt Malka's sons, were just like her, although Uncle Barasch didn't seem to care at all. Maybe that was why both Sammy's mother and father didn't like them. Sammy had heard his father complain that Aunt Malka wasn't at all like their wonderful mother, Sammy's grandmother, may she rest in peace. Although his father didn't say so in so many words, Boruch Levi was the perfect son precisely because he was just like his sainted mother. When Sammy fell and cried or shuddered over a bird run over in the street, his father admonished him, "Stop acting like your mother."

Sammy wondered why his father wanted him to wait.

He normally insisted that Sammy arrive at the synagogue early, before the service. Embarrassed and self-conscious, Sammy often had to thread his way alone to their seats on the eastern wall, facing the entire congregation. Everyone shuffled uneasily when Sammy took his place; after the services they praised him too ecstatically to his father for being a "good boy," which Sammy hoped was true, and for being "just like his father," which Sammy forlornly knew was certainly untrue and hopelessly beyond him.

Sammy also knew that for all their sycophantic respect, they didn't like his father any more than Rabbi Max did. The boy thought that Rabbi Max liked him, even though when Sammy entered the synagogue, the irreverent rabbi was apt to make some joke about the "degeneration of generations. Moses sent twelve spies into the Holy Land, but wealthy Boruch Levi can afford only one." The boy would blush and open a book to hide his eyes. Or he would stare up at the eternal light flickering red inside the glass globe that hung in front of the ark.

The thought of the small globe riding inside the supportive filigree crown reminded Sammy that earlier, when he was out on the balcony, he thought he had spotted a bird's nest in the hedge bordering the yard. Now he wandered across the narrow lawn to the hedge, which was at least twice his own height, and peered up through the leaves to see if he could identify the silhouette against the sky. The darkening dusk no longer provided the proper contrast, but the multitude of bugs that had come alive with the waning light held his attention. They swarmed within the interwoven, sheltering branches in seeming chaos, but Sammy understood that they knew when to move and when to rest and how to find their food and how to do all the things that bugs had to do. This alone was miraculous and wonderful. That they didn't have to scrub behind their ears for the Sabbath, clean their rooms, or have interminable Hebrew lessons after public school only increased his respect for the frail whirring creatures.

"Sammy, get over here now!" his father's gruff voice called.

"Yes, Pa." Sammy scampered back onto the sidewalk.

"What were you doing over there in your Sabbath suit?"

"I was looking for a bird's nest that I saw from the porch," Sammy answered quietly.

"That's how you prepare for the Sabbath? Looking for birds' nests?"

Sammy didn't respond; his father's questions often had no acceptable answer. He had prepared for the Sabbath, and he was waiting for his father without getting dirty, but his father's truth, to which Sammy was never privy, always seemed to be greater than Sammy's. Because he lacked it, he was forever doing everything wrong, angering his father.

"Is that how you prepare for the Sabbath?" his father demanded.

"I guess so," said Sammy.

"You guess so? What kind of fool are you?"

Sammy didn't answer. He wanted to take his father's hand—walking to or from the synagogue were the rare occasions when his father permitted him to do so—but he hesitated after this latest rebuke.

"I'm sorry," Sammy said appeasingly. For reasons

unclear to the son, his father found apologies absolutely necessary; it didn't matter whether they were sincere or even whether a person understood why he was apologizing.

As they reached the sidewalk, Sammy instinctively turned left toward Rabbi Max's synagogue.

"No," his father said, calling him back. "We're going somewhere else this Sabbath."

The bewildered boy automatically came back to his father. To Sammy's surprise, his father reached out to take his hand and held it in his hard, muscular one with a tenderness that made Sammy hope the new synagogue was far, far away.

Although the walk was not so long as Sammy would have liked, it was more pleasant than the route to Rabbi Max's; they strolled through their residential neighborhood of two-family dwellings and apartment houses without crossing any busy streets. As they approached their destination, his father looked down at Sammy and asked, "Do you know where we are going?"

"No."

"We are going to the Krimsker Rebbe's beis midrash. I used to pray in his beis midrash in Krimsk when I was a boy. You must be very well behaved."

Boruch Levi didn't look at his son as he spoke. He was busy intently examining the Krimsker Rebbe's three-story building, trying to discern whether there were any similarities to the rickety wooden one with all the windows in Krimsk. He hoped that there would be one very important similarity: a place for him now as there once had been.

# CHAPTER SEVENTEEN

CRIES OF "A MINYAN!" GREETED BORUCH LEVI'S ENTRY into the beis midrash. Now that a quorum was present, the cantor plunged into the afternoon prayer. Hebrew words spewed forth in a great rush like that of a bursting dam, suggesting that it was very, very late, probably too late for the afternoon prayer, even by the lax hasidic sense of time. Sucked into the temporal-spiritual rush, Boruch Levi and Sammy hurriedly took seats behind the nine other congregants, and Boruch Levi began praying from one of the many prayer books scattered about the tables. Reading hurriedly without much concentration, he was among the first to finish the silent devotion.

Continuing to stand, he surveyed the small beis midrash, which might be able to seat thirty or forty with everyone crowded together for the High Holidays. An adjacent alcove was closed off by a movable partition. At first Boruch Levi thought that might be the women's section, but it was completely dark, and he remembered that in Krimsk there had been no place at all for women. Probably

Reb Zelig's small but successful remnants/seconds business was conducted behind the enshrouding screen.

Originally Reb Zelig's commercial activity had surprised Boruch Levi; in Krimsk the rebbe had always refused to permit even talk of money in his beis midrash. In St. Louis, however, things were different. Almost everyone worked on Saturday, and since the rebbe could not accept donations that might have been earned in violation of the Sabbath, Reb Zelig, although no youngster, had reluctantly gone into business to assure the purity of the rebbe's funds. How unlike Rabbi Max's foolish bootlegging, thought Boruch Levi, but what smug satisfaction he felt dissolved with the realization that he, Boruch Levi, who now did observe the Sabbath, had never supported the Krimsker Rebbe in America. He felt like a deserting officer who returns to find that his troops have barely managed to survive without him, while with him they might have triumphed. In spite of having made the minyan, Boruch Levi didn't feel needed.

He looked around, hoping to discover some physical similarity to the beis midrash in Krimsk, but whereas there the room had been large, almost square, and filled with windows, here it was small and narrow, only a few windows gracing the walls, and those above head level. Boruch Levi examined the prayer hall for some glorious ritual object that hinted at the Krimsker Rebbe's greatness, but again he found nothing. Neither as large nor as grand as the synagogue he had presented to Rabbi Max, the St. Louis Krimsker beis midrash seemed inappropriate for such a great man as the rebbe. Then Boruch Levi suddenly realized that the two worlds of America and Krimsk were playing tricks on him again. The Krimsker Rebbe's beis midrash in Krimsk had been the most ordinary place in the world. Since the rebbe remained a constant in both worlds, this plain beis midrash in St. Louis was perfectly appropriate. The rebbe didn't need a grand, ornate converted theater, even if all the rest of America did.

Reb Zelig finished the silent devotion and turned to nod in appreciative greeting to the man who had made the minyan. Smiling in return, Boruch Levi marveled at how Reb Zelig had aged. His all-white beard and hair showed the wispy thinning that comes with age. But the vigor remained; the tough sinews in the sexton's neck were tight when he prayed. How old was he now? Reb Zelig had been no youngster back in Krimsk. Had his beard already been white when he left for America? Despite his excellent memory, Boruch Levi could not recall.

The Krimsker Rebbe suddenly finished the silent prayer and turned around. A startled Boruch Levi put his hand on his son's slight shoulder to steady himself. Unused to supporting his powerful father, Sammy twisted uneasily under the weight and looked up in apprehensive curiosity at his father, who was blinking in amazement at the man who had just sat down.

"It can't be," Boruch Levi whispered in astonishment. After seventeen years in America, the rebbe had not changed at all.

"The same. Absolutely the same. Like magic," he murmured.

He leaned down to his son and whispered hoarsely, "The rebbe. The holy Krimsker Rebbe. Do you see?"

Sammy saw the Krimsker Rebbe sitting hunched slightly forward with his hands on his knees.

"Do you see, Sammy?"

Sammy saw what generations of children had seen before him.

"Just like a frog," the boy whispered under his breath, but incredulous that the holy man resembled a frog, he had said it a trifle too loud.

"What?" his father asked.

Sammy was afraid to answer.

"A frog?" his father repeated, softly questioning his own memory. "Yes, a frog." The answer came from his very own youth so many years before, in a place so far away as to be in a different world. "Yes, that's what we all thought.

"The Krimsker Rebbe hasn't changed, has he?" Boruch Levi said to his son, his voice thick with remembrance and thanksgiving. He bent over and kissed his son's forehead.

"You're a good boy, Sammy."

Sammy felt his father's warm lips and blushed. He wasn't so sure that he was a good boy. After all, he had been preparing for the Sabbath with birds' nests and bugs. But he was sure that because of the holy rebbe, his father had kissed him.

For a long time Boruch Levi could not take his eyes off the Krimsker Rebbe. He didn't feel at all self-conscious about staring, since the rebbe seemed in another world (perhaps Krimsk?)—just as Boruch Levi remembered him.

When he finally switched his attention to the other congregants he recognized a few familiar faces. The cantor, melodically chanting his way through the afternoon service, sounded familiar, but was far too young to have conducted services in Krimsk. Boruch Levi realized that he must be Reb Muni's son, and when the congregation rose and turned toward the door to symbolically greet the Sabbath bride, Boruch Levi saw that he had guessed correctly, as an aged Reb Muni faced him. He recognized Nachman Leib Katzman and his younger son Shraga, but he was already familiar with them from using their shoe repair service. Nachman, always polite and hardworking, nodded to Boruch Levi.

"Pa, turn around," Sammy whispered urgently. Boruch Levi ceased examining the small minyan for old acquaintances and turned, facing across the quiet emptiness of the Krimsker Rebbe's ordinary beis midrash toward the door to welcome the Sabbath Queen. As he chanted the refrain into the evening darkness, "Come my beloved, to greet the bride—to welcome the arrival of the Sabbath," he felt as if he were welcoming a being no less personal and intimate than the rebbe and those old friends that he had not seen for so long in the secular, weekday world of America.

Sammy liked the Krimsker Rebbe's beis midrash much better than Rabbi Max's synagogue. No one stared at him. A quiet intimacy pervaded the smaller room. And above all, he leaned in delicious comfort on his father, who seemed more relaxed than ever before. Sammy hoped that this would last at least as long as the service in the synagogue, which dragged on interminably as his young stomach rumbled with hunger. All too soon, however, the final kaddish had been recited.

The few regular congregants rose and stepped forward to bow respectfully and murmur "good Sabbath" toward the Krimsker Rebbe, who remained seated next to the ark and acknowledged the greetings with ever so faint a nod. The hasidim then wished each other and Boruch Levi, too, a good Sabbath as they drifted slowly toward the exit.

Boruch Levi took Sammy's hand and stepped forward. Reb Zelig intercepted them with a Sabbath greeting, then Boruch Levi continued until he stood facing the Krimsker Rebbe directly across the table.

"*Gut Shabbos*, rebbe," Boruch Levi said quietly but very clearly.

The rebbe nodded. Reb Zelig rushed to the table.

"Boruch Levi, son of Naftali from Krimsk, made our minyan this Sabbath," the sexton announced.

Without any expression of recognition, the rebbe looked silently at Boruch Levi.

"Boruch Levi, the son—" Reb Zelig repeated, but the rebbe cut him short.

"What color is the river?" the rebbe asked Boruch Levi.

Fearing an embarrassing encounter, Reb Zelig stared at the floor. The rebbe knew that Boruch Levi's business was on the levee overlooking the Mississippi River. Although he had not been there himself, he had sent Reb Zelig years ago for some reason or other. The sexton could no longer recall whether or not he had gone inside, but the rebbe certainly remembered his report, for the rebbe never forgot anything.

Boruch Levi, however, answered without hesitation.

"Late this afternoon, on the eve of the Sabbath, it was a pale pink."

As he had left his office, he had glanced at the river, which reflected clouds floating in a late afternoon sky tinged slightly pink. Recalling how late it must be, he had driven quickly to police headquarters.

The rebbe sat up straight.

"Are you certain?" the rebbe asked eagerly.

"I'm certain that is how it appeared to me," Boruch Levi responded.

"Is something wrong with your eyes?"

"No, thank God. My eyes are fine." Boruch Levi paused.

"Then why aren't you completely certain?"

"Rebbe, I am completely certain that is what I saw, but since my visit to Krimsk this summer, I no longer trust the appearance of things here in America." Boruch Levi's voice quickened as he blurted out his strange, discomforting confession.

"I understand," the rebbe said.

"You do?" Boruch Levi asked, both relieved and surprised.

"Come. We'll discuss it upstairs," the rebbe said, rising from his chair.

The rebbe walked quickly to the interior side door and waited for Reb Zelig, but the sexton, thoroughly perplexed, was rooted to the floor. The rebbe had never invited any hasid, much less a former one, upstairs to sanctify the Sabbath with him.

"Nu?" the rebbe said, and Reb Zelig rushed over to open the door.

"Yes, yes," the sexton stammered in consternation as he motioned to Boruch Levi and his son to follow the rebbe up the back steps to the rebbetzin's kitchen.

# CHAPTER EIGHTEEN

SITTING ALONE IN THE KITCHEN, SHAYNA BASYA WAS surprised when a very powerfully built man and a slender young boy followed her husband into the room. She had heard only the rebbe and Reb Zelig climbing the creaky wooden steps. For a brief moment, she wondered if her husband knew that there were strangers following him, but when she saw that the sexton was behind them, she realized that was preposterous. The young boy, whose delicate face flushed with a quiet excitement, reminded Shayna Basya of her daughter Rachel Leah as a child. The bulky, powerful man did not appeal to her at all. She smiled at the boy, who, although pleased at the attention, shyly stepped behind his father.

The rebbe continued through the kitchen and on into the hall. Confused at what he should do with the guests, Reb Zelig stared wistfully after his rebbe.

"Some special prayers," he mumbled by way of explanation.

"Please sit down," Shayna Basya said to her guests.

"Oh yes, of course," agreed Reb Zelig. He looked at the rebbetzin in mild curiosity. Usually she fled into her room even at the mention of strangers.

Smiling at Sammy, the rebbetzin pointed to the chair next to her. The boy stepped from his father's shadow and shyly slid into the adjacent seat.

"Reb Zelig, aren't you going to introduce us to our guests?" the rebbetzin asked.

"Oh yes, of course," Reb Zelig stammered. "This is Reb Boruch Levi Rudman and his son. Reb Boruch Levi made our minyan this Shabbos."

Boruch Levi nodded, and Shayna Basya acknowledged him with a regal glance. Boruch Levi did not remember the rebbetzin's formal dignity. Under her dark brown wig, the color of ancient pianos and old, heavy desks, her face, although very much alive, had been creased with a myriad of fine, intersecting lines. At least, Boruch Levi thought, she has aged. Her pale eyebrows hinted that under her stiff, matronly wig, her hair was mostly white. Boruch Levi remembered the fidgety, disheveled rebbetzin rushing into the Krimsk market and then retreating in awkward, haughty arrogance to her house next to the beis midrash. In St. Louis, where Jews drove themselves crazy with memorial tea parties in manicured rose gardens, she was calmer and lacked pretense.

"What's your name?" the rebbetzin asked the boy.

"Sammy Rudman," he answered forthrightly.

The rebbetzin placed two caramels, one dark and one light, in front of him. "Eat them. They're very good."

Sammy hesitated and looked at his father. His father was very strict about not eating anything before the benediction over the Sabbath wine. But Boruch Levi himself didn't know what to say.

"Thank you, but we haven't made kiddush yet," Sammy said politely.

"Yes, I know, but the rebbe might not bless the wine for several hours. Women and children always had candies in my father's house, and he was the Grand Rabbi of Bezin," she added.

Sammy looked at his father, who nodded. After reciting the appropriate blessing, the boy popped the light caramel into his mouth.

"I see you like the light ones. So do I. Reb Zelig, would you please pass me the caramel box?"

Very pleased at having something to do, Reb Zelig moved with great alacrity.

With a regal movement, she deigned to remove a light caramel and place it into her mouth.

They all sat in silence as Sammy and the rebbetzin chewed their candies. Although he felt slightly uncomfortable, Sammy did enjoy the sweet. It was the very expensive kind that his father gave the police chief's wife when he gave the chief himself a bottle of whiskey for Christmas. Apparently, the Krimsker Rebbe and rebbetzin must be very important people. Although his father's stern, stubborn visage expressed disapproval of the rebbetzin, it was a very polite disapproval, and Sammy felt confident that he could safely eat the second caramel, since he would be receiving more.

"Occasionally, being a woman has its small advantages," the rebbetzin said aloud, and then she added, "Reb Zelig said that you have recently visited Krimsk."

Boruch Levi nodded.

"Did you have a good trip?"

"Yes, thank God," Boruch Levi said, trying to avoid a discussion with her. After all, he had come to see the Krimsker Rebbe. What possible use could he have for the rebbetzin? Still, she was the rebbe's wife, and Boruch Levi made a mental note to send Sammy over during the week with a box of good caramels. "Yes, I had a good trip, thank God," he expanded, meanwhile wondering why the wives of great men all ate caramels. The chief's wife did, and so did Yitzhak Weinbach's wife Polly. He reflected ruefully that his Golda had no appetite whatsoever for candies. He had always found that very sensible and admirable, but now he wasn't so sure.

"By any chance did you see my daughter, Rachel Leah, or her husband, Hershel Shwartzman?" The rebbetzin's voice had risen higher and was strained. Her throat colored, but not her face, as she fought to maintain her composure.

Boruch Levi was surprised that she, too, seemed to have no idea where they were.

"No, I didn't. I asked about them, of course, but no one seemed to know," he replied.

"Yes, I see," said the rebbetzin quietly.

It was clear even to Sammy that the rebbetzin was very disappointed and did not see at all. Her eyes seemed to quiver as if she were on the verge of tears. Hoping that she wouldn't cry, Sammy offered her his remaining caramel.

"No, it's for you," she said softly. She stroked Sammy's hand gently and said, "You know, you're a very good boy." She turned to Boruch Levi. "You must be proud."

Instead of answering, Boruch Levi jumped off his chair

and stood up straight. Reb Zelig, too, rose to his feet, murmuring, "So early!" and looked around in confusion as if hoping someone would explain to him what was happening. Imitating the men, Sammy slid off his chair and stood at attention.

Standing at the head of the table with a disapproving eye, the rebbe tapped the large empty silver kiddush cup. Reb Zelig didn't seem to understand what the rebbe was telling him and turned to the rebbetzin for help.

"Kiddush," she said. "The rebbe wishes to sanctify the Sabbath."

"Yes, yes, of course," the sexton mumbled in embarrassment as he ran to the cupboard for the wine.

Reb Zelig filled the cup to the very brim and then placed it carefully onto the rebbe's outstretched palm. As he balanced it uneasily, some wine slipped over the rim and in small rivulets streamed down the gleaming sides onto the rebbe's hand. Not seeming to care, the rebbe burst into kiddush. After he had finished, he sipped some wine and poured a small amount into little glasses, which Reb Zelig passed to Boruch Levi and to Sammy, who was still sucking his caramel. The mix of the wine and candy created a heavenly rich, syrupy taste.

Reb Zelig turned to bring a cup and bowl so the rebbe could perform the ritual ablution prior to blessing the braided Sabbath loaves.

"Wait. We'll talk first. Their family must be waiting for them. This is not Krimsk," the rebbe said.

At the mention of Krimsk, Boruch Levi moved forward eagerly to the edge of his chair. "Yes, this is not Krimsk," he repeated, as if it were a liturgical response.

"The river was pink this afternoon?" the rebbe asked.

"Yes, that's what I saw," Boruch Levi answered.

"But you do not trust what you see?" the rebbe inquired.

"No, I don't. I used to, but ever since I returned from Krimsk, most of our people here seem possessed. In Krimsk, where they are poor, they would never dream of working on the Sabbath, but here in St. Louis, where they are well off, they work like slaves on the Sabbath."

All of this came tumbling out; Boruch Levi had finally found someone who, he believed, could understand these things. He sat back, pounding his fist into his hand, then moved forward as if he had more to say. The rebbe, however, spoke first.

"And how does Krimsk appear when you are in St. Louis?"

"That's just the thing!" Boruch Levi exclaimed. "When I'm in St. Louis, Krimsk doesn't make much sense. I know they are far away from each other, but distance is only part of it. It's something else. They don't seem to be in the same world."

"How can they be? In America, there is no Sabbath," the rebbe said.

Boruch Levi sat thinking about the rebbe's words.

"Then they're not in the same world?" Boruch Levi mused aloud.

"Our presence brings them closer," the rebbe declared.

"Then they're not two different worlds?" Boruch Levi asked.

"Since there is no Sabbath here, think of it as Egypt, and you won't go too far wrong," the rebbe said.

"But I don't know anything about Egypt," the junk-man said in distress.

"All the Jews will learn. I can assure you," the rebbe replied, obviously bored with the topic. "Now tell me about the river, the Mississippi."

Boruch Levi sat still, trying to digest what the rebbe had said about Egypt.

"The river," Reb Zelig urged him. "The rebbe asked you about the river."

"Ah, yes," Boruch Levi said, bestirring himself. "I crossed the River Nedd when I took a walk to Krimichak."

"No—" Reb Zelig started to interrupt and explain that the rebbe had inquired about the St. Louis river, but the rebbe silenced him. Sensing something amiss, Boruch Levi paused.

"Go on," the rebbe urged. "What happened in Krimi-chak?"

"I met Wotek the herdsman. I couldn't convince him who I was until I told him that I left Krimsk when Grannie Zara died and the Angel of Death synagogue burned."

"What did he say to that?" the rebbe asked.

"He asked about the burning devil who saved the Torah."

Here Boruch Levi paused. He pictured again the ash-covered young man, Hershel Shwartzman, known as Grisha, who had emerged from the burning synagogue carrying the precious Torah. The rebbe had immediately declared Grisha a suitable groom for his daughter.

"And?" pressed the rebbe.

"And he said that it wasn't right that the Jews had burned the cats."

"You knew about that?" the rebbe asked.

Boruch Levi was surprised that the rebbe knew.

"Yes—no," he mumbled. "Yes, but that's not the real problem. It's that . . . It's uncomfortable to talk about it in America."

The rebbe rose and motioned for Boruch Levi to follow.

# CHAPTER NINETEEN

THE KRIMSKER REBBE'S VISION OF THE BLOOD RED
Mississippi when he came to America in 1903 had filled
him with awe and dread. Just as Egypt had once been the
world's most powerful nation, so America was developing
into the world's mightiest modern state. Into such important places God thrust his Jews. The insight that the simple
Jews must be on center stage filled the rebbe with awe. Awe
can inspire reverence, humility, and holiness, but the river
of blood filled him with recurring dread.

The Krimsker Rebbe had succeeded only too well in
leading his flock into the depths of the Exile. He had led
them into the modern Egypt! The Talmud taught that ten
measures of magic were given to the world; nine were
given to Egypt. With nine-tenths of the world's magic,
Egypt was the seat of witchcraft and demons, and pharaoh
himself was the universal source of impurity. His unswerv-
ing purpose was to cause the Jews to sin, thereby defiling
the holy nation.

The rebbe knew that the sojourn in the American land

of modern witchcraft had begun with his arrival at de-monic Ellis Island. America's sorcery proved quicker and more dangerous than the rebbe had ever dreamed. The rebbe had prayed that redemption would come quickly, with his wife the rebbetzin giving birth to the new Moses that they had conceived on that last fateful Tisha B'Av in Krimsk. But the large, florid-faced immigration official had glanced down at them with a row of shiny brass buttons on his tunic that flashed evil eyes upon the pregnant rebbetzin, driving the soul of the redeemer to heaven and leaving the holy rebbetzin's womb bare and barren. All of this the rebbe came to understand several months later, when the rebbetzin neither grew with child nor had her fertile cycle return.

In distant Krimsk the rebbe had dueled privately with the Polish witch Grannie Zara, just as Jacob had wrestled with Esau's angel. In America he faced sorcerous evil itself, abominable and ubiquitous. The material scale of America was unmitigated greatness; nothing was small. Endless trains slid over a monumental bridge that soared airily over the mighty Mississippi, greater than the pharaoh's Nile! A sure sign of magic, the rebbe knew, for the impure spirits cannot create anything smaller than a barleycorn.

And, most tragically, there was no Sabbath in America. How could there be? It was too busy; almost everyone worked on Saturday. The Jews of Krimsk had not come to America to rest; they had come to improve their lives. Through hard work anyone could become a Rockefeller, a Vanderbilt, or a Morgan. There was no tsar, and there were no violins; there was something much better: opportunity for those with ingenuity, intelligence, and no fear of hard work—especially on Saturday. No one worked harder on the Sabbath than the ex-Krimskers did.

America was a busy land; the Krimsker Rebbe knew that, but he also knew that such industry was only a superficial manifestation of the deeper reality—or the lack of it, for magic denied the deepest reality of all, God's total sovereignty over creation. The world was created to praise God, but there had been no time in the industrious week of creation. The world came to fruition on the first Sabbath, when every creature rested and praised the Creator. God and Israel testify to the sanctity of the Sabbath. The first six days formed three pairs; the seventh day, the Sabbath, remained alone and complained of her plight to God. He answered that the Congregation of Israel would be her betrothed. Since the reward for observing the Sabbath is inheriting the World to Come, the rebbe was not surprised that the American land of material magic seduced the Krimsk Jews into violating their holy Sabbath, thereby rejecting God's sovereign creation, denying the world its purpose, repudiating Israel's betrothed, and losing the World to Come.

All of this was nothing new. Ancient pharaoh had refused to permit the Jews to rest on the Sabbath, since he knew that was the day they studied scrolls telling of their redemption. In America they willingly worked and were torn away from the holy Torah, the fount of redemption, sanctity, and life itself.

The discovery that the lawless area across the Mississippi River from St. Louis, practically on the city's doorstep, was called "Little Egypt," and that its principal city was none other than Cairo, Illinois, confirmed the rebbe's theory of the neo-Egyptian exile.

The rebbe had arrived in America during Theodore Roosevelt's presidency. In keeping with biblical parallels, he anticipated that a "new pharaoh" would arise in America, whose "face would not be the way it was yesterday" and who would afflict the Jews. Taft and Wilson, however, had not led to any appreciable changes, and the rebbe began to suspect that he was too literal in his search for prophetic signs. After all, in busy, industrious America, the Jews already slaved on the Sabbath. True, they received financial compensation and no law said they had to, but nonetheless they served greed. They were, in fact, as dull as slaves. All they talked about was money—money as automobiles, money as buildings, and money as success.

The rebbe had long ago ceased holding personal interviews. He couldn't keep awake as one Jew after another who had more than enough to eat asked for his blessing for financial success. In America the Jews of Krimsk had become as boring as the goyim. It was a shame, because the Krimsker Rebbe himself was no longer averse to an interesting conversation. Especially about America. Although the Jews, enslaved to success, held no interest for the rebbe, impure America did.

The Krimsker Rebbe wanted to discover the essence of America. The rebbe was not confused by the hustle and bustle of the country. That was in some special splendid way American, but it was also recognizably Old World as well. No, for all the talk about new Americans, American whites and blacks were either mentioned in the Bible or known to the sages of the Talmud. The rebbe, with his keen kabbalistic instincts, turned to the indigenous American Indian, autochthon of the New World, for it was through creation that the kabbalah revealed the secrets of God Himself.

The Krimsker Rebbe had plunged into studying the Indian. He began by sending Reb Zelig to the city library for books. After he had exhausted the printed word, he sent Reb Zelig to interview eyewitnesses who had worked or, better yet, lived among them. The most promising were invited to visit the rebbe in his home. Eventually he demanded that his sexton acquire an automobile and drive him southwest of the city into the Ozarks to the Osage Indian reservation, where he could study his subjects at first hand, conversing with them and even camping among them for a few days at a time. However, the rebbe positively refused to spend a Sabbath among them, no matter how fast or how far Reb Zelig had to drive the Model T Ford to return them to St. Louis by sundown Friday night, when the Sabbath began.

Initially the rebbe encountered the beguiling theory that the Indians were one or all of the ten lost tribes of Israel—some form of primitive, open-air hasidim—but he rejected this after ascertaining two pertinent facts. None of the Indian tribes circumcised their children. In various biblical epochs circumcision had lapsed among the Jews, but the Indians' traditional ways precluded the loss of such a fundamental rite as the covenant of Abraham. Still, this was not the most convincing evidence. Their silence was more telling. This was such a salient characteristic that they were referred to as the "silent" red men. Often quiet for long periods, they spoke very little and to the point. Jews, in contrast, from Abraham to the hasidim, were a gregarious, noisy bunch.

The question remained: who was the American Indian? The answer would give the rebbe the key to impure, magical America itself and the knowledge that could help effect Israel's redemption from it.

The rebbe developed two theories. Either they were the sons of the concubines, or they were magic men. In Genesis it is written that after Sarah's death, Abraham took other women, but as his death approached, he decreed that only Isaac was to inherit the seed of Abraham. "But the sons of the concubines, Abraham gave them gifts and sent them . . . to the East, to the Land of the East." According to the Talmud, the gifts that Abraham bestowed upon them were the Impure Names of magic, witchcraft, and sorcery.

The latest "scientific" theories maintained that the Indians had migrated from Asia across the Bering Strait; the continents of America and Asia had then been connected by a land bridge. Thus they had arrived in the New World by a continuous migration to the East; America was none other than the Land of the East. In addition, they seemed to have faithfully remembered the Impure Names; the Indians were steeped in idolatrous, animist magic. Their chief was often the medicine man, who led such public rites. Magic and impurity suffused their lives. They were continuously chanting to spirits and inanimate objects, dancing around small idols, and offering incense sacrifices to all of them.

Their very names were imbued with such witchcraft—Running Wind, Singing Sky, Sitting Bull, Crazy Horse, Little Buffalo, Flying Cloud, Standing Bear, Don Eagle. At first the rebbe thought the names might simply be descriptive, but on further inquiry it became clear that they believed they were bestowing upon the receiver of the name specific forces inherent in the name. After the rebbe had participated in his first rain dance, they had spontaneously begun to call him Jumping Frog; that thoroughly convinced him of their magical powers. Magical or not, the Krimsker Rebbe thought their generous hospitality might well be a legacy of the patriarch Abraham.

The children-of-Abraham theory, however, did not explain the Indians' silence. Why should the sons of the concubines be more taciturn than other men? As Abraham's descendants, they should have been more loquacious than the norm, not less.

The Krimsker Rebbe's magic-men theory, which maintained that the Indians were living men created through magic, explained their silence very well. The talmudic scholar Rava created a man and sent him to his colleague, Rav Zeira, who spoke to him, but the man did not answer. Rav Zeira then said, "You are a creation of the initiated. Return to your dust." The Golem of Prague, the famous magic man created by the great Maharal in the Middle Ages, was similarly silent. The Talmud states that if it were not for their sins, the righteous could create the world. The Krimsker Rebbe understood that the talmudic teacher Rava and the medieval saint the Maharal, although righteous, certainly had sinned. Therefore they could not re-create themselves completely by magic. And that sin-induced flaw in their souls inhibited their ability to re-create precisely that feature closest to the divine, the soul of speech. For it was through the spoken word that God had created the world.

According to the magic-men theory, it was remarkable that the Indians could speak at all. Who possibly could have created such men? If the righteous could not create a speaking creature with the Pure Names, what infernal sorcerer conjured a speaking golem with the Impure Names? The thought of such a concentrated evil force made the rebbe shudder. Who was this pharaoh? Neither politics nor business offered a suitable candidate: Americans, even in the highest places, were all so lackluster.

Eventually the rebbe had hit upon a new idea. He posited that, indeed, an incredibly righteous man had created the Indians with the Pure Names, and the creatures, in their natural course of daily growth, had become corrupt and idolatrous. The Indian's evolution closely paralleled the creation of fragile Adam himself: Adam had been created as a good man with the potential—eventually realized—to do evil. The Indian was the new man, but since, as Ecclesiastes teaches, "There is nothing new under the sun," the New World creatures turned out to be remarkably similar to the corrupt old ones. With the arrival of the Jews from Krimsk, the New World had been incorporated into the Old World as the new and farthest frontier of exile. The Golem of Prague, too, had become violently dangerous— on the Sabbath, no less—and the holy Maharal had to remove from its forehead the aleph, the first of the three Hebrew letters imprinted there spelling "truth," thereby removing God's seal of truth and leaving the two remaining letters to form the word "death." The golem then collapsed into inert earth at his creator's feet.

The rebbe had turned his attention to war paint and other ceremonial tribal markings and decorations on the face and forehead. He consulted with Chief Don Eagle, Osage medicine man, but to no avail. The rebbe even went so far as to take bark pigment and paint the Hebrew word "truth" on Little Buffalo's forehead. Although it seemed to mean nothing to the medicine man and the other chiefs, as the Krimsker Rebbe erased the aleph, Little Buffalo, a most active and energetic brave, fainted. When he regained consciousness, he had a piercing headache that lasted for three months. The rebbe was not surprised and turned his search to paintings and photographs. He even spent two weeks in the museum, examining feather headdresses and Navajo blankets, which he came to find very appealing but devoid of any true kabbalistic markings, much less the overtly displayed Hebrew word "truth."

After his basic research, the rebbe still remained uncertain as to the Indians' identity. Although they were no longer a burning interest of his by 1910, he remained in touch with them, danced at their tribal celebrations, and even delivered a eulogy for Chief Don Eagle, in which he compared the late chief to the Master of the Good Name, the founder of hasidism, for the chief's remarkable combination of strong leadership, deep concern for his tribe's spiritual welfare, a simple, selfless humility, and a flair for telling a pretty good hunting tale. The rebbe's remarks were translated from the Osage and printed to some acclaim in the *St. Louis Post Dispatch*.

Subsequently the rebbe was invited to become curator of the museum's Indian collection, a position that he accepted, since it permitted him to examine the artifacts in storerooms and gave him access to private collections. He was also asked to join the Governor's Council on Indian Affairs, which he did not accept, since he once had heard the governor speak. Unlike the Indians, the governor was a man of many words, all foolish; there could be no doubt as to his natural human origins. Nevertheless, the rebbe's nomination to such a position brought glory to the general Jewish community and to the Krimsker congregation in particular.

Reb Zelig's seconds business prospered, boosted by the publicity. The community had already admired this example of thrift and commercial creativity, but now, in honor of the rebbe's noble Mosaic participation in American Indian affairs, even the aristocratic German Reform Jews, owners of the largest department stores, gave Reb Zelig preferential treatment in buying odd lots and closeouts.

The rebbe waited for the Messiah and the end of exile, but he did not wait idly. Fascinated by the development of flying machines, he suggested that Reb Zelig become a pilot and fly them down to the reservation, but by then the sexton was very busy with the odd lots business, chauffeuring the rebbe, and saying kaddish for Tsar Nicholas II, the last at the rebbe's uncompromising insistence. The rebbe did not press his sexton, and with his feet on the ground, he continued to sample less elevated products of the American cornucopia, starting each day with two of his favorites, Aunt Jemima pancakes—"I'se in town, Honey!"—and a drink of Postum—"What's in a cup?" Try as he might, and he tried Spearmint, Doublemint, and Juicy Fruit, he found the American passion for chewing gum a physical and spiritual abomination. It produced nothing but spittle and seemed to represent the most vulgar conspiracy of silence: the chewer's lips moved as if speaking, but no words emerged, as if mocking the soul of speech. He was equally depressed to discover that Harry Houdini, America's foremost magician, was a Jew, although he sadly admitted to himself that Houdini (Erich Weiss) did seem to epitomize the Jew in the New World.

Recent political events favored the magic-men theory of the American Indian. During this summer of 1920, the Republican Party had nominated Harding and Coolidge as their candidates for president and vice president. The rebbe saw at a glance that Harding was a pompous blowhard, but Calvin Coolidge, a man of so few words that he was known as Silent Cal, certainly was not. His minimal utterances— "The business of the United States is business" and "The man who builds a factory builds a temple"—revealed the essence of America.

Chief Don Eagle's death had dispirited the rebbe and left him anxious about America's leadership, but suddenly Silent Cal had appeared. Might Silent Cal not be the new silent-magic pharaoh? Furthermore, the rebbe perceived another astonishing national development: Prohibition promised to be a national madness. The number of sins in the world remained a constant, and if alcohol were added to the list, something else would be removed in its place, like extortion, or perhaps even murder.

These political and social developments left the rebbe with a powerful sense of expectation. Something was about to happen. The rebbe waited, following his daily schedule: Postum—"What's in a cup?" Might not the bitter cup of exile have been filled?—and Aunt Jemima pancakes—"I'se in town, Honey!" Might not the Master of Pure Names, the new Moses, be arriving in town any day now?

# CHAPTER TWENTY

A SMALL, SHADED DESK LAMP GLOWED IN THE REBBE'S study. Seating Boruch Levi at the table, the rebbe retired to the small couch in the shadows near the door.

"What book do you see on the table?" the rebbe asked.

"The Talmud," Boruch Levi answered.

"Kiss it," the rebbe commanded.

In the manner of a supplicant, the junkman leaned over until his lips touched the heavy leather binding in a votive kiss.

"Now you are no longer in St. Louis. Here it is Shabbos. —You were saying?"

"Yes, Rebbe, I knew what Wotek the herdsman was talking about in Krimichak, because that very night, before the Angel of Death synagogue burned, I had a dream about burning cats. Years later, after my mother's death, the dream returned. In the following dream my mother appeared, requesting me to keep the Sabbath. You see, rebbe, I have not always—"

With a disdainful flick of his hand, the rebbe cut short the confession. "Have you had this dream lately?"

"Of my sainted mother?"

"No, of the burning cats," the rebbe said brusquely.

"No, I had that only twice." Boruch Levi sensed that the rebbe knew all about the fiery death of Zloty, the witch's cat.

"On the eve of the Sabbath the mighty Mississippi was pink?"

"Yes, that's how it appeared to me."

"When you are looking at the river, you can believe your eyes, Boruch Levi, because the river reflects the heavens above."

Boruch Levi understood the implication: the rest of the time he couldn't believe his eyes.

The rebbe sat in silence. After several minutes, Boruch Levi mustered the courage to speak.

"The Jews in America seem possessed," he repeated.

"They are," the rebbe answered casually.

"To myself, I seem like a madman, a veritable meshuggenner both here and there. I don't fit in either place."

"No one does."

"Then what are we to do?" Boruch Levi cried quietly.

"Observe the Sabbath. Observe the Sabbath," the rebbe declared.

Boruch Levi nodded. He would certainly continue to observe the Sabbath, but he felt regret, even shame, for the past. He had rebelled against the rebbe and God, both here and in Krimsk.

"I ask the rebbe's forgiveness—"

The rebbe did not respond.

"Now that I have returned, I would like to serve the rebbe. If I can help the rebbe in any way—"

To his disappointment, the Krimsker Rebbe realized that Boruch Levi was a follower, not a leader. No, this was not Moses before him.

The rebbe stood up, terminating the interview. He motioned for Boruch Levi to return with him to the kitchen, and then he turned back to the junkman. "You must come to me with your problems. As for prayer, you will remain with Rabbi Max."

Boruch Levi was stunned by the decree that he must continue with the bootlegging rabbi.

"There I no longer feel that I am in the House of God," he pleaded.

"Then you must pray harder. This isn't Krimsk," the rebbe said and opened the study door.

As the rebbe entered the kitchen, Reb Zelig stood up and motioned for the boy to rise as well, but the rebbetzin put her hand on his knee and kept him seated next to her.

"Reb Boruch Levi, you have a very wonderful son," the rebbetzin said. "He's a pleasure to be with. And now you may stand for the rebbe." Laughing, she released Sammy's knee, and he stood up, flushing red with embarrassment.

"Sammy, I need a pilot," the rebbe announced. "Do you like wings? Do birds and bugs interest you?"

Tongue-tied, the boy blushed and looked down at the table.

"Sammy!" his father said sternly.

The rebbetzin took his hand gently in hers.

"Do such things interest you?" she asked.

Sammy looked at her hesitantly, then turned to the rebbe and said firmly, "Yes, birds and bugs do interest me very much."

"In what way?" the rebbe asked.

"Well," said Sammy, thinking about the bird's nest and the bugs in the hedge, "birds, because they fly. That's almost magical. Flying bugs are interesting, but in a different way. Bugs are so small and seem worthless, but they all work well together and seem to know just what they should do without any problem."

After this veritable speech, which had surprised even Sammy himself, he self-consciously turned back to the rebbetzin, who squeezed his hand in gentle congratulation.

The rebbe nodded in agreement, then said abruptly, "Gut Shabbos."

Reb Zelig was ushering them down the steps when the rebbe appeared in the doorway and called after them, "Boruch Levi, this time you will remember what I told you."

Ashamed of his earlier failure, he responded earnestly, "Yes, rebbe, of course. I give you my word."

"And, Boruch Levi, send Sammy to pray with us on the Sabbath. He belongs here. Do you understand?"

Before Boruch Levi could reply, the rebbe had disappeared. Smiling, Sammy continued down the steps after his father.

WITH SAMMY SMILING AT HIS SIDE, BORUCH LEVI pensively strolled home. He was pondering his encounter with the Krimsker Rebbe. The rebbe had received him, had even brought him into the family quarters to hear kiddush, and the rebbe certainly had understood his problem. That he didn't understand the rebbe's answers did not distress him; if he ever would be privileged to understand, it would take him a very long time. It was enough that the rebbe knew.

How did the rebbe know about the burning cats? Well, that was why he was a miraculous rebbe—even in St. Louis. But St. Louis wasn't Krimsk—the rebbe had stressed that several times—and one of tonight's surprises was that religion in America, although very weak, was not so simple. If everyone really was possessed, then why should things be simple?

Boruch Levi had wanted to confess his sins and to return to the rebbe's beis midrash as a humble, faithful servant. The rebbe had ignored both these needs and had decreed that he continue to pray with Rabbi Max. The decree stuck in his throat like a jagged bone. How was he to continue with that sassy bootlegger? Now Boruch Levi could no longer take away the synagogue building and humble the disloyal rabbi as he so richly deserved. If Boruch Levi didn't discipline him, Rabbi Max would become intolerable.

At least Sammy wouldn't have to grow up around Rabbi Max. That was some consolation, but indeed, very little. The rebbe seemed to prefer the delicate, almost feminine boy to his robust self. Still, shouldn't he feel honored that the Krimsker Rebbe had personally invited his son to attend the beis midrash?

Yet Boruch Levi hadn't liked all the attention that the rebbetzin had showered on his son. Sammy needed a firm hand. His wife Golda was too gentle with their son, and look what was happening. He was forever dreaming and eating caramels. But Golda herself didn't eat caramels. Maybe Sammy would be better off spending time with one who did. After all, the rebbetzin was no less than the daughter of the Grand Rabbi of Bezin and the wife of the Krimsker Rebbe. Sammy's answers had been very intelligent. He didn't say things like that at home. Perhaps he could develop very nicely at the rebbe's.

"Tomorrow morning, Sammy, after you have some juice, you will go straight to the rebbe's beis midrash for services. So pay careful attention to how we are walking, and you won't get lost."

Sammy was delighted at the thought of returning to the rebbe's intimate beis midrash. The rebbetzin was so pleasant; she spoke to him as if he were someone worth talking to. The rebbe was a little strange, but he was a very great man, and even he had spoken seriously to Sammy, although he had ended the conversation rather suddenly. The only other great man Sammy had met was the chief of police. But the chief wasn't really interested in Sammy, although he made a great show of asking the same silly question—What's a big boy like you want to do when he grows up?—every time they met. The only answer that the chief valued was "a policeman," and even when Sammy fibbed to please his father and gave the right answer, the chief never thought to ask Sammy to explain himself the way the rebbe had.

Sammy had never given much thought to what he wanted to do when he grew up—it seemed so impossibly distant—but piloting an airplane certainly appealed to him more than pounding a beat with a nightstick in his hand. It was uncanny that the rebbe had asked him about birds and flying insects, as if the holy man knew precisely that on the eve of the Sabbath, Sammy had been staring into the hedge. Most of all, Sammy liked the effect the Krimsker Rebbe had on his father. He was gentler, softer, and more affectionate than Sammy had ever seen him. At Rabbi Max's his father was all gruff churlishness, scrapping with people, barking at Rabbi Max, and grunting instructions at Sammy. He had hoped that tomorrow morning they would return together to the beis midrash.

"I know the way and won't get lost. Because I am new there, I would like to go with you again if we can."

His father's previous gentle tone had encouraged Sammy to risk the request. When his father didn't snap at him, Sammy hoped for the best, but when he didn't receive any answer, he didn't know what to think.

"No, Sammy, you will be going alone. He wants you there; you heard what he said about that."

Sammy felt tears spring to his eyes. He blinked rapidly, trying to stop the tears before his father noticed. Although the idea of praying next to his sturdy father always frightened him, for some strange reason he felt guilty at the thought of being alone with the childless rebbe and rebbetzin. Scared by the impending loss of his intimidating father and confused by such strange feelings, he gave in to his tears.

"That's not right," he sobbed.

His father looked down at him through his own distress.

"Sammy, quit acting like your mother," he said with a gentle tone that belied his words. "It's the rebbe's will. We must trust him, for he is a very holy man."

They walked on in silence under the soft glowing gas streetlamps.

"The rebbe seems to like you very much. It's a great privilege and honor. If you need any help, you can always turn to Reb Zelig. He will be glad to help you. There's nothing to cry about," Boruch Levi said, thinking that if there were, it was his having to pray with the detestable Rabbi Max and not Sammy's having to pray with the saintly rebbe.

As they approached their home, Boruch Levi noticed the hedge that had so fascinated his dreamy son earlier in the day and felt immediately that he was once again on more solid ground.

"Everyone seems to think you're such a good boy," he said gruffly, implying that unlike everyone else, he was not so easily misled.

Sammy's hand went slack in his father's, although his father's familiar, deprecating tone ended the melancholy confusion of tears. They had returned home.

"I hope they're right." His father's voice trailed off in a faint note of censure that was much milder than Sammy had expected. This good fortune, too, he attributed to their visit to the holy man.

"Come, we're late," his father said as he opened the front door.

Sammy raced up the stairs behind his father and finished only two steps behind him.

Golda, her narrow face pursed anxiously, met her family at the top of the stairs.

"*Gut Shabbos,*" Boruch Levi and Sammy said simultaneously.

"*Gut Shabbos,*" she answered nervously, the Sabbath greetings failing to alleviate her discomfort.

"Boruch Levi, Inspector Doheen has been here twice to see you. He came by after you had left for the synagogue, and I told him to come back a half hour ago. He did, but you still weren't home. I didn't know what to say."

As she spoke, she wrung her clean Sabbath apron in her agitated hands.

"What did he say?" Boruch Levi asked.

"He said that he must see you at once, even though it's your Sabbath. He's across the street at the chief's house, waiting for you."

"Did he say what this is all about?"

"No, just that you should come as soon as you can."

"If I'm not home by ten, leave the key under the mat and lock the door," Boruch Levi announced.

"But you haven't even made kiddush yet," Golda protested in her resigned but anxious manner.

"We heard kiddush at the Krimsker Rebbe's tonight. Sammy will pronounce the blessings for you. Leave a plate on the table," he ordered.

"Yes," she answered, but he was already halfway down the steps. She never could understand her husband's penchant for goyim with guns; the thought of all those brass buttons made her stomach quake. Not that it took very much for that to happen. What were they doing praying with the Krimsker Rebbe? Wasn't one rabbi, especially a bootlegger, enough for a family? As worried as she was about having her husband outside the house on the Sabbath, she was pleased to have Sammy alone so she could find out what they had been doing at the Krimsker Rebbe's. The rebbe and his wife were such strange holy people. She wondered whether they had seen the reclusive rebbetzin. But it was the Sabbath, and at the thought of her once hot chicken soup growing cold, she pursed her lips, shaking her head slowly from side to side in dismay.

# CHAPTER TWENTY-TWO

WORRIED ABOUT THE CHIEF'S HEALTH, BORUCH LEVI swiftly angled across the lawn. The chief was no youngster and really had no business at headquarters until he was stronger. Although the chief's house was only across the street and three doors down, Boruch Levi walked so quickly that when he stepped off the curb, he was practically running. Why shouldn't he? He loved the chief. Michael O'Brien was what an Irish policeman should be: courageous, loyal, hard-drinking, warm-hearted but tough as nails, and an understanding father to his men.

As Boruch Levi approached the first-floor apartment, he thankfully noted that there was no great rush of activity. The only official car parked on the street was Doheen's. Just in case the chief was resting, Boruch Levi knocked very softly. When no one answered, he knocked slightly louder. Mrs. O'Brien opened the door and welcomed him with her usual sad, slightly fearful smile; having a man leave every morning to patrol the streets with a gun on his hip was not like having a husband drive off to the junk shop. Boruch

Levi nodded with a sympathetic understanding that he bestowed on very few.

Doheen motioned for him to enter the dining room and then put a finger to his lips as Boruch Levi walked past the wide entrance to the parlor. Inside, the chief, in bathrobe and slippers, was dozing in his favorite easy chair with the newspaper crumpled in his hand. Boruch Levi nodded and joined the naturally dour inspector, who tonight wore an even gloomier expression than usual.

Respectfully avoiding the chief's chair at the head of the dining room table, the inspector positioned himself where the absent chief's right hand should have been. The two men pushed themselves slightly back from the table so they could face each other. Doheen gently put a brotherly hand on Boruch Levi's knee.

"We have a problem," he said softly.

Boruch Levi realized that it was serious; a full scowl gripped his solid features.

"What's wrong with the chief?"

The inspector shook his head. "It's not the chief."

Without relinquishing his scowl, Boruch Levi elevated his eyebrows in interrogation.

"Your brother-in-law, Bernard the cripple," the inspector said, as if he were delivering condolences.

"Barasch? I mean Bernard?" Boruch Levi questioned.

As if wishing to spare his friend the details, Doheen simply nodded.

"What happened?" Boruch Levi asked. "Was he in an accident?"

"I'm afraid he's mixed up in some bad business," he answered and paused.

"With the gambling?" Boruch Levi ventured.

"Yes. On the way home I stopped by his bookie, and right away I knew something was wrong. I make them all nervous when I come in, but when I mentioned your brother-in-law, he started squirming like an eel. It turns out that your brother-in-law had just walked in and put down two thousand. After your visit this afternoon, that stimulated my curiosity, and I took a little ride around town. I came across four other shops where he had placed an identical bet. In all, ten thousand dollars in cash."

"Ten thousand dollars?!" Boruch Levi repeated in shocked amazement. "In cash?"

"Yes, I'm afraid so," the inspector said, withdrawing from his inside jacket pocket a fat yellow envelope. He opened the flap to reveal the thick stack of crisp new bills inside. "Hundred-dollar bills all the way through. An even hundred."

"He's been betting like that?" Boruch Levi asked. The scowl had returned in its full sour majesty.

"No, that's just the thing. Until today, he's never bet more than a hundred dollars. Usually no more than twenty, sometimes fifty. But never anything like this."

Inspector Doheen tapped the envelope for emphasis. As surprised as Boruch Levi was, and he was very surprised, he couldn't quite believe that Malka had given that sum to Barasch, especially since she was worried about his squandering small amounts. Where had Barasch Limp Legs come up with such big money? The police probably didn't know that yet.

"What in the world was he betting all this money on?"

"Well, that's just the thing. He put it all on tomorrow's ball game." Here the inspector paused for emphasis. "On the Detroit Tigers. All ten thousand dollars on the Detroit Tigers. I know you don't follow the game."

No baseball fan, Boruch Levi didn't comprehend who or what the Detroit Tigers were, much less what the odds should be, but he knew very definitely that Barasch Limp Legs didn't know any more than he did. Someone else, however, most certainly did.

"Does this have anything to do with Matti Sternweiss?" he asked in undisguised contempt.

"I'm afraid that's the real problem. Do you remember those two young detectives who were in my office this afternoon? One of them had just come back from Chicago, where a grand jury is sitting and investigating last year's World Series."

Boruch Levi nodded, signifying that even he had heard about that affair.

"Well, it was fixed all right, and some of the jokers who did it are beginning to sing some very interesting songs, as they usually do to try and avoid imprisonment. Much of what they say has to be discounted—it's just so much slanderous malarkey—but there have been persistent rumors about Matti Sternweiss meeting with some of the big Jewish syndicate gamblers in the East. That didn't mean much to the young detective, since Sternweiss doesn't gamble himself, but it rang a bell with me because of what you had said. And now this."

Again he tapped the bulging yellow envelope.

"I put two and two together and came straight here to the chief. It's a bad situation."

"A very bad situation," the chief announced from the doorway, with a distasteful expression on his noble face.

Doheen and Boruch Levi both stood up, but the chief waved them back into their seats. Boruch Levi sat down, but Doheen helped seat his superior with all the gentle solicitude of a nurse. In recognition, Michael O'Brien nodded his handsome silvery gray head.

Although the bandage on the chief's hand was smaller —it had been an enormous gauze mitten—he looked old and shuffled when he walked. Boruch Levi felt ashamed that he was causing this wonderful man such discomfort.

"Very bad, indeed, Boruch Levi. They shouldn't mess with the game. Why it's the national pastime, sacred it is! If cards, dice, and horses aren't enough for them, why it's too bad. One of yours was the ringleader in Chicago, and now this in our town. That wouldn't look good. Would it now?"

The chief shifted in his chair as if such despicable, unpatriotic behavior physically pained him. Although Boruch Levi did not move a muscle, he felt equally uncomfortable. His unease, however, was slightly ameliorated by a towering rage and a desire to break every bone in Matti Sternweiss's baseball-playing body and mangle a few of the remaining straight ones in his fool brother-in-law's.

"What does the chief suggest?" Boruch Levi asked.

"Well, the best thing would be for our home team the Brownies to win. In an honest sport, however, that's impossible to assure. But we have to be certain that they'll play their hearts out and that nothing suspicious will happen. And we must be certain that there is no heavy betting on the Tigers; that way no one stands to gain even if the Brownies should lose, and consequently nothing is suspicious. You must get Sternweiss to convince the syndicate that it is all off so they don't bet. Those kinds of bets are usually made at the last minute, so if you get through to him, there should be time."

Boruch Levi nodded.

"You can tell him that we know everything. If you like, you can tell him that if something fishy happens tomorrow, we'll put him behind bars," Doheen said.

The chief nodded in vigorous agreement.

"It's the national pastime, and we aren't going to let those punks ruin it!" the chief exploded in a cry of indignation. Then he added more calmly, "We have a problem, Boruch Levi. You know how I admire your concern for family. But we all have a problem. The St. Louis Browns belong to all of us. Why, the very reputation of our fair city is at stake, isn't it?"

"I'll talk to him, all right," Boruch Levi said with all his stubborn determination.

"Sure you will," the chief responded optimistically. "That's why Doheen brought this directly to me. We can save everyone a lot of embarrassment and trouble." Then he dropped his voice and continued in his warmest paternal tone, "Boruch Levi, I don't have to tell you what you mean to us."

The chief held up his bandaged hand in salute. "You're one of us, and we want to protect you, just like you looked after us."

Boruch Levi modestly lowered his eyes.

"It's true, and we know that we can rely on you," the chief concluded.

Doheen nodded in agreement.

"I'll take care of it," Boruch Levi responded, accepting the chief's charge with a solemn dignity.

"Now take back all that money before it goes astray," the chief said jocularly.

Boruch Levi looked at the money but made no attempt to retrieve it.

Doheen cleared his throat. "Chief, Boruch Levi doesn't handle money on his Sabbath," the inspector reminded him.

"Ah, that's a fact. Excuse an old man's forgetting. Well, Doheen can keep it safely enough. I trust him more than I do myself, so you're no worse off than I am."

All three smiled at the chief's self-deprecating witticism.

"Wait—then you can't ride either, can you?" the chief asked solicitously.

"Sternweiss lives in the neighborhood, and I think he'll be home with his mother tonight."

"Good, but if you need any help, if you want to see someone or speak to someone who isn't in the neighborhood, just let Doheen know and he'll take care of it."

Doheen nodded agreeably.

"We have every confidence in you, but if it's very tricky and you can't solve it, then the police force will have to act at once in its official capacity. We have no choice. Doheen will remain here with me to find out how you make out. If you need our active intervention, don't hesitate. After all, I can't risk going anyplace dangerous without you, my boy! We have every confidence in you, don't we, Doheen?"

"Absolutely," the inspector said energetically.

"Thank you," Boruch Levi replied, deeply moved.

The chief reached out his good hand and warmly squeezed Boruch Levi's strong left hand.

# CHAPTER TWENTY-THREE

TRYING UNSUCCESSFULLY TO TEMPER HIS SCOWL, BORUCH Levi stepped into the hallway. Mrs. Sternweiss was genuinely flattered to find at her door the wealthy religious community leader, even with his usual scowl. She prayed in Boruch Levi's synagogue and appreciated his importance in both the Jewish and goyish worlds. But it was Boruch Levi's piety that particularly impressed her. There were other rich Krimskers in St. Louis, but unfortunately they were no longer very religious. In Krimsk he had been a poor little nothing—less than a nothing really, a half-orphan, and not very pious.

In America Boruch Levi had become very well-to-do, and amazingly enough, his religious and moral development matched his financial achievements. A friend of the most important men in the city, he wasn't the least embarrassed to observe the Sabbath publicly. Why, he even used his influence with the police department to have them deliver good pre-Prohibition whiskey to the synagogue. The patrolmen threw their great blue overcoats with the rows of brass buttons over the small kegs so no one should see what they were carrying. His Sufnitz wife, Golda, who made herself a little too simple for Krimsker tastes, was a very fine housekeeper. He had no choice but to marry a non-Krimsker. How could he have married someone who knew him and his family in Krimsk? No, he couldn't be blamed for that; indeed, he had never forgotten Krimsk. When Matti's father had died, Boruch Levi was in the house before nightfall to ask if they needed any help with the funeral arrangements. A friend like that was worth having.

Mrs. Sternweiss hoped that he might have some influence on her son. Yes, Matti was a good boy and always made sure to join her for Friday night's Sabbath dinner. Sitting in the chair of his late father, may he rest in peace, he made kiddush beautifully—when he was in town. Often, however, Matti was away. In fact, he wasn't in town because he wasn't very observant. And he wasn't very observant because he was a baseball player, which in itself wasn't so bad. Not that she understood it. It certainly wasn't as dignified as standing behind the counter in a kosher butcher shop or even running a store, but it was, thank God, an honest living. He didn't steal from anyone, and the goyim were all impressed.

No, that Matti's baseball kept him from observing the commandments wasn't the worst thing. As an old-fashioned mother she would have enjoyed a religious son, but this was America, and what could you expect? The younger generation went their own way. But even in America you had a right to expect grandchildren, didn't you? And that's why Mrs. Sternweiss objected to baseball. Matti was forever traveling, and he never got a chance to meet any Jewish girls. In Krimsk, Mrs. Sternweiss would have turned to a matchmaker. There were even a few in St. Louis, but they were for old people and new arrivals. None of the younger folk, much less a professional ballplayer, would dare use one. She needed an influential friend, both traditional and modern. No doubt Boruch Levi understood a widow's and orphan's needs. Why else would this good man have come if not to make a match?

"Forgive me for disturbing your Sabbath meal, Mrs. Sternweiss, but I would like to speak with Matti."

"We're just finishing. Would you like a glass of tea with a poppy seed cookie?"

"No, thank you. I would like to speak to him now."

"Maybe you have someone for him to see?" Mrs. Sternweiss asked, aware that the question was inappropriate, but after all, Matti was an only child, now orphaned of his father. If Boruch Levi had left the Sabbath table to arrange an introduction personally, it must be someone very special, and the mother was dying to know.

"Yes, I do," Boruch Levi answered, a note of surprise softening his flat business tone.

"Thank you, Boruch Levi, I can't tell you how appreciative I am," she said. "I'll call him at once." In her enthusiasm she quite literally began calling his name before she had even arrived at the entrance to the dining room.

A few moments later, Matti appeared, surly and distrustful. That suited Boruch Levi just fine; he didn't extend the short catcher any Sabbath greetings, much less a hand.

"Boruch Levi does have someone for you to see, darling,

don't you, Reb Boruch Levi?" Mrs. Sternweiss reassured her balky son in the most cheerfully didactic manner, as if she were addressing a very bashful, small child.

"Yes, I do," Boruch Levi affirmed.

"Who's that?" Matti asked suspiciously.

"The Krimsker Rebbe."

"The Krimsker Rebbe?" Mrs. Sternweiss exclaimed incredulously.

"Yes," he answered.

"Does he know someone?" she asked. Before Boruch Levi had a chance to clarify her question, however, Matti curtly asked, "Why?"

"Very pressing community affairs," Boruch Levi replied, and then added, "We have a problem," repeating Doheen's repetition of the chief's words. He felt on safe ground quoting the chief.

"Oh," Mrs. Sternweiss said in disappointment. "The Krimsker Rebbe."

"Would you please bring Matti a jacket?" Boruch Levi suggested.

Matti waited until she had disappeared into his room. As soon as he thought she was out of hearing, he asked aggressively, "What's this all about?"

"Community affairs; we have a problem, and you're going to help us solve it." He enjoyed adding to Matti's discomfort by keeping him in the dark.

"I have a game tomorrow, and I shouldn't be running around tonight. If you don't tell me what this is all about, then I don't go," Matti threatened.

"Oh, you'll go," Boruch Levi taunted him.

"I don't think so. He's not my wonder-working miracle man," Matti said sarcastically.

"Oh, you'll go, all right. And if you don't want to walk through that door, I'll put you right through that wall and drag you by your ears," Boruch Levi announced.

Boruch Levi stepped forward menacingly and stood with one foot in front of the other, as if he were preparing to assault the much smaller man, testing his head against the wall.

Although Matti did not give ground and tried not to reveal any fear, he was intimidated. He knew that Boruch Levi was fully capable of doing what he threatened. What really convinced him to walk amiably through the door was the junkman's near-maniacal baiting tone. This insulting, insufferably arrogant pillar of medieval piety would be only too pleased to do him bodily harm, and tonight Matti had every incentive, at least ten thousand of them, to play tomorrow's game against the Detroit Tigers.

His mother arrived with a suit jacket and tie.

"The Krimsker Rebbe wants to see my little Matti?" she asked in curious amazement.

"Yes, your little Matti is a very big man. He plays baseball for the St. Louis Browns," Boruch Levi deadpanned.

Mrs. Sternweiss nodded; she had never understood the game, all those people running to step on those little cushions—but it was true that the world went meshuga over the whole business. Why, Jewish children, even right in the synagogue, treated Matti the way they used to treat the rebbe in Krimsk.

"Maybe the Krimsker Rebbe has a nice Jewish girl for

Matti," she suggested. "Once he's there, it wouldn't hurt to ask."

"No one knows what the rebbe might think of," Boruch Levi answered in complete honesty.

He opened the door for Matti and said good-bye to Mrs. Sternweiss, wishing her a good Sabbath.

# CHAPTER TWENTY-FOUR

Uncertain as to the best route to the rebbe's—he hadn't been there in years—Matti hesitated. Boruch Levi promptly took his elbow and firmly guided him in the proper direction.

Offended at this custodial act, Matti asked derisively, "You're still playing policeman?"

"They tell me you're a thief. Ballplayer, you want to be a thief, rob a bank like a mensch."

No sooner were the words out than he regretted them. Boruch Levi had wanted to utilize the element of surprise. The less Matti knew, the less he might be inclined to run away. Above all, he didn't want a joker like Sternweiss to guess the reason for the visit before the rebbe knew about the problem.

What a bum this one is, Boruch Levi thought. And his poor mother thought I came to propose a marital match for her little jewel. He shook his head at such maternal innocence and filial abuse. He wanted to give Matti a few good slaps for that alone. Matti's smart mouth—just like vulgar Malka's—had prompted his intemperate response. As he thought of his own mother and sister, his antipathy for Matti increased and became a burning personal vendetta, his specialty.

"Your father's dying, and you're making a play for the nurse!" he had told Matti, who was obviously smitten with the day nurse, Penny Pinkham. "The beds in the hospital are for the sick, not for the sons of the dying to climb in with the nurses. You're a generous boy, Mattus, you want to leave a tip? It doesn't have to be yours; a box of candy is just as sweet."

Such disgraceful sick-room carryings-on had scandalized Boruch Levi; indeed, they still did. And Matti Sternweiss wasn't the only one. It was practically a plague, some social infection in the sick rooms that raged between the Jewish boys and the shiksa nurses. Boruch Levi was in very good health, thank God, but when he helped pay for a sick Jew's hospitalization, he made sure that it was in a Catholic hospital. The nuns weren't interested in the sick man's sons, and they didn't have anything better to do than care for the sick. They weren't thinking about their boyfriends, and they weren't running out to buy a new dress. Give them a box of caramels, and they would pray for you all day.

Boruch Levi continued with his calming thoughts of nuns and their fondness for caramels. The only disquieting aspect was the greatness it imputed to their husband, Jesus. Through his Irish friends he had learned a good deal about the church; Boruch Levi had even congratulated Doheen's family on their good fortune when their niece took holy orders. But Boruch Levi wasn't one to let theology bother him. Leave that stuff for the rabbis and priests, who had time for it since they didn't work in a junkshop or walk a beat, with the exception of that silly Rabbi Max and his rotgut. Even if Boruch Levi didn't believe in Jesus a lot of people did, and if not divine, he certainly must have been the equal of the chief and Isidore Weinbach. At any rate, those nuns deserved the caramels on their own merits, since they worked so hard. Boruch Levi really admired that. He could use a few like them in the junkyard.

In spite of Boruch Levi's stinging insults and accusations, Matti, too, was really very calm. Until Boruch Levi's outburst, Matti had felt like a schoolboy dragged along kicking and screaming against his will. Although technically he was still Boruch Levi's prisoner, now that he knew what this crazy business was all about, he had something to reflect on, and as long as Matti had something to analyze, he could remain very cool, indeed. He never concentrated so well as when the bases were loaded and the count had gone to three and two on the batter. With thousands yelling themselves hoarse, every player tensing up like a steel spring—why, Matti could even hear the home plate umpire's heart beating under his protective pads—Matti would analyze the batter. What kind of day was he having? What were his pitches? What would he be looking for? And his pitcher—what was he throwing? What did he have confidence in? Taking into account the field, the defense, the weather, the sun, the inning, the polish on the batter's shoe, any gossip he had gleaned from the newspapers, the locker room attendants or bat boys, Matti would choose a pitch and place his catcher's mitt just where he wanted the ball to cross home plate. More often than not, Matti was right;

because of that, Dufer and MacGregor each had a good shot at twenty victories. Yes, Matti liked nothing better than the full count in the bottom of the ninth, and tonight promised to be a squeaker.

Boruch Levi had come for him on the Sabbath, and he was taking him to see the Krimsker Rebbe. The only way Boruch Levi would get involved was through his brother-in-law, Barasch Limp Legs. Matti did not believe that Barasch would have willingly betrayed him, since Barasch's passion for Matti's pursuit had always exceeded Matti's own. No man, least of all a cripple, turns his back on a fiery passion like that. Barasch never would have told Boruch Levi. So it must have been his wife, that sly, hateful, horsey woman Malka. Deserting the peddlers in the junkyard, she had driven out the gate. Rejoicing that she was not around, Barasch had no idea where she had gone. "As long as she's not here, what do we care?" he had crowed, but obviously Matti had been right to care: she had driven out of the yard to see her arrogant, pious brother Boruch Levi. And what did he do after his sister's visit? Here Matti was not so certain; it depended on what information Malka had given him. Probably Boruch Levi had visited Barasch, but Matti was stumped; he couldn't imagine Barasch betraying Matti's passion for Penny Pinkham under threat, or that Boruch Levi's pious arrogance would permit him to strike a cripple.

But Boruch Levi had used the word "thief," so he wasn't coming just to warn Matti not to corrupt his brother-in-law. Boruch Levi definitely knew about the bet. Perhaps Malka had overheard them, or perhaps she had even found the ten thousand dollars and realized that something fishy was up: maybe someone had seen Barasch with so much money at the bookies. Might Boruch Levi know about the bet but not know which bookie held it and want to find out so he could recover the money? But that idea didn't make sense, because Boruch Levi knew that he could just beat it out of Matti, especially since Matti couldn't afford to sustain any physical injuries during the baseball season. There was no doubt that the rugged junkman was capable of inflicting such wounds. No, Matti suspected that the money was in Boruch Levi's hands. But why the Krimsker Rebbe? Matti didn't have an answer, but he did like the fact that Boruch Levi had come alone, for that suggested that the police didn't know. Matti wasn't certain of this, since he knew Boruch Levi to be very thick with the highest brass on the police force, but if they knew, they, too, preferred to handle it quietly through their loyal friend and admirer, and that was almost as good.

The final consideration was that Matti had committed no crime. Barasch Limp Legs had made a bet, which apparently was no longer with the bookie, so it wasn't even a bet. Since Matti had wisely not involved other persons, who could prove anything? So what if they had been found out? The police weren't involved. Unfortunately, Matti would not profit by ten thousand dollars. So it was unfortunate, but it wasn't so bad. Easy come, easy go.

As usual, the analytical exercise—Matti himself termed it an art—calmed him. His conclusions weren't very upsetting either. The odds certainly favored Matti, and that was all one could reasonably expect of life. The only thing that Matti couldn't fathom was the reason for their immediate destination. If Boruch Levi wanted to exert some moral influence upon Matti, why weren't they going to Rabbi Max, Boruch Levi's own rabbi and Matti's mother's spiritual guide as well? Why the Krimsker Rebbe?

Although Matti's entire success was based upon his personal maxim, What you don't know can hurt you, he welcomed tonight's enigma. He was very curious, almost eager, to see the Krimsker Rebbe. In recent weeks, and throughout the day, Krimsk had seemed to be falling out of the sky onto his head. The first thing this morning, he had had that crazy notion that the doomed mail plane had been bringing him a letter from Krimsk, and then all those old-fashioned thoughts about Jews and goyim as if he had been expecting a pogrom to start in the ballpark, not to mention Barasch's crackpot code about Beryl Soffer's match factory in Krimsk. Hadn't even the rebbe himself crossed Matti's mind? Something about the Krimsker Rebbe and his real Indians compared to the American League ones from Cleveland? Krimsk seemed to be falling out of the sky all right, just like that all-metal airplane spewing flame. The airmen had thrown out the mail sacks, saving them at the price of their lives. Lieutenant Max Miller rode his modern chariot into the fiery ground. What a terrible fate for such a noble talent! Such tragedy, even in America. Matti wondered if the Krimsker Rebbe knew about the postal aviator, may his soul rest in peace. There was nothing left for the farmers to do but pick up the letters.

"Did you bring back many letters from Krimsk?" Matti asked.

"Quite a few," Boruch Levi grunted.

"Have you delivered them all?"

Boruch Levi scowled affirmatively. After his threats and abuse, why was Matti Sternweiss so relaxed as to have nothing better to think about than Krimsk?

"I thought you might have one for me," Matti said, half joking.

"Who would write you?" Boruch Levi asked scornfully.

"No one."

"So?" Boruch Levi grunted.

"Boruch Levi, what was it like to return to Krimsk?"

Taken aback, the junkman continued walking in silence.

"Is it really a different world?" Matti asked simply.

"For most of us."

Out of the corner of his eye, Boruch Levi saw Matti nod in understanding, and he began to feel as though Matti was escorting him to an interrogation rather than the other way around.

"Did you see any airplanes over there?"

"No," Boruch Levi answered, wondering about everyone's sudden interest in airplanes. An hour ago the rebbe had been talking to Sammy about flying, and now of all things Matti Sternweiss was asking about airplanes in Krimsk! Might Matti be the pilot the rebbe was talking about?

Boruch Levi realized uneasily that his curiosity was overcoming his contempt. He no longer luxuriated in the overwhelming urge to bash Matti's face in. Had his disgusting brother-in-law Barasch Limp Legs corrupted Matti? But what difference did that make tonight? They all had a problem now; Doheen and the chief were waiting for an answer.

# CHAPTER TWENTY-FIVE

"Baseball is an important part of American life. Although it's just a game, it's not just a game; it's *the* American pastime. It's not like games in Krimsk. There only children played games. Here children play them, too, of course, but so do adults. The adults get paid to do it. It's a regular business. Mainly for the goyim."

Boruch Levi had been anxious to lay the problem at the rebbe's feet, but now he found that he did not even know how to begin. The rebbe was seated on the couch in his study. Boruch Levi and Matti sat in straight chairs at the table and had to stare uncomfortably through the light to see the rebbe. Persevering despite the difficulty, Boruch Levi tried to duck down slightly so that he could see whether the rebbe understood what he was saying.

"Various important cities have teams. Matti is a baseball player for the St. Louis team, the Browns. Not all the players do the same thing. Matti has an especially important job. He . . ."

Here Boruch Levi came to a lame halt. He really had

no notion of what Matti did in that foolishness where they all dressed like clowns with children's caps, but he felt it essential to explain just how terrible Matti's behavior was. Inviting help, Boruch Levi glanced quickly at Matti, but the player, who was short enough to view the rebbe, was staring intently at the holy man, not at all aware of Boruch Levi's predicament. The junkman felt his collar tightening around his neck and the sweat forming on his forehead, as if *his* behavior were in question.

"Matti is a special person in the game. He . . ."

Boruch Levi turned to Matti and heard a voice say, "He has been the St. Louis Browns' catcher, squatting behind home plate for the past three years."

Although Boruch Levi had not seen Matti's lips move, he still nodded appreciatively to him, since he had been expecting him to speak. Realizing that it must have been the rebbe who had spoken, Boruch Levi turned and bent under the lamp to find the rebbe sitting with his usual vacuous expression.

"Yes," Boruch Levi confirmed, but with a confused finality. Since the rebbe seemed to know everything about Matti and baseball, he really didn't know how to continue.

The rebbe, indeed, needed no explanatory lectures about baseball from anyone, least of all Boruch Levi. When Matti's late father had come to the beis midrash for help with his wayward son, the rebbe had dispatched Reb Zelig to the ballpark to find out exactly what Matti was doing. It wasn't easy, for Reb Zelig had no more natural affinity for the game than did Boruch Levi. The rebbe had to send him back to the grandstands time and time again until he could explain the fine points of the game. When he finally received the information, the rebbe immediately recognized that the butcher's gifted son had fallen to great depths of degradation.

The apparently innocent national pastime of the neo-Egyptian exile reeked of those vile sins for which a Jew must forfeit his life rather than transgress the commandments. In front of men, women, and children, they played the game in pajamas, veritable sexual lewdness. The communal chant of "Kill the umpire" was an invitation for the spilling of blood. The three white bases above ground symbolized the idolatrous Christian trinity. Only home plate, buried in the dirt, retained a suggestion of solitary unity, and there, thank God, Matti resided. There could be no doubt as to the depths of the idolatry, for Reb Zelig reported that every time a batsman scored a home run, the otherwise quiet, dignified customer seated next to the sexton would intone, "Holy Jesus!" and offer him a bottle of beer.

The rebbe realized, too, that baseball, like all powerfully seductive impurities such as the witch Grannie Zara, posed as life, when in reality it was death. Played by nine men on a side, together the two sides created the number eighteen, the numerological equivalent of the Hebrew word for life, chai, but in reality, just as with Grannie Zara, the two nines opposed each other and never could reach true life. That nine represented the symbolic number of baseball was confirmed in the regulation nine innings, during which the pajama-clad degenerates pranced about the three white bases (spitting upon home plate and striking it with their bats), while the paying customers aspired to "kill the umpire" and revered "Holy Jesus." It came as no surprise to the Krimsker Rebbe that they had baseball problems.

"What exactly is the baseball problem?" the rebbe asked.

"Rebbe, Matti is planning to cause the St. Louis Browns to lose tomorrow's game. He had my brother-in-law, the cripple Barasch, bet ten thousand dollars in cash this afternoon on the opposing team. Matti has been named in a Chicago grand jury investigation by big-syndicate gamblers as having planned to perform an illegal act."

"Is this true?" the rebbe asked Matti.

"Yes, basically it is, but not the part about the syndicate. They contacted me, and I turned them down cold, but the money, Barasch, and my intent to fix tomorrow's game . . . that's all absolutely true," Matti admitted in complete candor.

"Good," said the rebbe, nodding his head affirmatively. "This is what we have been waiting for!"

Matti and Boruch Levi were both completely taken aback, but it was Boruch Levi who burst out, "No, Rebbe, it's not good at all! You don't understand. The chief himself said that it's the national pastime, sacred. He said that if cards, dice, and horses aren't enough for Matti, why, it's too bad. The very reputation of our fair city is at stake."

Flushing red in angry agitation, Boruch Levi paused for breath.

"What else did the chief of police say?" the rebbe asked.

"He and the inspector said that in Chicago the goniff responsible for cheating in last year's World Series was one of ours, and that another Jewish cheater, right here in St. Louis, wouldn't look very good. The chief said that the best thing would be for the Browns to win, but above all, no heavy bets should be placed on the other team. Matti has to contact the syndicate and tell them the business is off. They warned that if something funny happens tomorrow, Matti and Barasch will wake up in jail."

Boruch Levi was relieved now that he had managed to convey the problem.

"If the syndicate isn't involved, then Matti's was the only bet," the rebbe said, turning to Matti for confirmation.

"Yes, that's right. There is no other bet. They don't know anything about it," Matti said.

"Then why are they talking about you in Chicago?" Boruch Levi asked.

"Because a man named Abe Levin met me in New York and tried to get me to fix a game, but I turned him down. Although I liked the idea, I didn't need him. I suppose he's in trouble and is trying to convince them that he is cooperating."

"It sounds suspicious," Boruch Levi insisted.

"I'm sure it does. In fact it is suspicious, but they don't know anything about tomorrow's game and wouldn't have any reason to bet on it. Since you picked up the money, there's no reason for anyone at all to bet."

"I didn't pick up the money; Inspector Doheen did," Boruch Levi stated.

"All the more reason for no one to bet," Matti said.

"I hope so," Boruch Levi replied, unconvinced.

"That is all the chief said?" the rebbe asked.

"They're waiting for an answer. If we can't stop this business right now, then they'll have to enter the case in their official capacity. They said that that would be very embarrassing for everyone. The chief himself said that if cards, dice, and horses—" Boruch Levi began to repeat himself, but the rebbe cut him short.

"When do you have to report to your friends?"

"Whenever we finish. The chief lives across the street from me, and Inspector Doheen will wait for me there."

Boruch Levi wondered whether he had to mention that, since the rebbe seemed to know everything, but he didn't want the rebbe to think that he had violated the Sabbath by driving or using a telephone.

"Oh, one more thing. They said that they would provide any help that I might need," Boruch Levi added as an afterthought.

"Have you eaten yet?" the rebbe asked Boruch Levi.

"No," Boruch Levi answered, thinking that was a ridiculous question, "but I'm not hungry."

"The first Sabbath feast commemorates the first Sabbath, when the world was created; it must not be delayed. Reb Mattus, have you sanctified the Sabbath and partaken of the first feast?"

"Yes, thank you, I have," Matti said.

"Good, that's most important. That's where we start," the rebbe said. "Reb Boruch Levi, please tell the rebbetzin that you have not eaten. You must concentrate on all the blessings to effect the divine unions."

Boruch Levi stood up to execute his rebbe's command, but he did so with a troubled heart; the rebbe didn't seem to understand the gravity of the situation.

"The Detroit Tigers had better lose tomorrow," he exclaimed.

The rebbe looked at him with his absurd wide eyes.

"That's the opposing team that Matti bet on. They're from Detroit."

"Tigers?" the rebbe asked, as if he had heard of them somewhere.

"Yes, teams have nicknames. St. Louis has the Browns and the Cardinals. Chicago has the White Sox and the Cubs. Detroit has the Tigers, the big striped cats."

"Yes, I know," the rebbe said.

"Oh," Boruch Levi replied. He was beyond embarrassment. How was he to know what the rebbe did and didn't know?

The rebbe stood up. "Thank you, Reb Boruch Levi," he said, pointing toward the kitchen.

After Boruch Levi had left, the rebbe carefully closed the door.

# CHAPTER TWENTY-SIX

WHEN YAAKOV MOSHE FINEBAUM, THE KRIMSKER REBBE, said that Matti's attempt to fix tomorrow's game was good, he meant it, for he was certain that Boruch Levi had brought him the American Moses. It was all so perfectly obvious, and yet who would have guessed? Certainly not even the rebbe, and he should have. Pharaoh's daughter had plucked Moses from the River Nile and raised him as her son in her father's royal palace. Who could have led the Jews out of Egypt? Not an intimidated, scourged slave but a proud free prince. Moses could contend with pharaoh because Moses knew the enemy as he knew himself; for indeed he himself had been the enemy as a member of the pharaonic house.

In America, however, the people were sovereign. Although the rebbe harbored high hopes for vice president Silent Cal Coolidge, the presidency just did not possess majesty. In America the people ruled; their royal court was the ballpark, and their princes were the players. Matti Sternweiss of lowly Krimsk birth had forsaken his people and had been raised in the populist pharaoh's palace, behind home plate, calling the signals in republican majesty.

"Come join me on the couch," the rebbe said to the majestic republican leader who could contend with the unholy adversary as an equal.

The small, shaded desk lamp threw a meager pool of light that barely reached their feet. Seated in the enshrouding shadow, Matti couldn't see the rebbe any more distinctly now than he had from the table, but nevertheless, Matti joined him. He had an inclination to reach out and place his hand on the rebbe's knee, physically demonstrating their bond.

"Why is it good, Rebbe, that I tried to fix the game?"

"Because it is only from the depths that we reach the heights."

"What are the heights?" Matti asked sadly, as if he wanted to believe but simply could not delude himself.

"Once you extricate yourself from the depths, you will be there," the rebbe said, almost cheerfully.

Matti felt that the rebbe had no idea who his uninvited guest really was.

"I didn't do it just for the money. I did it because of a woman."

"Sexual passion has great power; it always tempted our leaders. Here they worship plain money. Paper, not even real gold."

"Rebbe, she isn't Jewish," Matti protested.

"In Egypt, Joseph the Righteous was tempted by Potiphar's wife. He managed to escape, and so will you, Reb Mattus."

"I met her in the hospital when my father was dying,"

Matti whispered, humiliating himself. Boruch Levi had known the location of his true shame.

"Only after Joseph's death did the children of Israel descend into slavery's degradation. Of course, in America things move much more quickly. Here Joseph doesn't have to die before Moses appears. It's about time progress was applied to the spiritual realm."

Matti recoiled ever so slightly from the rebbe. None of his confessions disappointed the holy man; rather, he welcomed them almost as if they fulfilled specific prophetic criteria. Could the rebbe be suggesting that he, Matti, was the redeemer? Matti was flattered by the idea. Who wouldn't be? And it put his less than noble behavior in a good light. He felt great affection and appreciation for someone who, however mistakenly, could think so highly of him. Out of respect, he wanted to protect the rebbe from the dangers of such illusions.

"Baseball is such a silly game," Matti said.

"What did you expect from impurity?" the rebbe asked rhetorically.

Matti, however, treated the question seriously and carefully weighed his answer.

"Well, I expected . . . majesty, I suppose," he admitted, surprised by his own answer.

"That's exactly what it is. Was pharaoh any different?"

Matti thought the Egyptian business was mad, but he was fascinated by the neat logic of the metaphor. Baseball was silly because impure majesty must perforce have no real value. Baseball certainly was king in America. That's what had attracted Matti. Penny Pinkham, too. Insofar as she was attracted to him, it was because he wore the royal purple—or in this case, brown—robes of the American League St. Louis Browns. That was all very true—as far as it went.

"I think, though, you're making a mistake, rebbe," Matti said quietly.

"About what?"

"About me."

"In what way?"

"I'm a baseball-playing bum."

"What did you expect?"

Matti understood; the rebbe meant that an immoral action must degrade the actor.

"Perhaps I was drawn to such impurity because of the impurity within me," Matti suggested.

"No doubt you were."

"Then I think you have the wrong man."

"No, I don't."

"How can you be so sure?"

"An Arabian king far from Egypt who had heard of Moses' greatness wanted to see exactly what the great man looked like, so he commissioned an artist and sent him to paint a portrait. When the artist returned with the picture, the king called his ministers and advisers. The experts in physiognomy looked at it and said that this was the portrait of a mean, vile, base individual. They suggested that the artist must have painted a portrait of the wrong man. The artist, however, insisted that he had faithfully executed his charge and that the experts were mistaken. Deciding to find out for himself, the king traveled to see Moses; he discovered that the artist had perfectly portrayed the face of Moses and concluded that his experts were of little value.

When he told Moses the story, the great leader informed him that both the artist and the experts were correct. Moses confessed that indeed he possessed all the baseness that the experts had perceived in him, but that through willpower he had overcome his natural villainy and attained great virtue. He added that had he been born naturally good, then he would have had no more merit than a block of wood."

The story was appropriately inspirational, but it only depressed Matti further. In fact, the more he protested, the more convincingly the rebbe argued. Matti retained his doubts about the rebbe's ability to work miracles, but he had no doubt as to his intellectual abilities. As for Moses, it was all too fantastic.

"I can assure the rebbe that I will do my best tomorrow against the Detroit Tigers. Since no one but Barasch and myself knew anything of our conspiracy, I can't imagine that anyone else will bet heavily on the game."

"You don't accept what I am saying," the rebbe declared with a directness that made Matti squirm.

"I appreciate the Rebbe's confidence that I can and will become a better person," Matti said rather weakly.

"Why don't you accept what I am saying?" the rebbe persisted.

"Well, I'm just not Moses. For one thing, baseball isn't pharaoh."

"But you yourself said it was majesty," the rebbe reminded him.

Yes, Matti himself had said that. "But surely there are differences?"

"Such as?"

"For one thing, Moses received his charge from God through the burning bush."

Although Matti stated this definitively—after all, he had seen no bushes that burned without being consumed—the more he argued, the more he seemed to be admitting the possible validity of the rebbe's premise. And when Matti mentioned burning and consuming, Lieutenant Max Miller's flaming airplane came to mind. That, too, made Matti uncomfortable. For the first time in their interview, the rebbe had no ready response. Encouraged by the silence, Matti pressed his case.

"How can one possibly compare pharaonic Egypt with today's America? There are too many differences. I'm not Moses."

"The times and the places are different. You cannot be Moses, but that might not work against you."

"What can the Rebbe possibly mean by that?"

"You are right. You saw no burning bush, and God didn't speak to you. We are no longer in the age of miracles, and we are forbidden to rely upon them. God conversed with Moses before the Torah was given at Sinai. Now that we have been given the Torah, God talks to any man of Israel every second if we choose to examine his words. You, however, are more fortunate than Moses in one respect. God asked Moses to perform strange, innovative acts that Moses never dreamed himself capable of, but you, Matti, have already done once that which you must do again."

"I have?"

Matti had an excellent memory, but he didn't know where to begin searching it for some redemptive, Mosaic act.

"Yes, Matti, you must do it again," the Krimsker Rebbe persisted.

Matti struggled to recall this significant act that totally eluded him. Someone could put a gun to his head, but he wouldn't be able to provide a hint to the answer. The rebbe had been amazing him all night, but what really disturbed Matti was the violation of his usually successful precept that what he didn't know could hurt him. He strived to calm himself—that, too, had been another virtue—but he hadn't the faintest notion what past action could be relevant to his present situation. His heart beating wildly and his eyes blinking, Matti felt like a frog about to be impaled by a boy with a pointed stick.

"Do what?" Matti beseeched.

The rebbe turned toward him, took Matti's hands in his own, and brought his face so close that even in the dark shadows Matti could see the rebbe's eyes glowing with a fierce determination that seemed to originate deep within his holy being.

"Burn the cats!" the rebbe commanded.

Matti closed his eyes in fright and tried to withdraw his hands, but the rebbe's grip grew firmer as he rasped in hoarse fervor, "Burn the cats!"

The rebbe released him, but Matti did not open his eyes. He saw himself again as a boy in Krimsk, leaving Grannie Zara's burning cabin, where Zloty and the other cats were screeching as flames announced their fiery doom. At his side was Beryl Soffer's wife, the mad Faigie Soffer, accusing him of being a witch and wanting to put her hand into his pocket. And the craziness about the magic frog; that was involved, too. He could smell the pungent, fragrant smoke that hung in the hot, still air like suffocating drapes. Had he touched his pants now on the rebbe's couch, he would not have been surprised to find them once again soaked with urine. The furious cries of the witch's imprisoned cats had risen above the crackling, fatal flames as Matti and Faigie fled into the darkness.

When Matti opened his eyes—how long had they been closed?—he found the rebbe calmly sitting back as if he were asleep.

"Burn the cats," Matti murmured. "Grannie Zara."

"Yes, you have done it before. In Krimsk, when you were a child, you destroyed the instruments of evil and evil itself. You overwhelmed unalloyed impurity on Tisha B'Av, the very day when impurity rages in the world. Burn the cats. Then Grannie Zara's Zloty and friends, and now Detroit's Tigers. You have done it before, and you can do it again."

"Faigie Soffer thought I was a Jewish witch."

"Yes, she understood part of what was happening. From her point of view, she was right. Immersed in magic and superstition, she could not distinguish between purity and impurity. Similarly, pharaoh tried to imitate Moses' miraculous acts in order to reduce Moses to a mere sorcerer like himself. But pharaoh failed even when he thought he succeeded, for when Moses turned the River Nile into blood, he affirmed the heavenly host, whereas pharaoh's feat denied the divine agencies."

Matti grasped the rebbe's last point, but even in his confused state—he felt as if he had been uprooted—he was curious as to what the rebbe would make of the fact that Faigie had tried to seduce him. He dared not ask.

"When she tried to reach into your pocket to retrieve the magic frog, you abused her—" the rebbe began.

"But, Rebbe, I thought she—"

"Again, she was partially right," the rebbe said.

Matti tried to puzzle out what the rebbe meant, but again he was at a loss. "She was?"

"Well, she was not altogether wrong, just somewhat premature in her search. After all, if the photographs are correct, when you play baseball you squat down like a frog behind home plate with that rounded cage on your face and the large glove on your hand."

Short, stubby Matti could never have been a graceful gazelle in the outfield or a quick, sure-clawed cat in the infield. He had certainly noticed that there was something inherently awkward and froglike about catching; indeed, he was thankful for it. How else could he have succeeded in professional baseball? Some of his teammates even occasionally called him "Toad." According to the rebbe, Faigie was right: there had been a frog in his pants—him.

"Is there anything you would like to ask me?"

Matti's first reaction was to shake his head. He had heard more than he had ever expected to hear. What could he possibly ask? Krimsk had certainly fallen out of the sky all over him—frog, Zloty, Grannie Zara, and all!

"Rebbe?" Matti asked quietly. "I think I had an omen. Is the Rebbe familiar with the name Lieutenant Max Miller?"

"The postal aviator who crashed and died in New Jersey?"

"Yes." Matti felt no joy at the rebbe's omniscience. Had the rebbe named all of Penny Pinkham's childhood friends, Matti would not have been surprised.

"Did you know him?" the rebbe asked.

"No, I just read about him. There was nothing for the farmers to do except walk around in the field collecting the letters."

When the rebbe didn't respond, Matti turned to him.

"So?" asked the rebbe.

"So? It's such a tragic waste!"

"He wanted to deliver the mail by air, and he did. The mail went through, all of it."

"Does the rebbe think he died happy?"

"He fulfilled his mission."

Matti sat considering the strange idea that Lieutenant Max Miller had died fulfilled. "I don't think he was very happy."

"Do you think that he would have traded the life he had lived for another?"

"No, I suppose not." Matti reflected. "The newspapers said that many of the letters he saved were sent from Europe to people in the Midwest. I thought one might be from someone in Krimsk to me."

Matti spoke in a subdued, half-joking tone, but the rebbe answered in absolute seriousness.

"Now you know," he said.

"I do?" Matti asked.

"God has many messengers. Lieutenant Max Miller chose to be among them. You were right."

"I see," said Matti, "but how did you know about the plane crash?"

"I read the newspapers when I'm not on the reservation. But enough of this; now I want you to make a blessing with Boruch Levi."

Boruch Levi started to stand up when the rebbe entered the kitchen, but the rebbe told him to remain seated and to complete his Sabbath meal. Reb Zelig, however, did stand and remained at attention next to the rebbe's chair. Although the rebbe did not eat, he insisted that Matti recite aloud the appropriate blessings over the cake and tea so that Boruch Levi could answer "Amen."

"It is important that you two begin your relationship at the Sabbath table," the rebbe said.

Both Boruch Levi and Matti raised their eyebrows at this suggestion.

"Boruch Levi will be working with you," the rebbe said.

"With me?" Matti asked.

"Yes, he was trained by the chief of police himself and makes a very fine lieutenant," the rebbe said.

Boruch Levi nearly dropped his glass of tea. Suddenly, Rabbi Max appeared much less distasteful. Compared to Matti, Rabbi Max seemed positively attractive, even with the distillery in the synagogue, and Boruch Levi had not been commanded to serve Rabbi Max, merely to pray with him. Here was the Krimsker Rebbe ordering him to serve Matti Sternweiss, the baseball-playing clown, as he served Michael O'Brien, the chief of police. Why, just equating the two seemed a vulgar sacrilege.

"Matti, if you need any help in your holy endeavor, do not hesitate to call upon Reb Boruch Levi."

Matti's eyes met Boruch Levi's and he saw the same confusion that he himself must have shown when the rebbe told him he was the American Moses.

"Reb Boruch Levi, are you ill?" the rebbe asked.

"Yes, I think so, Rebbe."

The rebbe was not surprised. "What's the matter? Would you like to lie down?"

"Rebbe, no, it's—" Boruch Levi began.

"What is it, Reb Boruch Levi?"

"It's Matti," Boruch Levi said. He looked at the baseball player, who wore a sympathetic expression that seemed to encourage Boruch Levi. "He's a plain thief."

Boruch Levi was not one to say things behind a man's back that he would not repeat to his face. He stared directly at the man whom he had reviled. Not the least bit offended, Matti nodded in agreement and looked at the rebbe for a reply. Slightly embarrassed at having uttered such harsh remarks in the rebbe's presence, Boruch Levi turned slowly to face the Krimsker Rebbe.

"Do you wish to serve me or not?" the rebbe asked wearily, suggesting that Boruch Levi's contribution was welcome but not essential.

"Yes, but not him. I don't think the Rebbe understands who he is," Boruch Levi said very openly.

"You, who once received divine messages through your horse's backside, do not trust your rebbe." Yaakov Moshe shook his head mournfully at the deep enslavement that blinded his hasidim. "Reb Boruch Levi, yes, what you say was once true, but now it is so no longer. As for yourself, Matti Sternweiss is your only hope to bring St. Louis and Krimsk together."

"He is?"

"Yes, what you only dreamed about, he has already done."

"He has?"

"Yes, in Krimsk, when you dreamed of burning cats,

he actually did so. Here in St. Louis you again dreamed your dream of destroying evil. You must help him, because only he can realize it."

Boruch Levi looked incredulously at Matti, who, although embarrassed to have such things revealed, did not deny anything.

"I don't understand," Boruch Levi confessed.

"You don't have to, but let me remind you: pharaoh's advisers warned him that Moses aspired to steal his kingdom. They suggested that pharaoh test the child's nature by placing before the boy a shiny golden crown and a smoldering coal. Like any normal child, Moses reached for the crown, but the angel Gabriel guided his hand to the coal. Tonight you have guided Matti aright, and in return you shall be guided."

Boruch Levi saw for himself that Matti had changed in the short time they had been at the rebbe's. There was no trace of arrogance or rudeness; if anything, he could be described as humble. But what about tomorrow's baseball game? There was still the other team.

"What shall I tell the police?"

Animated, the rebbe sat up. "You must tell them the truth—that the Detroit Tigers will lose."

"They will?" Boruch Levi asked skeptically.

"Of course they will. It is a matter of holiness. On the holy Sabbath the impure spirits lose their powers. They are totally impotent. Whoever bets on the St. Louis Browns stands to make a fortune."

Boruch Levi did not wear his usual scowl; that would have been disrespectful, but he did look uncomfortable.

"Boruch Levi, you must not fear sanctity and the

Sabbath. For if you protect the Sabbath, then it will protect you," the rebbe said.

"It will?"

"Boruch Levi, have you ever dreamed of the chief of police?" the rebbe asked, slightly exasperated.

"No," said Boruch Levi.

"Of course not, because your dreams come true. You cannot serve them both. You dreamed of burning cats, and Matti will defeat the Detroit Tigers. Serve him, but beware of the police, for they are murderers."

"Oh." Boruch Levi gasped.

"Now, Matti, you must rest for tomorrow's test. You must remember that they had nothing to do but pick up the letters because the pilot succeeded in his mission."

Matti nodded.

"Boruch Levi, take him home so he can rest."

"Yes," Boruch Levi answered, but the rebbe was no longer listening. He had closed his eyes and was breathing very evenly and silently. Boruch Levi and Matti left the kitchen quietly so as not to disturb him.

# CHAPTER TWENTY-SEVEN

MATTI AND BORUCH LEVI WALKED BACK IN SILENCE. Matti wanted to apologize to Boruch Levi for embarrassing him, but he couldn't. That would mean explaining things that he himself didn't understand. Matti had arrived at the rebbe's as a failed cheat and had emerged as—what?— a prince of his people? It was more than a little confusing. Nor could Matti admit to his confusion, for that would only make Boruch Levi's job—difficult as it was—even more difficult. The only comforting statement that he managed to pronounce was, "You can rely on the rebbe." When Boruch Levi looked at him noncommittally, Matti added, "I'm sure of it," as confidently as he could.

Matti returned to his thoughts about the surprising connections between Krimsk and St. Louis. Everything that had seemed so new was suddenly not very new at all. Even Penny Pinkham, especially Penny Pinkham. Matti realized that she had been present in his Krimsk childhood fantasy; when he sat as the powerful Polish noble in his glorious manor house, she had been the blond princess at his side.

He smiled, remembering that even as a boy in Krimsk, he had realized that in the imaginary castle with its culinary splendor, milk and meat were never served together. As for Penny Pinkham herself, Matti no longer felt angry and hurt. She had proven to be as ephemeral as the blond princess. How could he blame her for not realizing his fantasies? She had made the right choice in Dufer; after all, a blond princess was entitled to serve milk and meat together to a blond twenty-game prince. The rebbe was right about that; baseball was America's majesty. Matti suddenly felt sorry for the real Moses. Like Matti, Moses could never have become a true prince in pharaoh's court. Had he remained, he would have been only a court jester. Moses had no real choice, and neither did Matti. Nor did Lieutenant Max Miller, according to the rebbe. Did anyone? Matti wondered. At any rate, Matti felt more comfortable with himself than he had for a long time. He did, however, have something on his conscience.

"Barasch was only doing what I asked him to do," Matti stated apologetically.

"He shouldn't have done it."

"I shouldn't have asked him."

Boruch Levi's lack of response suggested that Matti hadn't improved the cripple's position with his rigid, uncompromising brother-in-law.

"None of the money was his," Matti added.

As they passed under the silky glow of gaslight, Boruch Levi turned to examine Matti in disbelief. "None?"

"None. It was all mine. He refused to gamble with Malka's money."

"Then why did he do it?" Boruch Levi asked drily.

Matti realized that Boruch Levi didn't believe him. For a very good reason: Matti couldn't explain Barasch's motive.

"I don't know, but it, too, has something to do with Krimsk," Matti said.

Boruch Levi heard the uncertainty in Matti's voice—it was the same vulnerable tone in which Matti had spoken to the rebbe—and it inspired belief.

"I thought no one was further from Krimsk than America's Bernard Limp Legs," wondered Boruch Levi. Yet he believed Matti. Hadn't they all stumbled upon Krimsk in the streets of the New World? Why not Barasch Limp Legs, too? Cripples had all the more reason to stumble.

"For some reason, he wasn't so American in his dealings with me," Matti replied. Although he wanted to tell Boruch Levi about Barasch's unbridled enthusiasm for Matti's pursuit of the blond princess, he couldn't do so without betraying Barasch's confidence. Vulgar Malka was Boruch Levi's sister. Revealing Barasch's infatuation for wispy blondes wouldn't sit well with his puritanical brother-in-law.

"That's strange," Boruch Levi said.

"Yes, it is," Matti answered honestly. What did Penny Pinkham have to do with Barasch's Krimsk? His Krimsk had consisted of Beryl Soffer and his match factory. Then Matti suddenly recalled the one essential act that had slipped from his fine memory. He had burned the cats with Faigie Soffer, the wispy blond wife of Barasch's master. Matti understood: Faigie Soffer was Barasch's Penny Pinkham. Both Beryl's Faigie and Dufer's Penny were the master's wife and beyond Barasch's and Matti's reach.

"The rebbe understood all that, too!" Matti whispered.

"Understood what?" Boruch Levi asked.

Matti wanted to share his discovery, but that would be baring another man's soul.

"Understood everything that happened to me and everything I was doing," Matti answered. "I thought I knew so much, and I know so little."

"You understand the rebbe, don't you?"

"In some ways," Matti answered.

"Why did he say that the chief and the inspector were murderers?" Boruch Levi asked quietly.

Matti heard the disbelief in Boruch Levi's tone. Given the jolting shocks that Boruch Levi had absorbed tonight, Matti didn't want to add another. When he didn't answer immediately, Boruch Levi asked again, "Are they really murderers?"

"It's not who they are; it's what the world is," Matti carefully enunciated.

"I don't understand," Boruch Levi said plaintively.

"They may be as decent as you think they are, but in this distorted world—the world of Prohibition and syndicated crime and fixed ball games—a man licensed to carry a gun and sworn to enforce the law would have to be a saint not to abuse his authority. It really wouldn't be his fault so much as the fault of the way things are."

Boruch Levi remained silent for a while before he ventured, "So they're not really murderers?"

"Well, I suppose they're not to you and to me, but they are to the rebbe. He deals with life on a different level."

"Can we rely on him in our world?" Boruch Levi asked with a touch of embarrassment.

"Absolutely!" Matti replied reflexively, although he himself wasn't so sure. How could he be? Yet he had an overwhelming desire for Boruch Levi to have such certainty. Why? Did he think Boruch Levi desired it, or was Matti hoping to convince himself through another?

"He knows about baseball?"

"More than anyone I have ever met."

"He's a rebbe," Boruch Levi said, his confidence having returned.

"Yes, he is. For a while I had forgotten," Matti confessed.

"I did, too."

Having arrived at Matti's building, they stopped. A gaslight was not far away, and they could see each other clearly as they stood under the magnificent, broad-leafed, soaring sycamores that covered them like a great penumbral cloud. No longer strangers to each other, they sensed the night and their standing together against the encircling darkness.

"Would you like to come in for some tea or a drink?" Matti asked.

"What do you drink?"

"The hooch Rabbi Max sells," Matti said with a faint touch of irony that he should be offering Boruch Levi such refreshment on their holy Krimsker Rebbe's Sabbath.

"I'll send you over some good whiskey," Boruch Levi announced without his usual lordly, patronizing air.

"Thank you," Matti said, but he remained where he was and made no move to leave.

Aware of the rebbe's command to serve Matti, Boruch Levi asked, "Is there anything I can do?"

"No, everything is fine. It's just that a lot of unexpected things have happened tonight."

Boruch Levi nodded in agreement. "Do you want me to come in?"

"Yes, but I don't think you should keep the chief waiting," Matti said.

"I should see them. We'll make it some other time."

"I'd like that," Matti said, extending his hand. "*Gut Shabbos* and thank you."

Boruch Levi firmly grasped Matti's hand and warmly returned the blessing. As Matti turned to go, Boruch Levi said, "Matti, I'm sorry that I didn't bring you a letter from Krimsk."

"But you have already, Boruch Levi, and it's a very fine one at that. Thank you," Matti said.

Although Boruch Levi didn't understand exactly what Matti meant, he sensed that on some level it was true. With a newfound respect, even affection—Matti after all had assured him that the chief and Doheen weren't really murderers—protectively Boruch Levi watched Matti return home.

# CHAPTER TWENTY-EIGHT

A WEARY BORUCH LEVI CLIMBED INTO BED NEXT TO HIS sleeping wife. He began to toss uneasily as he wondered about everything that had already happened and was about to happen tomorrow. His mind kept returning to the chief and Doheen. His second meeting had gone very well, hadn't it? He wasn't sure.

Doheen had ushered the confident Boruch Levi into the parlor. The chief was seated in an easy chair, with a glass of whiskey on the lamp table at his side.

"Unless I miss my mark, I think Boruch Levi has good news for us," Doheen said in what was for him a veritable explosion of small talk.

"I had expected no less from our faithful friend, but good news is always welcome," the chief agreed.

Boruch Levi nodded and sat on the sofa next to Doheen, who also had a heavy whiskey glass by his side. He poured a generous one for Boruch Levi.

"Yes, relax a moment. I'll wager you've had a busy evening."

The chief sat back and sipped his drink. Boruch Levi eyed the short, massive, hexagonal glass in his strong hand. All precise angles and thick reflecting surfaces of mellow light and Irish whiskey, it was a match for his powerful grip. So unlike the way Jews drank from simple little shot glasses, balanced between thumb and fingers. He swallowed deeply and felt the fiery liquid coursing down his throat. It was too warm for a Jew to be drinking at such an hour, but the chief welcomed his participation. The Krimsker Rebbe had, too. So this was Irish kiddush, then, a secular sanctification, if such a thing existed. He would have to ask Matti about that. He might know. The thought of Matti warmed him almost as much as the liquor.

"We have nothing to worry about. The St. Louis Browns will win tomorrow," he informed them, speaking over his glass, as if the golden whiskey were his audience.

They both sat up with a sense of relief tempered by a veteran wariness at his innocent certainty.

"Can you be so sure?" Doheen asked.

"I can, but I might not be able to explain it. It involves men's souls and destiny."

Doheen smiled at the mention of souls; the chief did not.

"I can promise you that Matti Sternweiss will do his very best, and that no other unexpected bets will be placed on the Detroit team. He and my brother-in-law were in this alone."

"Good, that's the important thing," the chief said, sipping his whiskey. "Boruch Levi, *you* are very sure, but in these things a man can't be too sure. Do you think he might be pulling a fast one on us?"

Boruch Levi put his glass on the coffee table and shook his head.

"We trust you like a brother. But can you be so sure? I've been a policeman too long not to be a little apprehensive when the devil discovers a sudden impulse to do the Lord's work."

Not wanting to hurt his trusted friend, the chief said this gently, as if whispering to his dark whiskey.

"I've never been a policeman, but I do know my own. I know where he came from and where he's going. I give you my word."

"Boruch Levi, your word is golden with us, but these are earnest matters. Men can get killed in such affairs," the chief said, trying to instruct his young foreign friend in the ways of the wicked American underworld.

Boruch Levi flinched at the mention of death.

"Whoever bets on our home team stands to make his fortune. If you have a charity that needs some money, bet on our St. Louis Browns. I will insure you against any loss," Boruch Levi declared.

Boruch Levi stood up. How could he be any more forthright than that? He reached to take the chief's wounded hand in his. "Thank you for calling me about this. Don't worry any more about it. You must rest. We no longer have a problem. Trust me."

"Yes, I do, my friend," the chief said wearily.

Opening the door, Doheen had asked in a feverish whisper, "Boruch Levi, are you sure?"

"Absolutely," he had said with his stubborn certainty. And he walked into the mellow darkness that seemed to smell of Irish whiskey.

Things seemed to have gone well. Boruch Levi had reported good news, but they had remained doubtful. How could he have told them about the Krimsker Rebbe, Zloty the cat, and his own prophetic dreams? What was more, Boruch Levi didn't want to tell them—it wasn't their business—but he still resented their doubts. Things really hadn't gone so well. Just as the rebbe predicted, he couldn't serve them both. Boruch Levi never thought it would happen so quickly, much less that he himself would cripple the relationship. And what about the chief's remark that men could get killed in such matters? He tried to imagine what Matti might say about that, but a heavy blanket of weariness descended upon him. He rolled over, and within a minute he was snoring.

Although he was lying still in his bed, Matti's eyes were wide open. A breeze pushed the filmy curtains apart and revealed the great dark bulk of the sycamore trees. He could hear their stiff, hand-shaped leaves rustling. Yes, he thought, it was as if the rebbe had parted a curtain. Perhaps the rebbe's view of his future was suspect, but certainly he was right in picturing Matti's past as verging on folly. A folly of dishonesty, bogus romance, and fake identity that he could now expiate simply by helping defeat the Detroit Tigers—or, as the rebbe put it, by "burning the cats." That was an amusing analogy. And who was Zloty? Ty Cobb! How would the rebbe have worked that out? No, that would be no problem. The Krimsker Rebbe believed that nothing happened by accident: an unseen hand touched everything. Well, almost everything. What had Reb Gedaliah taught them as children? Everything depends upon heaven except the fear of heaven.

Staring through the open window into the dark, un-
formed night, Matti felt very much at ease. He couldn't
remember ever having experienced such a sensation of
well-being and relaxation. The world seemed so new and
mysterious. But best of all, it was his world. Was an unseen
hand tracing his destiny across this world, just as the invisible man inside the great black scoreboard posted the
results, inning by inning? What was there to fear in that
predestined game? It would be his life, his world. Not a
child's game, not an imagined romance, not a counterfeit
success. Tomorrow he could find out about his world, but
now he had a delicious sense of anticipation, the way the
first scent of the rich sweet cloud of bubbling fish broth
made his mouth water Friday afternoon before the table was
even set. He could hear the great scaly-barked sycamores
kneading the darkness with their stiff green leaves, but they
held no fear for him. He was secure, and with the indolent
comfort of a silky red apple ripening on a warm, smooth
tree in his boyhood town of Krimsk, he closed his eyes.

Shayna Basya's eyes were closed, but she was wide awake.
She was wondering why her husband had not made love to
her tonight. Her eyes were closed in the now rather forlorn
hope that the rebbe would kiss them in his special way.
Tonight things had seemed so very promising after the
rebbe had decided not to visit the savage Osage reservation. Since their American honeymoon began, they had
always spent the Sabbath together, celebrating the Sabbath
night of "holy unions," as Yaakov Moshe called it.
 She put her finger gently to her eyelid and felt the many
furrows. Although a myriad of fine lines crisscrossed Shayna

Basya's face with the geometric precision of a doily, they were not deeply ingrained. Testifying to her age, this ceaseless fretwork said little about her spirit. Indeed, Shayna Basya radiated a youthful sensibility, for she was something a doily could never be. Quite simply, the Krimsker Rebbetzin was a woman in love. From that final Tisha B'Av night in Krimsk when she lay in her husband's arms and Yaakov Moshe had called her by name, her loneliness had ended. When his name was mentioned, she felt a glow. When he entered the room, she found herself smiling, and when he held her and pronounced her name, the passion returned.

Ever since that night, she had felt more like a girl than a woman. When the rebbe announced that their daughter Rachel Leah was engaged to Hershel Shwartzman, a man she had neither heard of nor seen, she simply said "*mazel tov*," and when the rebbe announced their precipitous departure from Krimsk, she immediately began packing. The journey to America and the years in St. Louis were an extended honeymoon. The distance from Krimsk, the strange new American world, all these things that intimidated the other older Jewish women who hovered close to the sink and stove, Shayna Basya enjoyed. She delighted in the sputtering cars rushing down Delmar Boulevard in a never-ending procession, as if over the horizon God himself were taking them out of a great box and winding them up. Strolling in her neighborhood, she enjoyed the symmetrical sidewalks, the gas streetlights, and the friendly goyim who nodded at her when she went to the market, which was filled with every sort of forbidden food.

The broad green expanses of the city's Forest Park seemed fit for royalty. Downtown the great train station soared above the trains and men as if it were the first of the seven firmaments. The rebbetzin liked to wander through the massive department stores, square-windowed mountains that took up entire city blocks, where narrow aisles separated entire worlds. The metallic clang of the streetcar's bell and the klaxon beep of the automobile's horn aroused her to the strange but wonderfully frenetic world that rushed around her in never-flagging exotic energy. All so alien, so fantastic, and so perfect for a distant kingdom where she and Yaakov Moshe could live in privacy, love, and passion.

Two things, however, troubled her about America. She feared for the rebbe's life every time he visited the Indian camp. Black and white Americans did not intimidate her; in fact, many charmed her with their friendly openness and willingness to help. But the redskins seemed as bad as the goyim back in Krimichak or worse—even in the pogroms, the peasants didn't go around scalping people. The rebbe insisted that the Indians had ceased scalping long ago, but in the museum Shayna Basya had seen the tops of human heads hanging stiff and dry from a pole like hairy shrouds of death itself. She was convinced that no one who had once committed such horrible acts could ever reform. Some roads are so long that one can never turn back.

The great river that had given birth to the trading city also frightened her. This massive swirling river that drained the continent in mud-filled turbulence to the distant sea was appropriately called by an Indian name, Mississippi, the Father of Waters. She hated the mud color, for it seemed to her as if the silent, treacherous river had risen up and scalped the land of its soil.

She feared the Mississippi River for a more personal

reason: the rebbe wanted her to dip in it instead of the ritual mikveh pool that the community maintained in a perfectly well-heated building. Shayna Basya understood his logic. During their final five years in Krimsk, the rebbe had withdrawn mysteriously from the world into his study; there he had been locked in a titanic spiritual struggle with the forces of evil, locally embodied in Grannie Zara the Polish witch. Then, impersonating Lilith the demon queen, Shayna Basya had furtively visited him in the dark of night. Because everyone in Krimsk understood that the rebbe had withdrawn from his wife as well, Shayna Basya could not ritually purify herself in the communal ritualarium. There was no choice other than the River Nedd, where it flowed through the dark pond between Krimsk and Krimichak.

When she had told Yaakov Moshe how, during all those years she had been visiting him under the guise of Lilith, she had gone alone to dip in the Krimsk pond rather than use the town mikveh, the rebbe's eyes had lit up. Praising her courage and wifely virtue, he declared that such nobility must be transferred to the New World: she must dip in the Mississippi to regain her ritual purity. But she never did, for she never became impure. The manner of women had ceased a month before they had left Krimsk; otherwise she would not have been able to give herself to her husband that fateful Tisha B'Av night. And her fertile cycle had never returned. Thank God it had not, for the late-night pond had filled her with terror. Trembling, she had waded into the still waters that clothed her nude body in quiet purity. The thought of stepping into and submerging herself in the Mississippi's muddy, roiling waters, which rushed by the stone levee with such ravaging force, made her heart stop. She imagined that she would be swept away toward the dark bottom and there, turning over and over like a sunken wheel, rolled through a watery underworld for eternity.

Aside from the Indians and their ominous river, life was really very pleasant in untroubled America. When the hasidim who still frequented the beis midrash now saw her, they would ask deferentially whether they could be of service. St. Louis, however, was large, and the hasidim few, so the rebbetzin could float about freely like a tourist, unrecognized, unhurried, and unburdened by aristocratic obligations.

The warm, unassuming, almost playful woman who had so surprised Boruch Levi was not aware of how much she had changed over the years. The lack of pretense that was such a significant part of the change precluded thoughtful self-examination. After all, St. Louis was only a brief interlude in her life, a bubble in time, wasn't it?

Boruch Levi's son Sammy had pricked that bubble. In some mysterious way he had reminded her of her daughter, Rachel Leah. There was no physical resemblance, nor were their personalities similar; Rachel Leah had been very shy, religious, and withdrawn. But Sammy's sweetness and eagerness to please reminded her of Rachel Leah. Poor Rachel Leah had been the great recluse's daughter, alone and uncertain. She had so desired her father's love and approval. As a nonwidowed widow during the five years that the rebbe had secluded himself, Shayna Basya had been too busy to provide enough love. She realized now that the rebbe had responded to her need for Sammy by commanding the boy to pray at the beis midrash. The reb-betzin eagerly anticipated his visits. How would he look in a sweater when the crisp cool air of autumn licked at his delicate cheeks? What had Rachel Leah looked like when the first Krimsk frosts—they came so much earlier there—settled their chill on the world? She could no longer remember; it seemed so long ago.

As Shayna Basya lay in the darkened room with her husband sleeping soundly at her side, she wondered where her daughter and son-in-law were at that very minute. The rebbe's last words to Boruch Levi came to her mind. "There was nothing to do but pick up the letters because the pilot had succeeded," he had admonished. Suddenly Shayna Basya desperately wanted the rebbe to write Rachel Leah and Hershel a letter. Right now it was the middle of the night, and the Sabbath, too, but as soon as the Sabbath was over, he must write. Yaakov Moshe would know exactly what to say and how to say it. He was, after all, the Krimsker Rebbe, the most remarkable of men. A true pilot.

"Yaakov Moshe! Wake up! I must speak to you," she said fervently.

Almost impossible to awaken, he slept as though he were in another world. She climbed out of her bed and approached him. Facing the wall, he slept on his side.

"Yaakov Moshe, Yaakov Moshe," she called in a voice coarse with anticipation. As soon as the Sabbath was over, he must write the letter!

"Darling," she said softly as she pulled his shoulder toward her, rolling him over onto his back. Facing her, he opened his froglike eyes.

"Darling, I must tell you something right now before I forget. It simply cannot wait," she said, apologizing for waking him.

"Yes?"

"Yes," she said. "Now it is the Sabbath, but it will soon be over, and I want—"

"The holy Sabbath?" he asked slowly.

"Yes, the holy Sabbath. You were saying earlier that there was nothing to do but collect the letters," she began to explain.

"The holy Sabbath?" he asked again in wonderment.

"Yes, the holy Sabbath, when it is forbidden to write letters, but tomorrow night—"

"My pure Shayna Basya has awakened me to the holy Sabbath. The holy Sabbath is one-sixtieth of the World to Come, and we must effect the holy union. 'My love is mine and I am my beloved's . . .'" And, quoting the Song of Songs of Solomon, he drew her onto his bed.

With a feather touch, he traced the myriad of exciting lines on her closed eyelid with his tongue.

"Yes, my love, yes," she gasped as a wave of passion broke over the soft sands of memory, washing away her resolve and the field with its letters scattered about like fallen leaves.

# CHAPTER TWENTY-NINE

AFTER ALMOST EIGHT FULL INNINGS, THE ST. LOUIS Browns led the Detroit Tigers three to one. In the third inning Sisler had tripled off the center-field wall for one run, and in the fourth, with bases loaded, Matti himself had pushed a ground single through the infield to score two more. On the mound, Dufer had a live fastball and a sharp, precise curve. With any luck, Dufer should still have been working on a shutout, but in the sixth Cobb had walked on a pitch that Matti thought was a strike and advanced to third when Heilman lifted a blooper down the left field line that just managed to elude both the shortstop and left fielder. On a short fly to center, Cobb tagged up and hustled home, beating the throw by a step. Dufer struck out the next two batters. The Tiger score was very much a solo run. With Dufer in control, and only one more inning remaining, the Browns seemed to have a comfortable lead.

Secure in the anticipation of victory, the large Saturday afternoon crowd, once enthusiastic, now relaxed and gave more of its attention to sipping cold sodas, licking ice cream bars, and munching roasted peanuts. As the communal focus degenerated from the playing field toward more individual culinary perspectives, the crowd's voice became haphazard and sporadic. Some of these random calls reached the playing field. Although they seemed innocent enough, they made Matti uncomfortable. As he crouched behind home plate calling Dufer's pitches, he felt a sense of menace floating somewhere behind him. Ironically, the more pacific the crowd became, the more he felt threatened. He knew what every professional athlete knows: it is easier to play in front of howling anonymous thousands than a small recognizable few. The former aided concentration; the latter undermined it. Fear was too strong a word, but Matti was concerned that out of the purposeless crowd a voice might call to him, causing his mind to wander into the audience rather than remain on the field where it belonged. He feared Penny Pinkham's demure smile, but most of all, he wished to avoid Barasch's familiar horsey head tossed in greeting. When he returned to the bench between innings, he stared down toward the ground until he was close enough to focus on the dugout without seeing many of the spectators beyond. In the partially submerged dugout he was able to relax with either the boisterous roar or the almost soporific buzzing of the crowd floating over his sheltered head.

Matti always thought of the crowd as an enormous conglomerate dog, stretching the length of the grandstands. On its feet, roaring, barking, or snapping, it exhibited obvious canine behavior. Even the buzzing was doglike. Matti imagined that the beast had fallen into a stupor, poking its dull muzzle at the myriad of fleas that rose phlegmatically from its hairy hide, producing an insistent buzzing in the afternoon heat. As for the crowd's fickle affections and lack of patience, well, Matti never had liked dogs. They were stupid, flea-bitten beasts, and if indeed they were man's best friend as Dufer claimed, that didn't say very much for friendship or for man. Matti realized that the rebbe's peroration against the national sport applied perfectly to his own vision of the crowd: on a warm, sunny afternoon, thousands of seemingly pleasant, intelligent persons could innocently gather and create a great monster. So much for the great foundation of devoted fans that sustained the mighty pyramid of the American League.

As Matti lounged in the dugout watching the Browns listlessly take their turn at bat in the bottom of the eighth inning, he had no intention of examining the rebbe's ideas. Probably he believed them all, but this was no time for his beloved art of analysis. He must take care of first things first, and without any doubt the Browns' defeat of the Tigers was first and foremost.

The emotional luxury that Matti did indulge in was a feeling of self-satisfaction. He couldn't risk looking into the stands, but with equanimity he could glance around the dugout. To keep his pitching arm warm between innings, Dufer sat draped in a towel. Matti glanced at his partially shrouded figure. Let him win twenty games; let him have Penny Pinkham, too. Neither was for Matti, and he knew it. And if he reached for them, he would be destroyed. Chewing his bitter wad of tobacco, duplicity, and distrust, manager Zack Freeling stood with his left foot on the dugout step. How pathetic! A man Freeling's age getting ulcers over some kid's ability to throw or hit a silly little ball. As the Browns' batter drove a towering pop fly for what was certain to be the third out, the avaricious manager grimaced. Young, the Tigers' second baseman, moved a few steps back, shielded his eyes from the sun, and waited for the ball to descend on its preordained path into his glove, which it did. The Tigers trotted toward their dugout for their final chance at bat. The Browns stirred from their bench to take the field. Zack Freeling clapped his hands in encouragement, and Dufer dropped the towel from his valuable arm.

"Hey, Sirdy, let's get going," Dufer called out, but Sirdy didn't respond. "You ready, boy?"

Matti sat frozen, making no move to put on his cap and mask.

"Hey, Sirdy!" As Dufer leaned over and tapped Matti's arm, he noticed that his catcher seemed to be staring off into space.

"Sirdy, you all right?" he asked anxiously.

Matti continued gazing toward the outfield. He blinked slowly several times, like a frog closing its lidless eyes.

"Yeah," the catcher said. "I'm all right."

But he really wasn't. As he had watched the fly ball falling toward the infield, a glint of silver bobbing over the center-field fence had caught his eye. When he looked again, it wasn't there, but he was sure that he had seen it. As he passed Freeling, the manager stopped him.

"Just keep him on target."

Matti ignored Freeling and jogged out to home plate. He didn't think at all about the earthbound crowd. He didn't even hear the dull explosions as the children popped their empty peanut sacks, a sure sign that their patience had worn thin and the game was almost over.

Tossing his warm-up pitches, Dufer grew uneasy. Usually Sirdy hollered a steady stream of encouragement at him—"You can do it, relax, just play catch with me." Instead, Sirdy was silently staring past him into center field. Feeling nervous, Dufer even turned around to see if anything was going on there behind his back. Finding nothing, and hoping that he would capture Sirdy's attention, he turned back to flash his brightest, most infectious smile. Dufer smiled so broadly that his perfect, glossy teeth might have fallen out, but Sirdy didn't even respond to the wild abundance of charm. The umpire was motioning the Detroit Tigers' hitter into the batter's box when Dufer suddenly called, "Time!" and came halfway to the plate. Matti trotted out to meet him.

"Are you all right, Sirdy?" he asked.

"Why did you call time?" Matti asked, annoyed at the senseless interruption.

Chastened, Dufer shook his head slightly. "You seemed so quiet."

"Just get on with it!" Matti commanded.

"What are you looking at, Sirdy?" Dufer asked, his curiosity tinged by a dumb but very real anxiety.

"You want to win twenty games or not?"

"What do you mean? You know I do!" Dufer answered enthusiastically, welcoming the opportunity to make a definitive response.

"Then get going!"

"You bet!" Dufer pounded his glove with passionate determination.

"Play ball!" the umpire called.

"You bet!" Dufer answered the umpire.

He stalked back to the mound in a fury of indignation that he had not already won twenty games. Throwing blazing fastballs, he managed to strike out the first two Tiger batsmen on six straight pitches that popped into Matti's large padded mitt with the sharp crispness of gunshots, capturing the crowd's attention with their staccato report and putting to shame the percussion of the peanut sacks. The fans watched what was sure to be the final out of the game; Detroit's second baseman stepped into the batter's box, took a pinch of dirt to rub on his hands for a better grip, and turned to face the overpowering Charles Dufer Rawlings. All business, Dufer kicked the mound in menacing preparation, squeezed the ball ominously, and looked at Sirdy for the sign. To his dismay, he found the catcher crouched behind the plate, paying no attention to the game. Sirdy was staring at the cloudless sky as if he were expecting rain. Rattled by such inattention, Dufer stepped back off the rubber and looked up. A shiny metal airplane lazily droned over the ballpark.

"Good heavens," moaned Dufer. "You'd think he's never seen an airplane before!"

The pitcher pounded his glove in frustration and stepped back onto the mound. Sirdy wagged one short finger, calling for the fastball, and Dufer reared back to uncork a beauty. As his powerful fluid motion propelled him toward home plate, his masterful right arm beginning to catapult the baseball at nearly a hundred miles an hour, he saw to his horror that Sirdy was gazing up at the sky again, exposing his naked neck under the dark bars of the metal face mask and above the brown padding of the chest protector. Dufer was aiming his hard, lethal pitch at that pale white flower petal, which a moment earlier had been protected by Matti's poised mitt. Fearful of killing Sirdy, Dufer struggled to release the pitch prematurely, but his controlled, practiced motions made that difficult. At the last moment, he managed to roll his hand off the ball and it sailed away from home plate, driving in toward the batter's feet. The ball struck Young, the Tigers' batter, on his toe and careened down the foul line into foul territory, where the third-base coach fielded it. The batter, hopping on one foot, spun about in agony like a wounded whirling dervish.

"Take your base!" the umpire called perfunctorily and motioned the hit batsman to first base. Young dropped his bat, ceased his whirling, and began to hobble toward first base. Before he got very far, however, Zack Freeling came charging out of the Browns' dugout.

"It didn't touch him. He's faking! It hit the dirt first!" the manager bellowed indignantly.

Unfazed by the madly gesticulating manager, the umpire calmly removed his face mask, revealing a slightly weary, indulgent look. A few listless cries of "Kill the umpire" drifted out of the stands.

"It bounced on the ground first!" Zack yelled. He pointed to the dirt in front of home plate.

"No, it didn't," the umpire answered.

"Sirdy, show him where it bounced."

Matti walked forward several steps. As he crossed the naked dirt patch in front of home plate, Zack spun toward the umpire and began screaming, "See! That's where it bounced." Zack didn't notice that Matti, oblivious to the umpire and to his manager, continued walking onto the infield grass and gazed up at the sky. A thoroughly shaken Dufer came off the mound to join him.

"Sirdy, what are you looking up at that plane for all the time? Haven't you ever seen an airplane before?"

Dufer received no response.

"Say something, Sirdy!" he pleaded.

"The rebbe is nuts!" Matti muttered in dazed bitterness.

"Oh yeah?" answered Dufer, puzzled but happy that Sirdy had at last said something. He didn't know anyone named "Raby." Sirdy must have said "Baby," like in Babe. So he must mean Penny. Dufer certainly agreed. After all, hadn't the very same Penny Pinkham who said that she couldn't live without her Charles Dufer Rawlings refused his intimate affections? For that, she said, they would have to stand before a preacher. And she didn't even go to church as much as Dufer himself did!

"That's how women are, Sirdy," he commiserated.

Zack Freeling, having lost his futile argument with the home plate umpire, jogged toward the mound.

"It was an accident," Dufer said lamely, as if he were a naughty child appealing to his parent. "One more out and we got them," he added.

The manager looked at his muddled, not too clever pitcher, on whose performance his job depended.

"Yeah, sure," he nodded. He turned to the catcher: "Earn your pay, Sirdy. Settle him down and tell him what to expect." Zack wheeled back to the dugout.

Dufer stared at the dazed catcher. You would have thought that the pitch had hit Sirdy, the way he was staggering around unconscious on his feet.

"What's up, Sirdy?" Dufer asked.

"Lieutenant Max Miller," Matti answered, eyeing the plane overhead.

"Miller, he's not in the lineup, is he?" Dufer asked, mildly confused. With Sirdy, all he had to do was throw the pitch that Sirdy called for, right where Sirdy put his glove. He wasn't too good on names.

"He'll be here, all right," Matti answered quietly.

"Pinch hitter, huh?" Dufer asked.

"Play ball!" the umpire demanded.

Matti turned toward home plate, but Dufer stepped forward and grabbed his elbow.

"Hey, Sirdy, what are we going to do about it?" His handsome face writhed in ignorant frustration. Matti shrugged.

"What should I expect?" he begged.

"Flames," Matti said in stoic resignation.

"Great!" Dufer crowed. "I've got plenty of blazing speed left!"

He pounded his glove and sprinted back to the mound, saying to himself, "He wants flames. He won't even see it."

The crouching Matti certainly didn't. He might have, but suddenly the all-metal plane began to rev its engine and tilt forward to make a soaring, sweeping dive over the ballpark. Matti held his giant catcher's mitt over his head to shade his eyes against the bright sky above the plane. Aiming at the glove, Dufer dispatched his blazing fastball. As it came in high, Matti squinted painfully and brought his glove down. The ferocious pitch barreled into the un-suspecting umpire's thin chest protector with a dull thud, knocking him unconscious as if he had been pounded by a hammer. He fell in a black, dusty heap, grazing Matti's back with his head. Matti turned, picked up the ball, and threw it to Dufer, who was staring in horror at the flat black puddle, seemingly much too small to be the tall umpire he had just felled. "Jesus Christ!" Dufer whispered in fright. He looked at the ball as if it were a smoking gun.

A hush gripped the crowd; the ever raucous beast finally had grown mute in the face of catastrophe. The Browns' infielders and the other umpires came racing in fearfully. The team trainer, followed by a stretcher crew, arrived soon after. They straightened the body, rolled it onto its back, and began removing the face mask and not-very-effective chest protector. The trainer stuck strong smelling salts under the victim's nose. With the crowd agonizingly silent, the sputtering roar of the airplane overhead sounded loud and harsh, as if its propeller were cutting its way through the air, shredding it to bits in the process.

Finally, the umpire's foot began to twitch. The trainer called for a water bucket and towel. The cold splashing water revived him further. When he opened his eyes in mute, dull curiosity, like a fish plucked from the water into the strange horror of a dry atmosphere, no one bothered to tell him where he was or what had happened. He was too far gone for that. The trainer merely advised him that it would be all right. As he departed on the stretcher, his dusty little umpire's black beanie cap riding alongside like a sad reminder that its owner had once held his head upright, brief applause burst forth.

"Jesus Christ," murmured the Tigers' batter. "You can say that again," agreed the Browns' third baseman. The great Ty Cobb, who was swinging two bats in the on-deck circle to warm up, didn't even shrug as one of the other umpires hurriedly suited up in the face mask and paltry chest protector to assume his fallen colleague's duties behind home plate. "Play ball!" the new umpire cried with more loyalty than enthusiasm.

Bush, the Tiger shortstop, stepped up to the plate only to walk on four straight pitches, each a laborious herky-jerky effort on Dufer's part. Sweating, Dufer would have given anything to get the inning over with. Suddenly that no longer seemed possible. As destiny bore down on him in the ninth inning, he seemed to have forgotten how to pitch. His once-magnificent spray of hair hung limp and stale on his tortured, suffering brow. He squinted as if he were going blind when he looked at Matti for the sign, and pitched as though he had been beaned by the ball. When Ty Cobb reached out over home plate and hammered a fat pitch to left center field, the distressed Dufer looked relieved, as if he had been expecting worse. The two base runners raced around for two runs, tying the score. The throw from the outfield barely managed to hold Cobb to a triple. Determined and brutal, Ty Cobb stood on third base with an impatient, savage arrogance. His work wasn't finished yet; the score was only tied—and he would be the winning run.

Zack Freeling climbed out of the dugout, and the Brownie third baseman called time out as the manager trudged toward the pitcher's mound. Behind him the crowd howled and moaned with all the surly humiliation and disappointment of a mutt who has just had a juicy bone plucked from its lazy jaws. In a vengeful mood, Zack marched right up to Dufer, who wore a long, hangdog face.

"This has been the dumbest performance I've ever witnessed. Goddamnit, Dufer, where do you think you are? You want to pitch in the big leagues?"

Dufer slackly nodded his head.

"Well, you couldn't even pitch in Tulsa like this!"

The pitcher winced at the mention of the minor league town.

"What in blazes is happening here?"

"Sirdy keeps looking up at that little bitty airplane," Dufer said weakly, less by way of explanation than accusation.

"What?" Zack asked. He hadn't been expecting this. "What airplane?"

"That bright, shiny one up there," Dufer said bitterly, even a bit jealously, too, that Sirdy should find anything more worthy of attention than his fastball.

Zack and Dufer both looked up at the airplane. The manager spat in disgust and turned to confront his catcher, but Sirdy continued to follow the all-metal plane as it described lazy arcs in the sky.

"Sirdy, look at me, damnit!" Zack growled.

Matti looked at him.

"Do you know we're playing a ball game today?" he asked in sarcastic fury. "You're looking at airplanes! This is not a Sunday afternoon church picnic, Sirdy. This is a Saturday, and those are the Tigers, and you're being overpaid to catch a ball game that we should be winning. Do you know that?"

Zack saw the distant, troubled look in his catcher's eyes. Matti didn't respond to the stinging sarcasm, but nothing he could have said would have upset Zack more than his unexpected silence. That positively infuriated him.

"Holy smokes! Someone cast a spell on you, Sirdy? Are you bewitched?"

"A witch? What made you say that?" Matti asked in a weak and scratchy voice as if his throat were very dry and he were frightened.

"Jesus Christ, Sirdy. You look as if you've seen a ghost!" Zack said.

"You believe in those, too," Matti sneered.

Although Zack bridled at the short catcher's tone, he was pleased that Sirdy was paying attention.

"You weren't listening, Sirdy. I said this wasn't a church picnic and this isn't Sunday, the Lord's day, but I guess as a Hebrew you wouldn't know about such things," Zack said in undisguised contempt.

"I do know, and you're wrong. *This* is the holy day," Matti informed him very deliberately.

"This isn't Sunday, Sirdy," Dufer protested.

"No, it's not. That's why we're going to win this game," Matti informed the two men.

"Well, are you going to stop gawking at that miserable little airplane!"

"Yes, I am. Anyway, it will be leaving soon."

Dufer and Zack looked up. The bright monoplane stopped its acrobatics and droned off into the pale blue sky above the left field fence. They turned back to Matti for an explanation, but he was already squatting behind home plate, waiting for the game to resume.

"Okay, Dufer, just play catch with me, big boy. Nothing to it. Just like eating cake!" Matti called.

"Get him, Dufer, and you got twenty," Zack said and slapped his pitcher on the rump.

"You bet, skipper," Dufer said. "You bet." And he stared at his brainy catcher for the sign.

Matti called for the fastball. Dufer wound up and let fly for a strike that popped into Matti's glove like a bullet.

"That's it, baby! That's it!" Matti called.

Dufer, smiling, pushed back his cap and brushed his handsome hair off his shining forehead in triumph. He was back in the groove, only two more quick pitches away from ending the inning. Few in the ballpark would have disputed his confidence. Veach, the Tiger batsman, stood with a queer little smile, as if he had not seen the pitch and didn't expect to see much more of the next two.

Determined not to die on third, Ty Cobb realized that with Veach's impotence at the plate, there was only one way that he could score the winning run. As Dufer began his full windup, Cobb sprang off the bag and began a wild sprint in his effort to steal home and victory. Concentrating on his pitch, Dufer never saw him, but Matti, once again alert, picked up the charging figure out of the corner of his eye. Dufer's smooth delivery was quick and his pitch as fast as they come; Cobb couldn't possibly hope to beat it.

In a flash, Matti realized that Cobb intended to knock or kick the ball away in a jarring slide. The pitch blazed into his catcher's mitt. Clutching the ball firmly in hand, Matti lunged to protect home plate. For all his swiftness, Cobb was not a graceful runner, but he was an exceptionally powerful one. Churning like a locomotive, he bore down the line with singleminded ferocity. Assuming that Cobb would hook-slide with his flesh-raking spikes tearing into his mitt, Matti remained in a low crouch. Then at the final moment when Cobb committed himself, Matti could plunge to either side and block home plate. Cobb, however, continued his upright dash. When he was two steps away, Matti realized that his clever opponent was not going to slide at all and would make no effort to avoid the tag. He was going to barrel into Matti full force in a collision calculated to jar the ball loose. Matti was much too low to be able to meet the thrust of the great center fielder's sinewy body. Cobb might even attempt to kick Matti's mitt as if it were a soccer ball. Fierce, almost maniacal competitor that he was, Cobb was not above kicking a catcher or any other infielder in the head if he thought it could contribute to victory.

Seeing this mad, sprinting, chopping machine of spiked shoes, gouging elbows, and smashing knees one step away, Matti realized that his disadvantage was potentially disastrous. Surrendering to the imminent and unavoidable impact, he began to straighten up, but as he did so, he instinctively turned his body slightly to avoid what he calculated would be Cobb's leading knee. Cobb tried to swerve sufficiently so as to smash Sirdy with that malevolent bony instrument, but he was like a mad charging bull, and his momentum prevented him from adjusting. His knee merely grazed the catcher.

Tightly clutching the small, hard ball inside his mitt, which he held tilted forward like a blunt pike, Matti, slightly off balance, lunged forward and upward in a corkscrewing motion, trying to penetrate as harshly and deeply as possible into the underside of his opponent's sore muscles and ribs. Utilizing the brief moment before the charging Cobb would strike the inevitable punishing blows, Matti drove forward in his strange spiraling wedge, assaulting Cobb's lower left side. A jarring sensation immediately thrashed through his arms to his shoulders. Sore or not, Ty Cobb was all muscle and bone; there seemed nothing so soft as cartilage. Having made contact, Matti lowered his head, trying to pierce the iron rib cage. Straining to keep his momentum, he pushed his arms forward, forcing Cobb to impale himself on Matti's ball and glove before he could launch his own attack. A great pressure burst on his wrists and elbows, and his joints felt as if they were being hammered, but Matti stabbed and twisted the blunt instrument of his arms as deeply as he could.

Although he successfully maintained his position, Matti had no sensation of having inflicted any pain or damage before the indomitable Cobb was upon him. With an animal instinct, Matti knew that he must not drop the ball. Even as Cobb's forearm, swinging forward like a prizefighter's, struck the side of Matti's head with deadly accuracy, he was telling his body one thing—to hold on to the ball. Matti felt himself falling to the side when Cobb's trailing knee moved forward with the full force of his sprinting body to kick him in the groin. As a terrible searing pain tore through Matti, Cobb's talonlike spikes ripped ravenously at his shins and ankle. The merciless trampling ended as Cobb lowered his shoulder and butted into Matti's chest and stomach with the considerable velocity generated by his weight, speed, muscle, and mad passion for victory. Cobb now thrust his head and entire body upward, tossing Matti into the air. As Cobb stepped onto home plate, Matti was flying through the air backward in a curled, closed posture like a comma. This curve saved him both from dropping the ball and from the serious injury that would have occurred had he landed flat on his back or on his unprotected head. He absorbed the shock of crashing into the ground on his coiled back, rolling like a ball in a perfect back somersault and stopping with an abrupt jolt as his knees and feet hit the ground.

Out of breath, battered, bruised, and even bloodied where Cobb had smashed his head, Matti came to rest like a worshipful supplicant with the ball still enveloped in his clasped, extended hands. The umpire raised his arm and whipped his thumb above his closed fingers, screaming "Out!" so loudly that Matti heard him say "ow" before the roar of the crowd descended upon him like a gale wind. As the cheer continued, Dufer dashed in to lift him to his feet and lead him away to the dugout for the bottom of the ninth inning.

Matti collapsed onto the bench, and the trainer quickly helped him out of his catcher's paraphernalia. He leaned back wearily as they applied an ice pack to his forehead and eyebrow. Matti blanched at the burning sensation of the wet towel on his raw skin, but he welcomed the numbing cold that soon followed. At first he thought he imagined the low gentle soughing sound, but out of his uncovered eye he saw his teammates standing up and staring toward center field. Zack Freeling came off his perch on the dugout steps.

"Well, Sirdy, there's a sub in center field. You knocked Cobb out of the game."

Matti looked up at the manager.

"You stuck him right where he hurt, didn't you?" Zack said with admiration and a touch of contempt. Matti closed his eyes to absorb more of the numbing cold.

"Can you bat?"

"Yeah," Matti said.

After Zack returned to his station on the steps, Matti opened his good eye. He watched Smith foul off four or five pitches before striking out on a poor breaking pitch. Matti dropped the ice pack and began to climb out of the dugout to take his place in the on-deck circle.

"Hey, Sirdy, your leg is bleeding. Are you all right?" Dufer asked.

Matti paused and looked down at his ripped pants. His high woolen sock was suffused with a dark red.

"You ought to get it taken care of," Dufer insisted.

"This won't take long."

Matti knelt on the ground with his bat in his hands. He didn't even bother taking any warm-up swings. Very calmly and carefully, he studied the Detroit pitcher's encounter with the Browns' right fielder. Tobin lashed two line drives foul, took two pitches for balls, and lifted a high fly to deep center field for the second out.

As Matti stepped up to bat, ripples of applause began to traverse the grandstands, finally meeting for a brief moment of ovation. The crowd seemed to have little more strength or concentration than the Detroit pitcher. Matti couldn't care less about the crowd, but he was keenly aware of Morrisett's condition. The pitcher was tired. Smith, not a particularly good fastball hitter, had fouled off four consecutive fastballs before striking out, and Tobin had managed to get in front on the first two pitches. Moreover, Matti was willing to bet where that first tired fastball would be thrown. Whenever a pitcher or player got rough with Ty Cobb, he suffered instant retribution at the hands of

Detroit pitchers. If not, Cobb made life miserable for them, and no one could make life more miserable than Ty Cobb could. Matti stood covered in enough of his own blood to appreciate that. He also appreciated that no one in all of professional baseball played his heart out for a team and its pitchers the way Cobb did for the Tigers. Now that Morrisett had two outs, he could afford to waste a few pitches in order to avoid Cobb's wrath. Since Matti did not initiate the crash and had been bowled over, bruised, and bloodied, he didn't think that Morrisett would actually try to stick the ball in his ear. That would put Matti on first base, and Freeling might pinch-hit for Dufer, who followed Matti at bat. No, Morrisett would just brush him back with a tight inside pitch that would knock the bat out of his hands.

Matti took a warm-up swing and stepped to the plate, crowding it for all he was worth. As Morrisett raised his foot above his head, momentarily taking his eyes off the batter, Matti drifted back two quick steps away from the plate and dug in. The pitcher released the ball and Matti began his swing. The lackluster fastball arrived right where Matti's stubby hands had been but were no longer. Instead, he was guiding the bat through an extended arc designed to provide the maximum power. As the bat made contact with the ball, he increased his force by turning to the left, generating added leverage with the trunk of his body and pulling the ball toward the left-field line. He knew from the solid sound and light feel that he had hit the ball very well. Following through very deliberately, he concentrated on not lifting his head too early. When he finally did so, he saw that, unlike Tobin, he had timed it right; the ball was at least ten feet in fair territory and would easily clear the left-field fence for a home run. Jogging toward first base on his ritual uncontested circuit of the diamond, he could see the Tigers dejectedly heading for the clubhouse in defeat. As Matti reached second, the applause and cheers of the crowd reached a deafening roar that accompanied him all the way around to home plate. Turning languidly toward the Browns' dugout, he paused.

A band of cheering teammates surged out in wild fervor to congratulate him. A whooping, yelling, twenty-game winner raced ahead and draped himself in a bear hug on the short hero, knocking off Matti's beaked cap with his ecstatic leaps. Matti completely disappeared from view until Dufer in his wild exuberance bent down, clasped his arms around Matti's waist, and hoisted him straight into the air. As Matti suddenly reappeared, rising head and shoulders above his admiring fellows, a full-throated roar saluted him. A bruised, swollen Matti—hatless, the contusions on his head and cheek were bared for all to see—floated above the field in popular triumph. He wore an expression neither of joy nor of weariness but of somber, serious acceptance that recognized the thunderous adulation as his royal due. Acknowledging the acclaim, he lifted his arms in the ritual of victory. Cameras clicked; it was this picture that was to dominate so dramatically the Sunday sports section of the *Globe,* the city's largest morning newspaper.

# CHAPTER THIRTY

In front of his locker a very calm Matti sat on a stool in his sweatshirt and baseball pants, his injured foot immersed in a bucket of ice. The adulation continued around the unlikely all-star as newspaper reporters clamored to interview the catcher who had batted in three runs, including a tie-breaking, game-winning home run with two out in the bottom of the ninth inning. All this after having saved the game in the top of the ninth by stopping Ty Cobb from scoring in what the assembled reporters were already describing as the outstanding defensive play of the season.

How did it feel to get by Cobb? What did you think when you saw him coming? How did you manage to hold on to the ball? Were you surprised when Cobb didn't take the field? How did you feel when the ball cleared the left-field fence? Matti patiently answered all of these inquiries, stating that it always felt good when one was doing one's job well. The sportswriters seemed a trifle disappointed at his lack of enthusiasm in recounting his near-legendary exploits. (To become truly legendary, these exploits awaited only the writers' canonization in the next day's Sunday press.) Finally, a stark-naked Dufer joined them on the way back from the showers, rubbernecked at Sirdy's wounds, and announced, "You ought to see the other guy!" providing the ritual manic jocularity that the occasion so desperately needed.

Bill, the trainer, edged his way forward and announced that Zack wanted Sirdy to see the team physician, Dr. Williams, in the trainer's room. Matti excused himself. As he did so, Dufer called after him, "Hey, Sirdy, when you're lying down with that sawbones, you better guard home plate!" and grabbed his groin with both hands, pantomiming just what he meant by home plate. This wit brought forth a burst of appreciative guffaws and cheers that permitted Matti to exit on a manly note of joyous exaltation worthy of the hour. Everyone was more than satisfied; the players turned back to their lockers laughing, and the reporters rushed out of the clubhouse burning to share with the city's reading public the witty, stimulating, gallant world of the St. Louis Browns' professional baseball club, of which the press was such an important part.

"Let's take a look at it," the doctor ordered.

Matti sat on the edge of the padded trainer's table as the doctor examined the facial scratches and bruises.

"Not too bad," the doctor announced to Zack with a note of satisfaction.

This satisfied tone annoyed Matti. Dr. Williams had only one patient, the St. Louis Browns' baseball club, and only the well-being of that corporate entity concerned him. The team referred to him as "the company doctor," but Matti called him the "veterinarian" because the kindly, rumpled doctor with his easy manner and gray hair understood the necessity of fattening commercial beasts for slaughter. Even now, when the doctor examined Matti's eye for injury, he didn't look him in the eye. The catcher was just one of the herd who must produce.

"Let's check the foot, too, Doc," Zack proposed.

Matti lay down.

"Take your trousers off, it will be easier that way," the doctor suggested.

Matti unfastened his belt, and Bill, the trainer, helped him pull his pants off.

"Swelling isn't too bad. We'll continue with the ice, but we might need a few stitches here where the gash is."

The doctor delivered this unwelcome news very solemnly.

"Catcher, isn't he?"

"Yeah," Zack answered, "and you said Swede won't be ready for at least another week."

The doctor nodded thoughtfully.

"Sirdy's going real good, Doc. Wouldn't want to stop him now. Right, Sirdy?"

"The team needs him," the doctor announced sagely.

"He played a whale of a game today. We could use more like that," Zack informed the doctor.

"I imagine so," the doctor agreed, but it really wasn't clear what he was imagining.

"How does it feel, Sirdy?" Zack asked.

"It hurts, but the ice helps," Matti answered.

"Sure it does," Zack said curtly.

Zack wasn't at all pleased with the answer. He wanted no stitches so that Matti could catch tomorrow's double-header. The manager was trying to simplify the doctor's job by having Matti play down his pain. Matti wasn't terribly concerned about his leg—it wasn't all that bad—but he wasn't going to lie to play baseball. Those days were over.

"Well, we might avoid the stitches and keep him in the lineup. We could try taping it together. That might do it."

The doctor spoke slowly, as if he were weighing things very carefully.

"Good," Zack said quickly, encouraging him.

"But we would have to keep the ice on it and rest it as much as possible. Elevate it slightly and stay off it. Especially for the next few hours, to make sure the bleeding has stopped."

"If it's all right, I could stay here and rest for a few hours. I need a little rest," Matti suggested nobly.

"Sure, we could do that. Bill will stay here with you as long as you like. We could have some supper brought in from the grill. Maybe even a little something in a brown paper bag, too. On the club's account, of course."

"But I want you to stay off it for several hours, Sirdy," the doctor insisted.

"Until it's dark?" Matti suggested.

"Yes, if that's all right," the doctor said, as if he were agreeing to bad news. What red-blooded American all-star would want to celebrate victory in the trainer's room?

"Then it's settled. I'll remain here until well after sunset," Matti declared.

"That's the spirit, Sirdy," Zack said approvingly.

"We've got a good man here," the doctor announced.

"A ballplayer," Zack said.

"Forget the booze," Matti added.

"Not even suds?" Zack asked.

"Not even suds," Matti answered.

After cleaning the wound, the doctor tightly taped the edges together. Matti felt the pressure and the cold of the ice packs. He lifted his head to see his foot encased in tight sterile wrapping like a mummy. What he needed was a few neat stitches and time to heal, not the bright sheath of adhesive sticking to him like a false skin.

"With a little luck, we'll have you behind home plate tomorrow," Dr. Williams said, proud of his artistry.

"Yes," affirmed Matti.

"No doubt about it," Zack said. "If you want anything, ask Bill."

Matti nodded. Zack and the doctor disappeared for what Matti knew would be a private conspiratorial conference in the manager's office about his slightly elevated and thoroughly mummified foot.

On their way out of the clubhouse, players ducked in to wish him well or to give a few words of encouragement. The Browns weren't going anywhere this late in the season, and most were not overly concerned about a minor injury, even if it meant someone would be behind home plate who was not a trained catcher. Dufer solicitously asked whether he could help. Most concerned was Mack MacGregor, who needed two more victories to become a twenty-game winner. He was scheduled to go for the first of those triumphs in tomorrow's doubleheader.

"Can I drive you home, Sirdy?"

"You want to tuck me in, too?"

"I need you, Sirdy," Mack said seriously.

"Not as much as you think, Mack," Matti answered in sober honesty.

"Are you kidding? You know the hitters," Mack protested.

"You could learn them."

"I haven't so far, have I?"

Matti didn't respond.

"Hey, Sirdy, can I ask you something?" Mack requested, filled with curiosity.

"What do you want to know?" Matti answered without committing himself.

"What were you looking up at that little airplane for?"

"I thought the pilot was somebody I knew," Matti said.

"Well, Sirdy, I hope it doesn't come back tomorrow."

"I don't think there's any chance of that."

"I hope so. I've got a big game coming up," Mack said.

"We all do, Mack," Matti corrected him.

"You never let us down. Not you, Sirdy."

Matti didn't answer. Lying on his back, staring at the ceiling, he seemed absorbed in his own thoughts. Feeling ignored as Dufer had earlier, Mack glanced around uncomfortably.

"We're going to get them tomorrow, aren't we, Sirdy?" Mack asked, trying to promote the proper bubbling optimistic mood.

"Mack, would you trade your life for another?" Matti asked seriously.

"Heck no! I love throwing baseballs," he answered without hesitation.

"Then you don't have anything to worry about."

"Gee, that's great!" Wanting to leave on this enthusiastic, upbeat note, Mack added, "I better let you rest so we'll be ready. Take care, Sirdy." Mack tapped Matti's shoulder in affectionate farewell. "See you tomorrow, Sirdy. You sure had a great game!" he crowed and left.

Only the cleanup crew and Bill remained in the locker room. Stools scraped, a wet mop flopped onto the floor, and Matti began to think.

A great game, and only he, the hero, was left with his mummified foot. The rebbe wouldn't be a bit surprised that as a souvenir of his lack of faith he now lay with a foot resembling that of a dead pharaoh. The game had gone very smoothly until the airplane appeared at the end of the eighth inning. He had put the rebbe's fateful predictions out of mind. All at once the airplane appeared, and everything seemed to unravel. Losing confidence in the rebbe, Matti was left with chaos. He was certain that the airplane was going to nose over and plunge into a fiery crash. With any luck the all-metal plane would explode and bury itself in center field; without any, it would incinerate the grandstands in a mushrooming ball of flames in America's greatest aviation disaster.

Matti had looked up helplessly at the plane; there was no thought, no analysis, just impending disaster with Matti staggering beneath, no more able to influence matters than a simple blade of grass. Planes fall out of the sky, men die fiery deaths, and there isn't even any mail for the survivors to read. In his loss of faith, he had cried in despair, "The rebbe is nuts!" As an ill omen presaging the great catastrophe, the baseball kept falling from the air, striking innocent men, plunging them into agony and deathlike unconsciousness.

Matti dimly recalled looking around and finding limp bodies scattered around like unread letters with their addresses
rudely smudged.

The unlikely person of Zack Freeling had saved him
from the debilitating lack of faith. Zack's anti-Semitic
mouthings bespoke evil—not the impersonal evil of an
amoral chaos, but a virulent evil of willful hate and illusion
that necessitated its opposite, good and reality. Matti then
turned toward that reality—the holy Sabbath day, when
evil spirits and Zack's ghosts were impotent illusions—just
as the rebbe had taught him. When the vicious Ty Cobb
had sent him flying head over heels, Matti had seen fiery
stars that convinced him of his success in "burning the
cats." Just like Zloty, Cobb had torn at his legs, bloodying
them with his razor-sharp claws. The home run had demanded concentration, but it had been preordained when
Matti had seen the stars. For Matti, too, was to become a
star. Indeed, he already had by successfully tagging out Ty
Cobb in the collision at home plate.

Lying on the trainer's table, Matti supposed that the
home run following so closely after the defensive play
illustrated the rebbe's teaching: all one had to do to reach
the heights was to extricate oneself from the depths. Matti
had literally risen to the heights. As they lifted him above
the cheering crowd, he had seen everyone clearly. Penny
Pinkham stared at him in worshipful, lascivious excitement, for whomever the beastly crowd worshiped excited
her. Liberated from her whorish, idolatrous passion, he
turned to see a confused and fearful Barasch, the blood
drained from his horsey face. Surveying this scene, Matti
sensed how it felt to be a prince of the people, but the

royal house of the American League ruled a nation of idolatry, sexual lewdness, and bloodshed. The Sabbath had
saved Matti from such seductively vile temptations. He
therefore welcomed the absurd medical treatment that
permitted him to rest and to faithfully observe the remainder of the Sabbath as he once had as a boy in Krimsk. This
meant that he could not drive his car: sparking the engine
violated the prohibition against kindling fire. He did not
want to turn lights on or off; he did not want to handle
money; he did not want to use the telephone. The rebbe
had told Boruch Levi, "If you protect the Sabbath, it will
protect you." Matti was in debt; the Sabbath had protected
him, and it was only fair that he protect it. Now was the
time to start.

Bill stuck his head in.

"Sirdy, can I get you anything?"

"Yes, my hat, please," Matti answered.

"Your hat?"

"Yes."

"But you don't wear one."

"My baseball hat," Matti informed him.

"What do you want that for now?"

"To wear," Matti answered.

"In here?"

"Yes."

Bill returned with the baseball cap and watched Sirdy
promptly put it on his head. Since he was lying flat on his
back, the hard long beak poked straight up into the air.
Matti was aware of the trainer's disapproving look. That
was fair enough: what need did a naked player resting a
taped ankle have for the official team hat of the St. Louis

Browns? But Matti needed the head covering to offset the foot covering. The mummified foot belonged to pharaoh; the covered head belonged to the rebbe. Had he been sitting in the rebbe's beis midrash, he would naturally have covered his head as tradition demanded. The hat represented man's finiteness before the infinite Master of the Universe above. In that sense, the cap sat comfortably on his head. Matti was fully prepared to proclaim the infinity of the Holy One, and he fully appreciated his own limitations. Unfortunately, he appreciated them all too much. Perhaps his new awareness might help him effect his own personal redemption, but the Krimsker Rebbe intended something far grander. The rebbe was talking about nothing less than the redemption of the Jews by Matti, the modern Moses. Could Matti believe such a thing? He just didn't know.

Moses had been the most base of men; only through his struggle to subdue his overwhelming evil inclinations had he developed into a man of great virtue and prophetic holiness. The story about the king who had sent an artist to portray Moses explained the paradox of man—how he could be both so sordid and so marvelous—but it also troubled Matti and convinced him that his limitations were an insuperable handicap. Matti just was not, nor had he ever been, sufficiently evil. All he had wanted was to be a baseball player, earn some glory, win some money, and marry a beautiful girl. His one illegal enterprise really wouldn't have hurt anyone except a few bookies, and it wouldn't have hurt them very much. What would the royal advisers discover in this portrait? Matti tried to be as honest as he could. They might say that he was an intelligent, greedy, clever, grasping, slightly larcenous fellow, but certainly not very imaginative or insightful. Such a description wasn't much to be proud of, but in all honesty neither was it sufficiently vile, base, or evil as to suggest greatness. The story of Moses demanded the reality of an outstanding human personality. In reality Matti was a second-string baseball player, and given every generous interpretation, he wasn't more than that when it came to evil. So where did that leave him? Well, it left him on the trainer's table with a sore foot and a desire not to violate the Sabbath.

Matti could barely recall the last time he had wanted not to violate the Sabbath. He had observed the Sabbath for several years in America because his father had insisted on it, but he had stopped at the first opportunity. In fact, in his last year in Krimsk, he had not been very enthusiastic about either practice or belief. When he had burned the cats with Faigie he had already ceased believing the way the rest of Krimsk had. Otherwise, he would have been as afraid of Grannie Zara and Zloty as they were and would never have gone near the witch's house. Matti had heard there was a lady ritually purifying herself by dipping naked in the Krimsk pond, and he had set out to discover her identity. Instead he had met Faigie Soffer, who, unaware that Grannie Zara had died earlier in the day, was on her way to consult the witch. Matti had mistaken her for the naked lady, and she had mistaken him for a witch. Together they had burned the cats and the cottage.

Last night Matti had heard from the rebbe that Grannie Zara had possessed evil powers and that Faigie's hysterical suspicions too contained some truth.

Matti reached down to discover what he might have in his pocket now, and found to his naked embarrassment that he was without pants. What would the rebbe make of that? The lewdness of baseball? No, Matti had conquered his lust for Penny Pinkham and for the glory of the Hall of Fame. The rebbe would certainly have some ingenious interpretation of his nakedness that would augur well for Matti as Moses, but Matti didn't want to hear it.

Although he wanted to follow the rebbe out of the ballpark, he was not prepared to follow him back into the beis midrash; he did not accept the rebbe's cosmic view. Fortunately, it was the holy Sabbath; Matti had no desire to rush back and report to the rebbe. He did want to speak to Boruch Levi about some kind of business, and above all he wanted to tell Barasch that everything had gone the way Matti had really wanted it to. Matti felt responsible for the pale, bloodless Barasch. He had uprooted him from his comfortable life. After dreams of Penny Pinkham, could Barasch ever return to Malka? Maybe the rebbe could speak to the unhappy cripple. And what about Matti and the rebbe? Would the rebbe accept Matti as a simple hasid? All these things troubled Matti on the trainer's table, but as long as the Sabbath lasted he was safe. For the moment he could do nothing but observe the Holy Day, which, after all, was the day of rest. Puzzled by how he would resolve these various concerns, he celebrated the Sabbath in the traditional manner by falling asleep.

# CHAPTER THIRTY-ONE

ALTHOUGH MATTI DIDN'T HEAR BILL'S VOICE, HE DID feel the trainer's gentle touch stirring him into wakefulness. Matti slowly opened his eyes to see the lightbulb glowing brightly above the table. He blinked a few times, finally turning away from the fiery spot.

"What time is it?" he asked, groggy with sleep.

"After nine o'clock."

"Is it dark outside?" Matti asked. His voice was still rough, but his question was sharply focused.

"Yeah, sure it is. You've been out like a light for over four hours. Zack just called again and said to be sure and wake you, otherwise you wouldn't sleep at night. You got to be rested for tomorrow's doubleheader."

Matti sat up and dropped his legs over the table onto the floor.

"How's the foot?" Bill asked with the professional interest of one of Zack's most trusted employees.

Matti really hadn't noticed. His first concern had been to make sure that the Sabbath was over. He tested his foot gently on the floor. Very little pain and hardly any swelling.

"It's still there, but it doesn't feel too bad."

Bill nodded. "I kept the ice on it."

"Thanks," Matti said. "I guess I kept you here pretty late."

"That's what I'm paid for," the trainer said. His voice expressed a pride in his job that belied the modesty of his words.

"Well, thanks. I appreciate it."

"Don't mention it."

Matti eased himself off the table and stepped gingerly on the taped leg. To his surprise, although he felt the tight adhesive, he could walk normally. Cautiously, he put the leg in front of him before sitting on his locker stool.

"I'm thirsty. You have anything to drink around here?"

"I ordered supper for you. I could put some fresh ice into the Coke; it's been standing around for a couple of hours."

"Yeah, I'm dry as a bone."

The trainer disappeared. Matti looked around. All was still. Orderly. Too orderly. The lockers tightly closed, a stool placed precisely in front of each. The four legs rotated to form an imaginary square parallel to each locker. Matti glanced down; only his own stool destroyed the perfect, fearful geometry. In the quiet, almost ominous emptiness, he felt himself both an intruder and a stranger. When Bill arrived with the soda, he drank it all before the cooling ice had any effect. Dressing quickly, he hurried past the regimented, silent stools and stiff lockers. In a few moments, Bill would see to it that his stool, too, had joined the dumb, still ranks. He stepped into the dark night and paused. The warm air seemed spontaneous and alive.

The trainer, who had followed him in order to lock the door, said, "Great game."

"Thanks," Matti said, but at the moment he was more excited by the open, undulating night.

"See you tomorrow, Sirdy."

"Maybe," Matti said. Without looking back, he crossed the street to start his car. He spun the crank, welcoming the explosion of sparking energy as the engine turned over.

Driving toward home, he savored the feeling of being the last player out of the clubhouse; it suggested his dedication and professional pride. But no sooner did he have such thoughts than he felt ashamed. How could he enjoy such a total falsehood? It was as if the feelings of his former self were surfacing to confuse him. He had remained because he did not want to violate the Sabbath, and he had not relished his stay in the locker room at all. As he drove through the city streets, he suddenly realized why he had fled as quickly as he could from the room's brutal, orderly artifacts. The place had reminded him of Grannie Zara's cottage with its deadly, suffocating harmony. Yes, and the uneven sound of the sparking engine had been sweeter than the cheers of the crowd or the screeches of the burning cats.

Perhaps it wouldn't be as easy to change his life as he had thought. Look how Barasch Limp Legs had reverted so pathetically to the old snorting gracelessness of the Krimsk factory yard. Matti had meant to contact him first thing, but in his hurry to leave the clubhouse he had forgotten. He considered calling from a telephone in a drugstore or restaurant on the way home but then rejected the idea. He didn't welcome anyone overhearing, and he had a lot of explaining to do. Maybe his mother would be at the neighbor's—that would be best. She wouldn't be expecting him tonight. He rarely came home before midnight on Saturday nights.

Certainly the rebbe was expecting him. He had saved Matti and was at the very least entitled to a courtesy call, but Matti did not have the energy or the certainty to confront the forceful Krimsker Rebbe, not after what had happened in the ballpark today. He needed a little more time to think things through. If he went to the Krimsker Rebbe's house, he would be inviting the rebbe's guidance, and he knew what that would be. He remembered that on the way home last night, Boruch Levi had expressed doubts about the rebbe. He suddenly had a strong desire to discuss his own future outside baseball with the junkman. The solid, hardheaded Boruch Levi knew and loved both Krimsk and America; so did Matti, didn't he?

His fears about changing his life remained. To allay them, Matti concentrated on his driving. On the busy thoroughfare, the swirl of bright headlights and soft red taillights looked as if the stars of heaven swarmed in the city's streets. But tonight as he watched them, all Matti could think of was that he didn't have any stars to steer by. The bright lights of baseball had irrevocably dimmed, fading from view, but he feared the prophetic constellations that the Krimsker Rebbe saw rising on the horizon. With his considerable faculties for observation, he concentrated on the swirling vehicular lights that enveloped him, but to his disappointment, none of them guided or accompanied him. Turning to the right, to the left, slowing down, passing him, stopping, not following his route westward, invariably the other cars abandoned him. Alone, he arrived in the West End in front of his apartment building. The light in the kitchen told him that his mother was home.

Matti opened the door but remained in the shadows of the living room so that he could tell his mother about his bruises before she saw him. When she entered the room, he quickly said, "A good week," the traditional greeting uttered upon the conclusion of the Sabbath. She stopped short and stood hesitantly.

"A good week to you, darling," she said softly and then added, "It's dark in here. Why don't you turn the light on?"

"Well, I got a few bumps and bruises in today's game. They look worse than they are. I wanted you to hear my healthy voice before you see them."

"Are they so bad?" she asked fearfully.

"No, not if it's your own face. They're really nothing. But if it's your child's face and you worry about him and whom he will marry, then it must seem worse," he answered.

She was anxious to see for herself and moved to pull the string on the light.

"No," Matti said. "Let's go into the kitchen. While you take a look, I can eat supper."

"You didn't have supper yet?" Her voice revealed the fear that nothing other than serious injury could have kept him from eating.

"No, I didn't feel like riding on the Sabbath, so I stayed at the ballpark until after dark. I fell asleep, or I would have been home earlier."

In the well-lit kitchen, his mother served him cold chicken and cursorily examined his bruised face. She exhibited the ritual revulsion, but he could see that the bruises didn't really worry her. As a boy he used to return with far worse.

"Not so bad, thank God," she said. "You want some salad?"

"No thanks."

She sat down across from him.

"Is everything all right, Matti?"

"Yes. It was a rough game."

"You seem different," she said timidly. She tilted her head slightly to the side, as if the aroma of destiny were a much sharper smell than she had imagined.

Matti stopped eating and put down his knife and fork.

"I am, Mom. Isn't that what you always wanted?"

She nodded quickly. "I didn't really think it would ever happen. It seemed to be asking too much. But last night—" She stopped in midsentence. "I almost forgot. Boruch Levi called a half hour ago and said that he had very good news."

Good news to Mrs. Sternweiss could only mean one thing: a wife for her only son. Matti, too, was very receptive.

"Good news? Did he say what it was?"

"No, but he said that he wanted to see you tonight if you have time. He seemed much friendlier than last night."

Matti started to get up, then thought better of it. "I'll finish, then I'll call him."

"You shouldn't keep him waiting," she said.

"No, it's better this way," he answered, since he realized he would be going out.

Fifteen minutes later when he made the telephone call, Sammy answered. He seemed to have been expecting him.

"No, Mr. Sternweiss, I don't know what he wanted to tell you, but right after he called you, he went over to the police chief's house. He said if you called to tell you that he wouldn't be there very long. Shall I tell him to call you back?"

"No, Sammy, tell him I'll be in touch," Matti said pensively.

When Matti didn't end the conversation, Sammy spoke.

"Mr. Sternweiss?" he asked, hesitantly requesting permission to continue.

"Yes, Sammy?"

"That was a terrific picture of you in the *Globe* tonight," he said, wanting to compliment the star of the game but uncertain whether it was appropriate for a mere child to do so.

"Thank you," Matti said graciously. He still didn't hang up.

"Good night, Mr. Sternweiss."

"Good night, Sammy," Matti said and finally hung up.

He continued to sit by the phone.

"Boruch Levi wasn't home?" his mother inquired.

"No, he'll be back soon. I think I'll pick up a paper, then drop by to see him."

"You don't know what the good news is?"

"Not yet." He smiled. "But we'll find out."

"Pooh, pooh, pooh," she said to avoid the evil eye.

Matti laughed.

"Don't wait up for me. I might be back late."

"You need some rest," she said.

"Yes, I certainly do," he agreed good-naturedly.

# CHAPTER THIRTY-TWO

WHEN MATTI DROVE AWAY FROM THE CURB, HE NOTICED in his rearview mirror that another car, a rather large one, switched on its lights and followed him down the street. In no hurry, he leisurely turned the corner and made two more turns through the quiet, residential neighborhood until he arrived at Delmar Boulevard. Unlike the myriad of lights that had abandoned him earlier, the automobile continued to follow him. Matti turned onto the main road, easing himself into the flow of traffic, but he made a point of checking in his mirror to see whether the large sedan turned right, too. Matti was pleased to see that it did. Since Matti was going only two blocks down to a drugstore, that meant that he had won; the other auto had followed him all the way.

Since he wanted to call Barasch, he passed the local newsboy hawking the morning *Globe* at the first intersection and continued down the long block. Near the drugstore the street was solidly parked. Matti slowed down and turned into a side street. Thinking it was rather late to be calling Barasch, he parked and hurriedly ran back to the store.

Burt, the elderly proprietor, wearing his customary gray smock with black garters on his sleeves, was behind the marble counter serving a high school couple two ice cream sundaes. He had that weary look in which his droopy eyelids sagged a little more than usual, as if they were pulling down the shades on the day's activity. Ray, the teenage helper, was dragging an oversize metal bucket, sloshing soapy water onto the floor. Matti caught Burt's eye and pointed to the cubbyhole of an office behind the prescription counter where he often called Penny, and more recently Barasch. For a second he wasn't sure whether Burt had seen him, but as the elderly man continued to scoop vanilla ice cream, he nodded at Matti, who went behind the prescription counter with its maze of bottles and great metal cash register. In the office, he carefully closed the door behind him.

Matti anxiously listened to the distant reverberations of the telephone ringing in Malka's messy kitchen above the junkyard. When a child answered, he became hopeful. Matti asked to speak to the boy's father and waited for Barasch, but instead he heard the sly, slovenly voice of Malka.

"Hello," Matti said as confidently as he could. "May I please speak to Bernard?"

He heard no more than a quiet click as she hung up. Matti stared forlornly at the earpiece, then rang the operator to try again. Once more the same ringing and the same voice.

"Malka, this is Matti Sternweiss. Please don't hang up. I would like to speak to Barasch about something that is extremely important to all of us." He paused for a moment but didn't receive any response. "I know you don't like me, and I understand why. Believe me that things have changed for the better. Until now I have been misleading your husband, and I would like to tell him that it is all over."

He paused for an answer, but she remained silent.

"Malka, I'm sorry about what I did to Barasch. May I please speak to him?" he pleaded.

"Drop dead, you bum," she answered simply in her crafty, measured tones and hung up.

Matti hung up sadly and sat back for a long minute, reflecting on her response. He couldn't blame her. He couldn't promise to return Barasch to his St. Louis self, but Matti knew that for his own sake he would have to try. If he really wanted to speak to Barasch tonight, he would ask Boruch Levi to call and have Malka put her husband on the line. At any rate, he might mention that Malka had hung up on him and hear what Boruch Levi had to say about it. Matti left two nickels on the desk and opened the door.

Well into his mopping, Ray had left a dry pathway for Matti that led past the soda fountain. The surrounding wet tiles glistened with a shiny splendor under the bright overhead lights. A trace of a quick, quiet shadow flickered across the shiny reflective tiles like the fluttering of dark wings. Matti glanced up to be sure that this almost imperceptible shadowy rhythm beating its way toward him was not a product of his imagination. He watched the four large blades of the electric ceiling fan silently stirring the air. He even closed his eyes for a moment to discern whether a breeze reached his face. Disappointed, he opened his eyes and began to follow the dull, dry way left especially for him.

"Had a great game this afternoon, Mr. Sternweiss!" Ray called out over the swishing of his large, wet mop.

Matti nodded. As he passed the soda fountain, Burt

lowered his head a bit in a respectful seconding of his helper's statement. In the mirror on the wall behind Burt, Matti could see the high school sweethearts, thoroughly enraptured with themselves and their ice cream. They were carefully spooning so that each bite was accompanied by a helping of rich, hot fudge and an even thicker adoring glance that encompassed their confections and themselves. They were blind to Burt's drooping eyelids and tired stance; they didn't see Matti staring at them in the broad mirror; they didn't hear Ray working his long hairy mop in great bubbly swaths across the floor; and they had no idea whatsoever that the stiff wooden blades of the ceiling fan spun endlessly through the air above them. Matti turned from watching them and smiled at Burt. The older man nodded in gentle agreement; a brief indulgent smile creased his face, revealing the slightest trace of envy at such romance and innocence at closing time.

Matti continued around the freestanding cosmetic counter in the center of the store. Through the open double doors he could see the random lights of the automobile traffic on Delmar. He wondered whether Boruch Levi had returned from the chief's house. Matti wasn't in any hurry; if Boruch Levi wasn't home, he might disturb the rest of the family. He was curious, however, as to the good news. Normally, he would attempt to analyze the situation and try to figure out what message the chief of police wanted Boruch Levi to pass on. Times were, however, no longer normal, and Matti had no desire to analyze or even to guess. He would find out soon enough. He was more curious about his new life, but that too would take time. By the door he felt a slight breeze, but he couldn't tell whether it was generated by the fan inside or was wafted through the still darkness facing him.

"Gee, Mr. Sternweiss, aren't you going to buy a paper? It has some picture of you!" Ray exclaimed, breathing heavily, with beads of sweat clinging to his forehead.

Matti had forgotten all about it.

"Yes, I think I will," he said gently.

He took a thick edition off the bulky stack on top of the glass cigar counter and dropped a dime into the smoothly worn heavy wooden bowl.

As he stepped outside, he scanned the front page. There didn't seem to be any particular good news, or any particular bad news either. He turned down the tree-lined side street toward his car. In the deep darkness, he shuffled instinctively through the various Sunday sections to the one that had always been of such great importance to him. Approaching his car, he came into the golden pool of a softly glowing gas streetlight. The banner headlines across the top of the sports section proclaimed, SIRDY STOPS TIGERS. It seemed so long ago. He was faintly surprised that it didn't say SIRDY BURNS TIGERS, but he realized that then it would have to read MATTI BURNS TIGERS, and it couldn't possibly say anything other than Sirdy. That was the way it had to be, but he preferred the finality that "burns" implied. "Stops" sounded all too temporary, as if the Tigers would have another chance at Matti, or worse, at his old self, Sirdy. Well, well, thought Matti as he lifted the page slightly to get a better look at the large photo centered so dramatically under the headlines.

He remembered floating above them all in triumphant weariness. He recalled his lack of exuberance and joy, but he was surprised and mildly disappointed to discover that in the picture he wasn't wearing his hat. At his moment of glory on the holy Sabbath day, he paraded bareheaded under the vault of heaven. That was appropriate to Sirdy, all right; but the somber expression of victory was all Matti.

It was during such considerations of self that a voice softly called, "Hey, Sirdy." Matti wasn't the least bit surprised, and for the briefest moment he thought that the newspaper itself was speaking to him. He glanced up over the sports section to see a slender man with a wide-brimmed fedora pulled low over his face. In the street a large, vaguely familiar sedan with its lights off stood double-parked. Matti glimpsed someone behind the wheel, but he turned from the car to the man in the shadows, who stood as if he were holding or presenting something. Matti lowered his newspaper so he could see what that might be. Even in the soft yellow gaslight, the all-metal chrome automatic gleamed brightly, but that paled in comparison to the brilliant, fiery flash that exploded from its barrel, first once and then again in lethal, incandescent bursts.

As Matti fell, he threw the sports section aside. He had no sensation of hitting the ground, but as he lay staring at the gently glowing light, he heard the noise of running feet, and then without any warning, he had a rich, sweet taste in the bottom of his mouth, as if he were slowly dissolving the hard candies of his youth. A sedan door slammed, and a motor accelerated in a muffled roar as the large automobile abandoned Matti. But he never heard it, for he was listening to the sound of many voices crying, "Thank you, Reb Mattus!" and he was answering, "Blessed art Thou, O Lord," even though tears flooded his eyes.

The ambulance arrived within an hour, but it really made no difference. The driver saw the two holes in the chest and realized that even if they had been there when it happened, the victim could not have been saved. After they stowed the body in the back, there was nothing else that they could do except to wander over the dark lawn collecting the various sections of the morning paper.

# CHAPTER THIRTY-THREE

THE BRILLIANT SUN STOOD DIRECTLY ABOVE, ITS SHADE-limning rays revealing nothing of the cortege's direction as each vehicle sat tightly hiding its own shadow. But the measured pace, the dirgelike cadence of the muffled engines, the rigid geometry of the long automotive line, all told the destination: onlookers removed their Sunday hats and bowed their bared heads in the blazing light at the shadow of death. The seemingly endless procession of the largest Jewish funeral St. Louis had ever seen rolled slowly and irrevocably west on Delmar Boulevard toward the cemetery beyond the city limits. Where churches released their congregations, hundreds stood respectfully in Sunday finery with beads of sweat dotting their foreheads and often with tears of anguished tribute for their city's slain hero, who had refused to betray their trust and affection.

Those fans hoping to catch a glimpse of Sirdy's St. Louis Browns teammates were disappointed, for after escorting the casket as honorary pallbearers at the funeral parlor, they left for the ballpark. They had all attended: a stern-faced

Zack, a bewildered Mack, a tearful Dufer with an equally lachrymose Penny Pinkham on his arm, a mournful but ever-solicitous Bill, who offered St. Louis Browns smelling salts to anyone who was faint. They followed the plain wooden coffin to the hearse, boarded a special bus for the ballpark, and arrived in time for batting practice.

Everyone who watched the somber journey to the cemetery saw the chief of police's automobile, and they might have noticed His Honor the Mayor in his large Pierce-Arrow. They certainly couldn't miss the police motorcycle escort leading the procession. Approaching a busy intersection, the lead outrider momentarily sounded his siren. At the unexpected wail on a quiet Sunday morning, people turned their heads two blocks away, half expecting to see a bank robbery in progress.

Riding with Mrs. Sternweiss in the limousine immediately behind the hearse, Boruch Levi heard the intermittent blasts with all their frightening, violent implications. He harbored no illusions as to the criminals' identity: for him they were not anonymous. Although he was angry, the subject did not interest him; Matti was dead. His square jaw set in stoic mourning, Boruch Levi stared out the open window and wondered anxiously what the Krimsker Rebbe would say by the grave.

Boruch Levi had offered the rebbe the honor of speaking first at the funeral parlor, but the rebbe had announced that he would speak at the cemetery. Boruch Levi explained that in St. Louis eulogies were delivered in the spacious, well-appointed auditorium, where everyone could sit comfortably instead of standing under the broiling sun, but the rebbe responded that he would be brief. Boruch Levi suspected that the rebbe did not want to speak at the funeral parlor because he would not be the sole speaker. Yitzhak Weinbach had insisted that Rabbi Dr. Emmanuel D. Morgenstern, dean of the city's Reform rabbinate, speak, too, since it was to be a communal funeral. Boruch Levi had consented—with the public dignitaries and the press attending, someone had to be sure to express the appropriate Jewish sentiments—but he had sandwiched the pompous Rabbi Doctor between a European-born Conservative rabbi and the nondescript chaplain of the Jewish Hospital. Predictably, the various speakers had all acclaimed Matti's courage, passion for justice, love of America and its glorious national pastime, noble contribution to national decency, and general sobriety. In stentorian tones they mourned his untimely death and decried murder most foul. Matti had proven so worthy of America's blessings, Rabbi Morgenstern explained, and now we must continue in Matti's footsteps with our faith in justice and love of country unabated as he would so certainly command.

After such flowery speeches, Boruch Levi half feared and half hoped that the Krimsker Rebbe would get up and tell the truth. But what was the truth? That Matti had gone too far and couldn't escape unscathed? That Matti had done penitence? That the greed of the police had killed him? That Boruch Levi's own boastfulness had incited that greed? That the grand funeral was a self-serving, hypocritical farce?

Mrs. Sternweiss stifled a sob, and Golda, Boruch Levi's wife, took her arm in comfort. Golda seemed less nervous at funerals than she did at any other time, as if the tragic moment itself could never equal her perpetual trepidations.

Whatever the truth, Mrs. Sternweiss had reason to mourn; she had lost her only child. Boruch Levi looked back out of the rear window. Reb Zelig was at the wheel, and next to him sat the rebbe, looking as if he were asleep, but Boruch Levi knew better.

Boruch Levi turned back to notice that there were no more spectators. There were no more sidewalks either. They had left the city with its pedestrian amenities and were entering the pastoral county. Occasional roadside stores intruded—lonely reminders of the city among the meadows, trees, and farms. It wouldn't be long now. Boruch Levi had given instructions for the hearse to stop at the cemetery's great wrought-iron gates.

"What would the rebbe like us to do?" Boruch Levi asked.

"Have the hearse pull inside the gate. I'll speak out here," the rebbe instructed.

When the great crowd gathered around the entrance, the rebbe stepped from his car. Standing on the running board, he could not command their attention.

"Lift me up!" the rebbe ordered Boruch Levi and Yitzhak Weinbach.

"What?" Yitzhak Weinbach stammered.

"Lift me up. Put me on the roof of my automobile."

"Oh," responded Yitzhak Weinbach.

Boruch Levi was already hoisting the rebbe into the air when Yitzhak drew closer to help. The rebbe planted a shoe firmly on his shoulder and, with the powerful Boruch Levi still propelling him upward, nimbly skipped onto the roof. At the sight of the Krimsker Rebbe in his long black coat and beard apparently floating above them, the large throng grew suddenly quiet and attentive. The rebbe paced the length of the roof before turning and addressing them.

"You are stunned, saddened, even shattered by the death of Mattathias Sternweiss. Not long ago, he felt the same way about the death of Lieutenant Max Miller, the distinguished postal aviator. Matti was wrong. The aircraft's fiery explosive crash was terrible, but it was so terrible precisely because the man had been so high in the sky. The fall was catastrophic, but others will follow, and eventually one will succeed. Matti was wrong, and so are you. Matti ceased to mourn Lieutenant Max Miller. Matti Sternweiss was a pilot. He flew higher than any of us. His crash was catastrophic, but eventually, but eventually . . ." The rebbe's voice broke. He lifted up his arms as if imploring heaven. Words failing to express his desire for salvation, he stretched toward heaven, even leaping toward it, only to be drawn down by merciless gravity. He landed with a dull thumping on the automobile roof, only to leap again and again. Then he stopped and covered his face with his hands. Tearfully, he looked out at the sea of faces and spoke in strong, confident tones.

"We must mourn, but not for Matti. He served holiness. Forget the fancy talk. We mourn today for ourselves and the Shekinah, the presence of the divine. Moses has contended with the overseer and lost. We remain in bondage to impurity. Let us mourn." The rebbe promptly sat on the Ford's roof as if already mourning the bondage of his people to impurity. He crept froglike toward the edge and slid off quietly into the pool of upturned faces. Boruch Levi managed to catch him and keep him from stumbling.

Yitzhak Weinbach poked his head between the rebbe

and Boruch Levi. "What do we do now?" he implored in a whisper meant only for them.

The rebbe did not answer immediately. He seemed distant and preoccupied. "What do we do now?" Yitzhak Weinbach beseeched.

"Do we have a choice? Bury him," the rebbe answered matter-of-factly.

# CHAPTER THIRTY-FOUR

THEY BURIED HIM IN A GRAVE JUST LIKE ALL THE others; they had no choice. But the crowd that buried him was not the same crowd that had halted at the cemetery gates to listen to the rebbe. Curious, fearful, seeking the thrill of proximity to someone touched by a more articulated, glorious fate, they had come as spectators—respectful to be sure, but observers, hoping to be touched by that dramatic tragedy that was the life of Matti Sternweiss. Without quite understanding the rebbe's words, they watched him leap toward heaven only to fall back to earth, and in some mysterious way they accepted his command and fell with him into mourning. As a community of mourners they somberly followed the simple wooden casket to the grave. Pained, mute, and contemplative, they heard the first shovelsful of hard, dry earth thumping upon the coffin lid with the hollow echo that announced the lifeless void within.

The Krimsker Rebbe's words touched everyone. Even those few who were already mourners when they arrived at the cemetery experienced fundamental changes. Bedraggled, ungainly, wild distraught eyes rolling in brute terror, Barasch Limp Legs hobbled, inarticulate in his pain. Indeed, he had refused to attend the funeral. With the help of the children, Malka had trapped him in the junkyard, wrestled him down from a pile of tires where he teetered like a delirious scarecrow, and stuffed him into the passenger seat of the pickup truck. Afraid that he might bolt at a stoplight, she drove with one hand on the wheel and the other on his coattails. She loaded the boys onto the back, where their red heads glinted in the sun like identical spools of copper wire. Inside the cab, Barasch slumped down like a hopelessly collapsed auto chassis, wrenched askew and ridiculously bent. Malka released her grip on his dirty coattail; such a junk heap as Barasch seemed incapable of motion.

At the funeral parlor, she took his arm and dragged him along. Like a wreck under tow, he bumped about, offering no resistance. Much to her surprise, at the sight of the simple wooden coffin, salty tears trickled from Malka's small, squinty eyes. She could not have cared less about Matti; the news of his death had even brought a sly smile to her rapacious lips. But as she stood by Matti's coffin, she had the sinking feeling that her beloved American husband Bernard, the courtly dandy, lay dead inside the box in front of her, and that she was left with the shabby Krimsk remains called Barasch. Bending his head, he stared with wild, rolling eyes at his legs of differing lengths. When he was led by Malka or his sons, his shoes scraped like an old horse collar being dragged back to the barn. He shuffled to the cemetery gates when the Krimsker Rebbe climbed onto his automobile and began to speak, and Barasch listened.

Barasch had hoped that America could succeed where

Krimsk had failed. Ever since the early morning telephone call telling them of Matti's murder, Barasch had been reliving the nightmare of Faigie's return visit to his hut in the Soffers' factory yard. After three years' absence, she appeared one summer's night in his doorway right after he had gone to bed. Barasch believed that he was dreaming as usual.

"I'm here," she said.

"Faigie?" he whispered incredulously.

"Yes, may I come in?" she asked.

"Of course," he answered and started to get up.

"No, don't get out of bed," she said.

He pushed back the cover so that she could join him, but instead she settled herself into the worn easy chair at the head of the table.

"Barasch, my life is in your hands," she said.

"I love you. Only you," he whispered hoarsely, feeling all the desires of his three celibate years descending upon him.

"Then you will do what I say," she responded.

"Yes, yes. Whatever you say."

He started to rise.

"No, stay where you are. I'll only be a minute," she protested.

"Only a minute," he agreed, asking no more of his goddess.

"You must leave Krimsk," she stated.

Her voice was not sharp; indeed, it was delicate and soft, but definite, as if she had planned her words very carefully.

"We are leaving?"

"No, you are leaving. You must go."

"No," he said. "I can't leave you."

"You must. You know you must."

"Why?" he asked in simple innocence.

"You don't know why?"

"No," he answered in tremulous fear.

"The baby looks like you."

"Moses?" he asked. "Like me?"

Although he had thought the child might be his, he had always thought of the baby as *hers,* the child of the divine Faigie.

"You must leave," she repeated.

"Where will I go? What will I do?" he asked in total consternation, like a child who is asked to perform a feat far beyond his juvenile abilities.

"You will marry Malka and go to America," she said simply, as if she were asking him to pass the salt.

"No," he begged plaintively. "I must be near you. Only you."

"I cannot leave my marital bed," she declared.

"No," he insisted with spirit, refusing to believe that his dream of Faigie's return had come true—but as a nightmare.

"If you are not married by the Sabbath and on your way by the end of the month, I shall be dead," she stated with unmistakable certainty.

She stood up.

"Do you understand?" she asked.

"How can I?"

"You must live, Barasch," she pleaded.

"Faigie, Faigie," he moaned.

Barasch took his bride Malka into exile far from his beloved. Faithful in an alien land, he accepted his lost love's decree that he must live. In this epic struggle, he effected the miraculous metamorphosis that fascinated, delighted, and filled Krimsk with an unbounded pride in Barasch, themselves, and their new country. A country where, if gold did not literally lie in the streets, it wasn't too far from the truth, for the old scrap metal, bottles, rags, and paper that did lie in the streets need only be dragged into Malka's junkyard to be converted into riches. Riches that were real and could purchase fine shirts, elegant cuff links, shiny shoes, spanking clean spats, silk ties that even a regal monarch might envy.

But such riches could not satisfy Barasch, for he had a hunger that could not be sated by gold in the streets. He dreamed of gold in the hair, of his divine Faigie. Through Matti's love for Miss Penny Pinkham, Barasch came to believe that in America such a dream could come true. But the telephone had rung, and that, too, had ended in a nightmare, even worse than the original, for it meant the death of dreams. How could a cripple live without a dream? He descended into the yard to join the other maimed junk, bent, sprung, and useless, but Malka, used to turning junk into gold, had plucked him mercilessly from the mountains of rust and worn rubber, stuffed him into her truck, and brought him to the cemetery gates.

There he heard the rebbe's amazing words. He heard that he was correct to mourn, but also that he was correct to dream. Matti had been a pilot who was courageously flying into the future. Although Barasch had failed in Krimsk and Matti had failed in St. Louis, one day—some day—a new pilot would surely succeed. And so golden Faigie was right: he must live. Although that commandment seemed so harsh, he must try.

Malka didn't notice, but as the rebbe spoke, little by little Barasch's bent head lifted off his chest. By the grave, Malka's eyes were dry, but Barasch was weeping. The tears flowed in tragic dignity. On the way out of the cemetery, Malka noticed that Barasch dusted his jacket and straightened his collar.

Boruch Levi had been anxious when the procession arrived at the cemetery gates, but when the rebbe asked to be lifted to the roof of his car, he had responded with alacrity, for in that commandment he heard all the old authority and certainty of the Krimsker Rebbe. Indeed, it reminded him of the rebbe ordering the benches to be overturned on that final Tisha B'Av in Krimsk. The communal mourning experience in St. Louis could only be compared to the magical evening prayer in Krimsk that followed the rebbe's jumping on his table with the little idiot boy, Itzik Dribble.

As they followed the coffin onto the cemetery grounds, Boruch Levi felt an unexpected surge of pride in his noble rabbi, the holy Krimsker Rebbe, who had worked the miracle of mourning at the largest Jewish funeral in the city's history. Boruch Levi almost luxuriated in that sense of community and pride that radiated from Matti's coffin. Krimsk and St. Louis had never seemed closer; for the first time they seemed to inhabit the same world. The blocky Model T Ford even looked like the rebbe's dark, ugly table in Krimsk. Matti lay dead, but even in failure, the rebbe had succeeded. Let these modern Jews hear a real rabbi! It would do them a world of good. His advice about "forgetting the fancy talk" spoke to the depths of the junkman's soul. The rebbe's words that others would succeed where

Matti had failed made poor Matti's death seem less tragic. It was, after all, part of a process that was certain to succeed.

Boruch Levi had arrived at the cemetery mourning the world and himself. He had felt threatened by an all-encompassing chaos: Matti, an irrevocable failure; the rebbe, a useless artifact; and the police, murderers. The other night Matti himself had not quite understood what the rebbe meant by calling the police murderers. Poor Matti never did receive the "good news" that Boruch Levi had to deliver. It was just as well, since the good news wasn't very good at all. Matti had won a fortune and lost his life. Boruch Levi wasn't sure what his relationship with the chief and Doheen would be, but some of the boiling anger had subsided. When the rebbe said that Moses had struggled with the overseer and lost, Boruch Levi realized that they were all involved in some grand drama beyond anyone's comprehension—except for the rebbe's, but even he had his limits: he could not control events and he understood them fully only after the fact. If America was Egypt, well, then everyone was performing a role beyond himself, doing things he had to do. It was all very confusing and impersonal. Why, the chief and Doheen had never even met Matti. Since someone would surely succeed where Matti had failed, it wasn't as if anything so final had occurred. But poor Matti was dead. That was final enough.

When Boruch Levi had called Isidore Weinbach, Isidore was deeply saddened at the tragic news, but he was also aware that the funeral would spare him his annual necessity and embarrassment, the memorial tea party for his late father. His wife Polly didn't welcome his Krimsker brethren into their elegant mansion, and the Krimsker community refused to eat anything in his nonkosher house. Since he shared both attitudes, he didn't know who offended him more. The only one who emerged from the affair with any honor was his late father, who had had the decency to die in the warm summer weather when one could invite guests for a garden party, or in this case a memorial gathering, absurd as it was. Isidore encouraged the idea of a great communal funeral, since that would completely obviate any need for his hosting Krimsk to little cucumber sandwiches in his rose garden. He was even willing to foot the bill. Yitzhak, now Isidore Weinbach, was the wealthiest Krimsker in the world. Unlike Boruch Levi and several other "Yiddish millionaires"—what do you mean, he's not a millionaire? He's got twenty thousand dollars in the bank!—Isidore Weinbach was worth over five million dollars.

A great Jewish communal event offered the added reward of diluting any honor accorded to the Krimsker Rebbe. Isidore Weinbach had never forgiven the rebbe for his affront on that final Tisha B'Av in Krimsk, when he had refused to honor his daughter Rachel Leah's engagement to the then Yitzhak Weinbach. The rebbe's accusation that the matches produced in Weinbach's match factory had been responsible for burning the Torah never made much sense. The loss of Rachel Leah could be tolerated easily; Yitzhak hardly knew her, although if the truth be told, there was something wistfully ethereal about her that in her absence proved haunting. But rejection as a son-in-law was an unforgivable offense to the then-young industrialist's pride.

Isidore, too, had left for America, with the ruffian Boruch Levi as his traveling companion and bodyguard, and as they say in America, "He had showed them," turning his original investment into a considerable fortune, marrying into an old Reform Jewish family. His wife Miriam-Mary-Polly Friedberg had built him one of the city's most palatial homes.

The home was the problem: the goyim and the Reform Jews didn't consider it his, whereas all of Krimsk did so, in a very real sense; hardly anyone visited *him* in his own home. Only the boorish Boruch Levi, who for all his undisguised contempt for Polly, the trayf kitchen, and the botanically unique rose bushes (Polly had been assured that only the Mellons and Rockefellers had anything comparable) did visit, and he came precisely because it was his, Isidore Weinbach's, home, and that was where Isidore was to be found. Isidore didn't really like Boruch Levi, but with no brothers and few disinterested friends (the idea of loyalty among them was laughable), he had come to value the penitent junkman's blind loyalty and sincere selfless concern for his well-being. Who offered him anything like that, even if it came from Krimsk along with the rebbe's insult?

The American Reform rabbis certainly didn't show him any respect. After all, Isidore spoke with a Yiddish accent, lacked any formal education, and above all, maintained the incurably obsolete custom of his father's *yahrzeit,* the memorial reception. The last distressed his wife Polly, and Isidore wondered whether the other two deficiencies might not also, but he supposed that the memorial service was the only one that she believed she could do something about. Or imagined she could, because Isidore, so compliant to almost all her wishes (he had asked her not to serve ham on the Sabbath) and still so very susceptible to her considerable American charms, steadfastly refused to give it up. At least once a year Krimsk visited him at his home, if not in it, and they had known his father, may he rest in peace.

Isidore had the wisdom to know that any further renunciation of himself wouldn't help his standing in Polly's world. The real problem would arise when Isidore's daughter asked him to stop. It would be more difficult to explain to her than to her mother that his facility for making money—upon which their world was based—was just as much a part of Krimsk as the memorial service for his father. Polly believed that her husband was a cosmopolitan mercantilist whom fate had dropped into the primitive cultural embarrassment called Eastern Europe. He knew better; the rag-filled Krimsk marketplace with its unshod horses and malnourished cows had spawned him.

Since Isidore was already obligated to say the mourner's prayer for his father this Sunday, Boruch Levi decided that he should do so at graveside for Matti. Isidore welcomed the suggestion insofar as he could thus slight the rebbe and honor the great Reform rabbi, Morgenstern, through Krimsk itself. It seemed the perfect investment; he couldn't lose.

Things had gone very well. Everyone had turned out for the event. The entire city—the mayor, the police chief, and all the newspaper people—gathered in full force. Isidore was concerned that he would be photographed and appear in the newspapers saying the memorial kaddish. It was one thing to represent Krimsk in St. Louis. It was quite another to *be* Krimsk! He considered having Boruch Levi request that out of respect no photographs be taken in the cemetery proper. That was his only concern as they arrived at the cemetery gates. If the Krimsker Rebbe wanted to speak there, well, that was his error, because there wasn't a podium. He wouldn't even be seen, much less heard.

Isidore Weinbach had been horrified when the rebbe asked to be hoisted onto the automobile roof. When the rebbe proceeded to plant his shoe on Isidore Weinbach's shoulder as if it were a stone or ladder, his fears and embarrassment increased. Once again, just as he had done so publicly in Krimsk, the rebbe seemed to be walking all over him. He wanted to run and hide, but the crowd was as thick as a carpet, and there was no room to move. A captive, he had to listen to the rebbe. When the rebbe finished, Isidore-Yitzhak accepted the rebbe's command to mourn for himself. Isidore was a pilot trying to guide Krimsk into Polly's world. He was on a lonely mission that could not succeed on its first run, but it was, as the rebbe suggested, an essential, noble one that would some day succeed. But what was Isidore-Yitzhak to do now? And where was he to mourn for himself, in the house or in the garden? Or maybe somewhere else altogether? In such confusion he had turned to the rebbe and asked, "What do we do now?" and had received the rebbe's answer that they had no choice but to bury Matti. Isidore accepted that, too. As he followed the coffin to the freshly dug grave, he was determined to intone the mourner's kaddish loud and clear in the hope that he would command the attention and respect of the newspaper photographers.

Proudly erect, even with the imprint of the rebbe's shoe on his shoulder—perhaps because of the imprint of the rebbe's sole—he had stepped forward to begin when he felt a gentle but firm hand on his elbow and turned to find Reb Zelig restraining him.

"It's only fair," the white-bearded patriarch admonished gently, "that if I say kaddish for pharaoh the tsar, I say it for Moses, too. After all, I killed them both."

Before Isidore could begin to comprehend his words, much less respond, the noble white-bearded sexton had begun to intone the memorial chant with a stentorian clarity, and the cameras clicked.

# CHAPTER THIRTY-FIVE

MANY PAUSED RESPECTFULLY BY THE GRAVE, BUT eventually everyone exited through the great cemetery gates. The reporters and news photographers left first. They drove away quickly, but the mourners whom they had deserted understood; after all, they were fleeing the cemetery for another deadline. The many mourners drove back slowly through the green county. At first the riotous green of summer foliage seemed an inappropriate contrast to their image of Matti's raw grave, but by the time they reached the city, they had forgiven the trees and grass their intemperate outburst of life and had come to accept that this, too, was the way of the world.

Returning to their various worlds, they resumed lives they had left earlier in the morning. But they remained mourners all that day, quietly harboring their hearts' sharp pain amid the casual Sunday world around them. No one went to the ballpark because no one felt like it, which was just as well. The St. Louis Browns played with no signs of life and lost both games of the doubleheader. Ty Cobb, wrapped in tape like a mummified Tiger, exacted his revenge by burying Matti's former teammates with three home runs. Immediately after the final out, the Browns descended into the tomb of the speakeasy below the grill to hide and to drown their sorrows. By the time they emerged, darkness had descended mercifully onto the world, and they could go home in anonymous privacy. The darkness that shrouded the ballpark also blanketed the cemetery, covering the gaping brown wound of Matti's grave. But most of all, the darkness eased the mourners' agony. The earth had turned, the sun had set, and this was no longer the unrelenting day in which they had buried Matti.

Boruch Levi paused outside his house in the enveloping darkness. After the crowds and ceremonies of mourning, it was good to be alone momentarily in the night. But there was still some unfinished business. As he stepped off the curb onto the hot tar, Boruch Levi felt the warmth of the day leaking slowly into the night. No, he thought, the murderer was only the man with the gun or the one who hired him. As for the rest of us, well, only the rebbe knows.

Boruch Levi saw that the chief's salon and dining room were dark. Nevertheless he knocked on the chief's door.

"The chief had a long, hard day. That hot sun tired him out," explained Doheen, who met Boruch Levi with a somber look appropriate for a mourner, but Boruch Levi recognized in it the inspector's natural mien. The man really should have been an undertaker. He led Boruch Levi into the kitchen. On the table was a heavy paper bag. It contained something bulky and unrestrained, pushing indiscriminately against the sides. Boruch Levi felt as if he were identifying the corporeal remains of Matti Sternweiss. And all because the chief and Doheen had believed Boruch Levi.

On Saturday morning the inspector had driven to the very same bookmakers from whom he had confiscated the money on Friday evening; only this time he bet all of it on the St. Louis Browns. Out of respect for Boruch Levi's guarantee, he placed an additional ten-thousand-dollar bet for himself and the chief. That wasn't all; after Barasch's bets and Doheen's confiscation of them, the odds had moved to eight-to-five in favor of the Tigers, so Matti had won sixteen thousand dollars for the ten thousand bet. The total "good news," including his original bet, consisted of the twenty-six thousand dollars waiting for Matti. The bookmakers who lost so heavily to Inspector Doheen, however, had seen things somewhat differently. Unable to revenge themselves on police brass, they did so on the man they believed had set them up. Along with the money, there was a bullet waiting for Matti.

"That was some funeral," Doheen said respectfully. "It's all in the paper."

Boruch Levi nodded.

"You want some coffee?" the inspector asked.

The junkman shook his head. Awkwardly, they eyed the bag.

"You better count it," Doheen advised.

"No need for that," Boruch Levi answered.

"We all make mistakes," Doheen replied.

Knowing just how fatal Doheen's mistakes could be, Boruch Levi sat down and started counting. The stacks of bills that gave such an organic impression inside the bag seemed lifeless and lacking all substance in his hands. The more abstract and impersonal they seemed, the better Boruch Levi liked it.

"It's all here," he announced.

"Let me tie it up for you. It'll make it easier."

The inspector returned the bills to the bag and folded it into a neat package before tying it together with string.

"There," he said, "just like a Christmas gift." Realizing how inappropriate the reference was, he amended it by adding, "or a birthday present," only to realize that was even worse.

A grimace of embarrassment crossed his face. He turned to Boruch Levi.

"I'm sorry. I'm very sorry," he said in simple honesty.

"I know. I am, too," Boruch Levi said and shook the inspector's hand.

Boruch Levi picked up the package.

"Take the newspaper, too. I bought several. It has a quote from the chief."

Doheen folded the *Globe* and slipped it into Boruch Levi's hand.

Wearily, Boruch Levi dragged his burdens across the street and up the steps to his home.

The string-tied package looked less ominous on Golda's kitchen table. She looked at it in curiosity, but Boruch Levi didn't enlighten her as to its contents. If she knew that twenty-six thousand dollars in cash lay on her table like a loaf of stale bread, no one would get any sleep. Golda herself would have an ulcer by morning.

"Matti left some unfinished business that I have to take care of," Boruch muttered. Golda clucked nervously at the mention of the tragedy.

Sammy stared curiously at the package. He had heard his father climbing the stairs and expected him to be carrying something much bulkier and much heavier. The boy's interest in the object ended abruptly when his father put the newspaper down.

"May I read it?" he asked eagerly.

His father nodded and turned to make a telephone call. Isidore's butler answered, and Boruch Levi gave his name. In a moment, Isidore himself came to the phone and greeted Boruch Levi.

"Did you get it?" he asked.

"Yes. There was more than we expected," Boruch Levi answered guardedly; Golda was listening.

"How much more?" Isidore asked with keen interest.

"Six," Boruch Levi answered briefly. His friend understood that he couldn't talk openly because of Golda and Sammy.

"Good. That makes a fine sum to invest for Mrs. Sternweiss," Isidore said. "At least she won't have any financial problems. You'll bring it to my office tomorrow?"

"Yes," Boruch Levi replied.

There was a pause.

"Is there anything else?" Isidore asked.

"I thought that we should let the rebbe know what we are doing. As a matter of respect."

Boruch Levi was aware of Isidore's ambivalence toward the man who had had no desire to become his father-in-law.

"Yes, I suppose so," Isidore consented.

"Would you like to join me in telling him about it?" Boruch Levi asked.

"What do you think?" Isidore asked his friend.

"I think that you will be making the investments, and you should be there to receive his blessing," Boruch Levi said without hesitation.

"Yes, I think that would be a good idea."

"I'll call Reb Zelig to make an appointment."

"Good."

"Tomorrow in your office, I'll give you the time."

"Did you see the morning paper?" Isidore asked with some interest.

"No," Boruch Levi replied, wondering why Isidore should mention it. "But it's right here. Sammy's reading it."

"Things went very well today. There are some interesting photos. Take a look."

"I'll do that right now, Isidore. Good-bye."

"Boruch Levi?" Isidore asked.

"Yes?"

"Thank you for calling. Thank you for all your calls. I appreciate them." Isidore hung up.

The wealthy realtor was not given to emotion, and Boruch Levi felt a warm glow. He also felt good about the rebbe. Perhaps some things could be done here in St. Louis that couldn't be done in Krimsk.

"Sammy, tell me about the newspaper story," Boruch Levi requested.

Absorbed in the article, the boy didn't answer. The father joined his son at the table and gently touched the child's arm.

"Sammy, are there any interesting photos?" he asked.

"Are there? Just look!" the boy said excitedly.

Sammy turned back to the front page to show his father the large, black-rimmed St. Louis Browns' publicity photo of Matti. In his baseball cap and with his self-conscious tal-mudist's smile, Matti looked almost handsome. Boruch Levi saw in that tragic picture all the foolishly noble aspirations of Krimsk in America and understood Matti as he never had before. For a moment, he almost gave way to tears.

"Forgive me, Matti," he whispered.

"What, Pa?" Sammy asked.

His father simply shook his head, and Sammy flipped to the back page where the story was continued.

"Look," Sammy said proudly.

His hands raised to heaven, the rebbe stood on the auto roof addressing the rapt crowd of mourners. The shot, taken from a distance over the crowd, captured the magical sense of the rebbe's inspired flight before he fell in mourn-ing. The second picture portrayed mourning, pure and noble. Reb Zelig, eyes closed by tears, chanted the kaddish of faith by the grave.

"Look, that's you!" Sammy cried.

Boruch Levi followed Sammy's finger into Reb Zelig's shadow, where he and Isidore stood. Isidore looked hag-gard and anguished, but to his disappointment, Boruch Levi looked sad but composed. He had the feeling that he was staring at some unfeeling stranger, the way he thought the chief had appeared at the cemetery.

"Does it say what the chief said?" he asked.

Sammy skimmed the columns and then began to read, "'He was a great patriot and a great American, who refused the blandishments of evil and played his heart out for our St. Louis Browns,' said a deeply saddened chief of police, Michael O'Brien."

The boy stopped reading.

"Is that all?" Boruch Levi asked, hoping that the chief, in spite of his unfeeling look, had said something other than "fancy talk."

"There's more here, Pa," and the boy read:

"'He was the smartest man I ever met in baseball, his death notwithstanding': Zack Freeling, St. Louis Browns' manager.

"'He was my best friend in baseball. He introduced me to my fiancée, Penny Pinkham. We were going to ask him to be our best man': Dufer Rawlings, twenty-game winner.

"'We shall miss his bat in the lineup': Thatcher Jones, pitcher."

Boruch Levi was no longer listening. Even had he known who the other speakers were, he wouldn't have paid attention. It was unfair to expect more, but it was all just fancy talk. That's what they wanted from the press. Isidore was right; the three photographs told more about the funeral than they had any right to expect. He found the one of Reb Zelig exceptionally powerful. Affectionately, he tousled Sammy's hair as the boy continued reading.

The rebbe's line was busy. Instead Boruch Levi called his sister Malka to remind her of her promise to give her sons Hebrew lessons. One of his nephews answered, and Boruch Levi asked to speak to the boy's mother. After a few minutes, the child announced that his mother and father had gone to bed and refused to open the bedroom door. Telling his nephew to have Malka call him at his office in the morning, Boruch Levi hung up. The very night following the funeral, too; what a slut, he thought. Those kids will need all the instruction Reb Zelig can give them.

He tried the rebbe again but still didn't get through. He toyed with the idea of driving over to speak to Reb Zelig in person, but decided not to. It was almost ten o'clock. It had been a long day for everyone. Neither the rebbe nor his sexton were youngsters. And out of loyalty to Isidore, Boruch Levi didn't want to go to the rebbe's home without him. Again the telephone operator told him that the line was busy. A glance at his pocket watch told him that it was already ten o'clock.

"Sammy, it's time for bed," he said with a touch of his usual gruffness.

A flush of excitement on his tired features, Sammy neatly folded the newspaper and got up from the table.

"That must have been some funeral," he said.

His father merely nodded. As Boruch Levi pulled the light cord, the funeral didn't interest him; that was over. What did interest him was why the rebbe's line was busy. As he stood in the dark, he wondered: who, instead of Boruch Levi, was speaking to Reb Zelig?

# CHAPTER THIRTY-SIX

BORUCH LEVI NEED NOT HAVE WORRIED. NO ONE WAS speaking on the rebbe's telephone. Like a pendulum that had grown weary, the earpiece dangled off the cradle. Earlier in the day, all the newspapers had wanted to interview the rebbe. Community leaders wanted a word with him, or at the very least, called to congratulate him on his wise words. These calls had finally ceased by the evening. Reb Zelig thought that he might finally have some peace, but he was wrong. During the evening prayers the phone began to ring incessantly. Racing up the steps immediately after the final kaddish, Reb Zelig was overwhelmed with unending requests for audiences with the rebbe. Every Jew from Krimsk wanted to speak with "his rebbe," and almost every other Jew who attended the funeral or had read the papers wanted to meet the "Grand Rabbi of Krimsk" (thus the newspapers had referred to the rebbe at Isidore Weinbach's prompting). It was as if nightfall had created a new world of supplicants in need. Reb Zelig politely took their names and asked them to call back later in the week.

After the list had grown to more than a hundred petitioners, he left the receiver hanging off the hook and went to see the rebbe. Although he loyally took the names with him, Reb Zelig was really interested in speaking to the rebbe about his own future. The rebbe, uncharacteristically, had not appeared in the beis midrash for the evening prayers. Reb Zelig half expected to find him asleep in the study. If so, he would awaken him to say the evening prayers. That would be a shame because Reb Zelig was more anxious than he had ever been in his life to speak to his rebbe.

The rebbe's eulogy at the cemetery had inspired Reb Zelig to intone the most powerful kaddish the city had ever heard. The rebbe's words had put Reb Zelig's life together and, of course, resurrected his confidence in the rebbe himself. The sexton had wanted to speak to the rebbe as they drove home from the cemetery, but that would have been inappropriate and disrespectful to Matti. Now the sun had set, and a new day had begun. Now was the time to tell the rebbe that he, Reb Zelig, was ready; the rebbe need mourn no longer.

The rebbe's words had elucidated several mysteries, not the least of which was the rebbe's having called him the tsar's murderer. All that talk about airplanes—the rebbe had wanted Reb Zelig to become a pilot and had asked Sammy if he wanted to fly—had mystified him, too, but now he understood. The rebbe had invited Reb Zelig to become the pilot, but not comprehending the real intent, Reb Zelig foolishly had refused for lack of time. Instead, the rebbe had turned to poor Matti, who had failed. Greatly to his credit, Matti had understood and had tried to complete the dangerous mission. As far back as Krimsk, Reb Zelig should have saved the Jews, in which case the tsar would have become a righteous man, and all Russia would have been saved from the murderous Bolshevik Revolution. Reb Zelig was years late, but he was finally ready. Proud and fiercely determined, he walked from the kitchen to the rebbe's study door. He knocked respectfully but with a clear clarion tone—and received no answer. He knocked again, louder and more insistently. The rebbetzin stuck her head out of her door to see what all the fuss was about.

"Rebbe, it's me, Reb Zelig!" he called.

The rebbetzin disappeared into her bedroom, and Reb Zelig remained alone in the hall. He must be asleep, thought Reb Zelig in disappointment. He turned the knob and slowly opened the door to find the study pitch-black. He reached for the cord and pulled the light. Momentarily the sudden flash blinded his aging eyes. When he could see again, he was surprised to find his rebbe sitting on the couch wide awake and staring at him as if he, Reb Zelig, were mad. In addition, the rebbe was cradling his head as if he were in severe pain. For a moment Reb Zelig was uncertain, but he quickly regained his composure, stood nobly erect, and announced, "I am ready." Receiving no reply, he moved directly in front of the rebbe, as if reporting for duty, and repeated more loudly and aggressively, "My rebbe, I am ready!"

"Ready for what?" the rebbe asked derisively, as if there were no way to get rid of this madman other than by humoring him.

Undeterred, Reb Zelig answered in strong, confident tones, "Ready to become a pilot!"

"Why in the world would *you* want to do that?" the rebbe asked in genuine curiosity.

"To save the Jews," Reb Zelig wanted to answer, but he

thought it circumspect to use the rebbe's own code. "In order to fly the rebbe down to the Osage Indian reservation."

"Have you been getting enough sleep?" the rebbe asked.

"Yes, I think so," Reb Zelig answered, taken aback at the question.

"Does your head hurt?" the rebbe asked.

"No, not at all," Reb Zelig replied.

"Well, mine is killing me. I would appreciate it if you would stop pounding on doors and screaming like a maniac," the rebbe said.

"I'm sorry," the sexton apologized.

"You will not enter again without receiving permission. Is that clear?" the rebbe snapped.

Reb Zelig nodded.

"Good," the rebbe said, dismissing him with a flick of his wrist.

"But what about my flying?" Reb Zelig asked.

The rebbe stared at him strangely.

"I am ready to become a pilot," Reb Zelig pleaded.

"Are you crazy?" the rebbe asked soberly. "At your age, the vehicle that comes after an automobile is a wheelchair."

The rebbe turned away. Reb Zelig, crushed, left the study, leaving the door open behind him. As he passed through the kitchen toward the steps to his room, he didn't even notice the telephone hanging off the hook. Nor did he fully realize that he had dropped the list of supplicants into the large wastebasket beneath the sink.

If Boruch Levi was in the dark about how to contact Reb Zelig, he had guessed completely right about Malka and Barasch.

Barasch had left the cemetery determined to live. As soon as he returned home, he washed, shaved, and dressed more elegantly than he ever had. It wasn't easy. Even if the striking butterfly that emerges from the cocoon bears no resemblance to the homely caterpillar that inhabited it, who knows whether the graceful butterfly still possesses the bumptious heart of the caterpillar who spun its insular, earthbound cocoon? And if it does, what can the butterfly do to satisfy its displaced heart's yearnings? Fly faster, higher, alighting on ever more beautiful and colorful sun-bathed blooms—light, air, breeze, sweet purple violets, pungent red roses, perfumed sticky honeysuckle—and never quite succeeding. But forever trying, and Barasch knew that he must try.

Malka had witnessed this emergence with delight and increased desire. More than willing to give Barasch the opportunity to try, she invited him into the bedroom and locked the door. That very night after the funeral, she raised the blanket. Barasch entered and tried to bury himself in her robust, living flesh lest death claim him. In a land far from his love, he struggled for his life and called the name of his wife, "Malka, Malka, oy, yoy, yoy!"

The rebbe had wanted to call Reb Zelig back to close the door, but the pain in his head was too acute. He received minimal relief by cradling it in his hands. He was about to cross the room to close himself off when Shayna Basya walked in.

"Close the door," he commanded.

She complied immediately and turned to greet her husband. When she saw him on the couch cradling his head, she gasped and fell back against the door. She had not seen him sitting like that since he disappeared for five years into his study in Krimsk for his self-imposed exile. She was afraid to speak.

"Would everyone stop banging on the door? My head is killing me," the rebbe complained.

Although fearful, the rebbetzin was pleased that he had spoken first.

"I'm sorry," she said. "Can I get you anything?"

"No, I don't think anything will help."

Suddenly she had an idea. "Would you like me to make you some Aunt Jemima pancakes and a cup of Postum?"

The rebbe looked at her as if she, too, had gone mad.

"Have you been getting enough sleep?" he asked.

"Yes, why?"

"It's the middle of the night. Those are breakfast foods," he explained.

Shayna Basya didn't know quite what to say.

"I was hoping the night was over," she said simply.

He looked at her closely. "So was I, but it is not. It has only begun. But that is not why you came in."

"Yes, you're right. I came to ask you something I meant to ask the other night when you were talking about Krimsk. Yaakov Moshe, I want you to send for our daughter Rachel Leah."

The rebbe didn't answer, but he did sit up as if he felt some slight relief to his agony. This encouraged the rebbetzin.

"Heaven knows what is happening in that Bolshevik land. She must come here," the rebbetzin announced.

"No, she cannot come here now."

"Why not?"

"We buried him in the afternoon. Now our children must wait for the Messiah with all the others."

"I am not interested in the Messiah, Yaakov Moshe, I am interested in my daughter."

"That will delay his coming."

"Write her and tell her of the Messiah," Shayna Basya suggested.

The rebbe didn't answer, but he appeared to be weighing the idea.

"Yes, the Messiah," he repeated.

"Just write. Is that asking too much?" the rebbetzin demanded.

"There is nothing to ask," the rebbe said definitively.

"But you will write?" she implored.

"It is hard to know," he said sadly, but not without feeling.

The rebbetzin left, closing the door behind her.

Yaakov Moshe, much to his surprise, felt somewhat better.

"There is nothing to ask," the rebbe repeated to himself. After all, the only question worth asking was the color of the river, and now the rebbe did not need to ask Boruch Levi the color of the mighty Mississippi. It was red, blood red, but not miraculously so as in the first plague. No, the taskmaster had slain Moses, and the river flowed with the redeemer's blood. Red with blood; there was nothing to ask. The exile would be long and hard. Blood had been spilled. Idolatry and sexual lewdness could not be avoided either. All must wait, and all must suffer.

The rebbe was mystified that his head felt better. The river was blood red, but something was happening in the city that was redemptive, and in his agony, that gave him courage. He tried with all his powers to concentrate on what that might be, but all he could discover was a voice faintly calling in the night. He remained mystified. Was it the lonely Shekinah? He could not discern that it was the voice of Barasch calling the name of his legal wife. The only thing that the rebbe could discern was the color of the Great Indian River—murderously blood red.

# THE LETTER

FOR YEARS THE REBBETZIN DUTIFULLY PLACED POSTUM and Aunt Jemima pancakes before the rebbe at the appropriate time, in the morning, and Yaakov Moshe dutifully consumed them. After breakfast the rebbetzin placed pen and paper on the rebbe's desk; but even though he spent long hours alone in his study, the rebbe never touched them. When she encouraged him to write to their daughter Rachel Leah in Russia, he would nod agreeably and explain, "When the time is right."

There were moments when the rebbetzin thought the time might be right. In 1923, after Warren Harding died and Silent Cal Coolidge entered the White House, the rebbetzin noticed that the pen and paper had been used. But one morning the rebbe pointed with disgust at a campaign picture in the newspaper of Calvin Coolidge posing in an Indian warbonnet. In the background, his chauffeur and limousine waited to whisk him away. "An impostor, a fake," the rebbe declared angrily and stalked into his study.

The next morning Shayna Basya again found the writing materials untouched.

They remained that way until 1927, when Charles A. Lindbergh made his historic solo flight across the Atlantic. "The Spirit of St. Louis," the rebbe mused conspiratorily, savoring the name of the heroic aviator's crafts. "Our son-in-law Hershel Shwartzman could fly it back here for him," he suggested, picking up the pen. The rebbetzin didn't respond. As far as she knew, Grisha couldn't pilot a plane. Even if he could, Lindbergh had flown solo; there wasn't any room in the "Spirit of St. Louis" for Rachel Leah. It made no difference, however, for the rebbe suddenly ceased writing when the newspaper worshipfully referred to Lindbergh as the "Lone Eagle." "A trayf bird, grasping impurity," he pronounced, sadly shaking his head. Despairing of his ever writing to their daughter, Shayna Basya stopped providing him with pen and paper.

In 1936 Reb Zelig fell ill and died. On a steamy summer day, they buried him next to Matti Sternweiss. Upon returning from the cemetery, the rebbetzin opened the icebox for a cool drink.

"Would you like something?"

"Yes," the rebbe answered, sweat covering his smooth forehead with an unbroken watery film as if he had just surfaced from a deep pool.

"What?" she asked.

"A pen and paper," he demanded.

"Whatever for?" she asked.

"If I don't write now, the letter won't arrive before Rosh Hashanah, the New Year," he explained matter-of-factly.

The rebbetzin followed him into the study and presented

him with pen and paper. "Thank you," he said, and began writing at once.

Fifteen minutes later, she was sipping a cool glass of water at the kitchen table when the rebbe returned with the letter.

"That was quick," she commented.

"Sixteen years, and you call it quick," the rebbe said, slightly bemused.

"Would you like a drink?" she asked.

"A beer, please."

She looked up in surprise. The rebbe had never shown any taste for the beverage.

"Yes, Prohibition is over," he stated.

She placed the cool bottle on the table; at once a fine mist shrouded its dark surface. She pushed the letter away so it wouldn't get wet.

"Thank you," he said, but she didn't answer.

She was staring down at the envelope addressed to her son-in-law. Prohibition had ended in St. Louis. The rebbetzin wondered how her daughter and son-in-law were welcoming Rosh Hashanah, the New Year, in Moscow in 1936.

ALLEN HOFFMAN, award-winning author of the novel *Small Worlds* and of a novella and short stories, was born in St. Louis and received his B.A. in American History from Harvard University. He studied the Talmud in yeshivas in New York and Jerusalem, and has taught in New York City schools. He and his wife and four children now live in Jerusalem. He teaches English literature and creative writing at Bar-Ilan University.